HOTEL MORGUE

HOTEL MORGUE

Janet Laurence

A Perfect Crime Book

D O U B L E D A Y

NEW YORK LONDON TORONTO SYDNEY AUCKLAND

A Perfect Crime Book
PUBLISHED BY DOUBLEDAY
a division of Bantam Doubleday Dell Publishing Group, Inc.
666 Fifth Avenue, New York, New York 10103

DOUBLEDAY is a trademark of Doubleday,
a division of Bantam Doubleday Dell Publishing Group, Inc.

Library of Congress Cataloging-in-Publication Data

Laurence, Janet.
Hotel Morgue / by Janet Laurence. — 1st ed.
p.   cm.
"A Perfect Crime book."
I. Title.
PR6062.A795H67   1992
823'.914 — dc20   92-20566
CIP

ISBN 0-385-41912-0

To my brother, Michael Duffell,
one of the world's greatest hoteliers

Acknowledgements

I owe many thanks to a number of people. Tony Elliott, proprietor and Managing Director of the delightful and luxurious hotel, The Greenway Shurdington, Cheltenham; Kit Chapman, Managing Director of his family's hotel, The Castle in Taunton; David Ward, who was Managing Director of The Stafford in London and my brother, Michael Duffell, for many years Managing Director of The Ritz Hotel and The Stafford, all have been most generous with advice and information. Detective Inspector Neil Thompson and Detective Sergeant James Mallon of the Avon and Somerset Constabulary both patiently answered many questions about police procedure. And my husband, Keith, bore all the trials and tribulations of the writing, including during our holiday, with great patience and good humour. Others, too numerous to mention, contributed various details which helped me tell this story. All errors must be laid at my door, not theirs. The Greenway influenced my description of The Manor Park but its owners and personnel are quite different and the Hotel Morgan is completely imaginary. Other than actual named places, you may look in vain for the landmarks mentioned in this book and all the characters and their actions are imaginary. Their names and experiences have no relation to those of actual people, living or dead, except by coincidence.

Chapter One

The fish was innocent. It lay appetising and succulent, little curds of freshness clinging to the firm white flesh. The villain was the sauce.

'Brill in champagne, lemon and thyme sounded interesting, creative,' said Darina Lisle plaintively. She tried another mouthful, unable to believe the first had tasted quite so dire.

Her companion poked the offending food with his fork. 'To suggest even non-vintage had anything to do with this is an insult to any self-respecting bottle of bubbly. And why is the sauce this odd gluey consistency?'

'It must have been thickened with cornflour, and far too much at that. The same heavy hand added the thyme; this is practically a whole branch!' Darina's fork lifted a small stalk thickly clustered with tiny green leaves, then dumped it back on the plate and went for a sliver of lemon peel. 'And look at this. More pith than peel, thick enough for marmalade and unblanched; far too bitter. The champagne, if there is any, doesn't stand a chance. Such a pity because the fish itself is delicious; it really is a crime.'

Her gaze moved restlessly round the dining room, flicking over round tables clothed with long pink tablecloths and comfortable chairs upholstered in checked shantung that toned with swagged curtains trimmed with fringes, tassels *and* contrasting linings. The assured designer finish bore little relation either to the rest of the hotel or the food they were being served. It had to be one of the worst meals Darina had ever been offered.

They had chosen the chef's special menu; at first sight it seemed to offer exceptional value. The country culinary scene must be looking up if a small hotel in the heart of rural Somerset could think it worth decking out its restaurant in such style and offering such an imaginative menu.

Alas, imagination outstripped ability. A first course of avocado and mango with tarragon cream appeared with a splodge of stiff cream cheese flecked with dried herbs, an unappetising accompaniment to thick slivers of the two fruits.

Darina had given up her attempt to eat it. 'It needs a dressing,' she said, laying down her fork. 'As it is, it's quite, quite . . . ' she hesitated, slanting a quick glance at her host.

'Disgusting?' he offered, dead pan.

'Thank you, darling, definitely the *mot juste*.'

He raised an eyebrow. 'If bad food means you call me darling, I must bring you here more often.'

'If I have understood correctly, you want me to invest in this hotel, in which case I would be here permanently.'

'Which would mean a set menu of endearments,' he leered cheerfully at her across the table.

'If I was here permanently, you wouldn't get served a dish like this!'

'Have you finished?' asked the waitress, surveying their plates of half eaten food. 'I told Chef it wouldn't go. I mean, avocado and prawns is one thing but no one round here wants stuff this fancy.' She cleared away the remains of the starter, brought the main course then stood leaning negligently against an attractive dresser, picking bits of dirt from under her fingernails.

Three other tables were occupied. Two businessmen were eating the steak the set menu had offered as an alternative – for a supplement. Their tongues flashed more busily than their forks. One was a big man with a large growth behind one ear; his companion was smaller with a weasel face and a habit of rapidly blinking his eyes and pointing his fork to emphasise his remarks.

The other two tables were each occupied by a single diner. A thin man ate his set meal with solemn intensity, his eyes wandering round the room, examining every detail of the décor and his fellow eaters. The other loner was a podgy man with soft skin and a pleasant-looking face. Mouse-fair hair crept in sticky clumps across a shiny pate. Darina was interested to note he was served soup and shepherd's pie, neither dish having been included

10

on the menu they had been offered. And either his food was better than theirs or his tolerance greater, for he ate with relish, using a piece of roll to wipe up the last of the meat juices from his plate.

'Didn't you like it?' asked the waitress, removing Darina's scarcely-touched plate of fish.

'Sorry, I can't say I did,' she confessed.

'The gentleman over there didn't finish it either,' the waitress indicated the thin man on his own. 'Chef's going to be awfully disappointed.' The prospect did not appear to worry her; a round, beaming face shone out from below a quiff of bright yellow hair. 'Pudding or cheese and biscuits? There's ice cream or Chef's special fig tart with blackcurrant coo, coo, ooh . . . I knew I'd never remember what it was called.'

'Coulis?' offered Darina.

'Right! That's it, fig tart with blackcurrant coulis.' She gave them an extra bright smile and stood waiting, with their dirty plates poised in one hand.

'William?' Darina looked across at her companion.

'I'll choose safety and the cheese and biscuits.'

'Coward! I'll go for the fig tart.'

'Right you are, then.'

Out of the corner of her eye, Darina noticed the plump man watching the waitress walk across the room, hips swaying, the tight black skirt wrapped around her ample behind. She disappeared through the service door and the man returned his attention to what looked like apple crumble.

The cheese offered was more than respectable, an excellent farmhouse Cheddar and Coleford, a subtle blue cheese made from sheep's milk. The fig tart was another matter.

'Honestly, William,' said Darina after her first mouthful. 'You can't seriously suggest I could be interested in going into partnership with an outfit that calls this good food?' She pushed the flat circle of pastry topped with slices of fig overlaid with a purple goo across her plate with a disdainful flick. 'It not only looks like cardboard, it has the consistency and taste of cardboard and the blackcurrant kills any flavour of fig.'

Her companion was a tall young man of about thirty with dark curly hair, silver-grey eyes flecked like a herring and an engaging smile.

11

'You can't judge a hotel entirely by its food.'

'In my book it's one of the most important features. Food is basic, it's a necessity of life, if it's inedible people are not going to be interested in beautifully swagged curtains and if it's really good, they will put up with uncomfortable chairs and poor decoration. And just why do we have this wonderful looking dining room when the waitress hardly knows her job? We ordered sparkling mineral water and she's produced still. The salt and pepper have been left on the table and she seems to be totally ignoring those people over there. And just why does the rest of the hotel look as though the Fifties are still with us?'

'Come on, you weren't born in the Fifties!'

'Even I can read colour supplements. Admit it, it's true.'

'Tony Mason bought the place a year or so ago. It was a residential hotel then, full of senior citizens (don't you prefer the French term, *troisième âge*?) who'd retired to the West Country. But he believed it could be turned into a luxury country hotel. The dining room and kitchen were his first project.'

Darina gave another swift look around her. 'I can see the décor matching his ambitions but whatever happened to the food?'

'Ulla says— ' started William.

'And who is Ulla?'

'Ulla is *la patronne* and it was when I was talking to her that I got the idea you could be interested.'

'Yes, explain just why you thought I could want to invest money in a place like this?' Darina's tone was not encouraging.

William flashed her a quick grin. 'Haven't you been wittering on ever since we first met about your ambition to own a country hotel? Aren't you trying to sell your expensive Chelsea house to raise the capital to acquire one? Weren't you saying only the other day that even that didn't look like raising enough money for the sort of place you wanted? Well, when I heard that the Hotel Morgan was looking for a partner to inject some extra capital in this place, I immediately thought of you.' He looked like a puppy proudly offering a pair of slippers, blind to their chewed edges.

'You mean,' Darina regarded him thoughtfully, 'you mean you take my ambitions seriously?'

'Do you doubt it?'

'When you use that tone of voice, yes.'

'What's wrong with my tone of voice?'

'It's unctuous with a "if I humour her maybe she'll realise what a daft idea it all is" quality.'

Her grey eyes looked steadily into his and his smile faded. He reached for her hand, closing round it firmly, even though she offered no resistance to his grasp. 'Look, darling, I do take you seriously. Heaven knows, I've seen enough of you in action to realise that you have enormous talent and determination. You made a great success of your catering business and I reckon you're at the top of your profession. But you can't expect me to welcome you taking on a project that will totally involve you, possibly take you away from this part of the world, which would certainly mean I would find it difficult to see you. This seemed to offer a good compromise.'

'Compromise?'

'It's nice and near so we could meet when I'm off duty, and you'd be in partnership, sharing the responsibility of running the place.'

'So I'd be able to drop everything whenever you wanted?'

He groaned and released her hand. 'Don't take that attitude, you know that's not what I mean.'

'It sounded very like it. Look, I accept that as a Detective Sergeant of police you don't have a nine-to-five job and your social life is often non-existent. Why can't you accept that a hotelier or caterer operates under much the same system?'

The hand holding hers tightened its grip. 'Darina, darling, marry me and give up the whole idea.'

Her eyes widened and she sat quite still for a moment.

'That's a bit sudden.'

'Now don't say, "How you startled me!" You know what I feel about you and during the last few weeks I've come to believe you might feel the same. So isn't marriage the natural next step?'

'Which would mean me giving up my job and settling down to be a housewife?'

'You wouldn't have to give up entirely, you could do odd parties and things.'

13

'Odd parties and things!'

'Well, wouldn't being my wife be more important? And then there'd be children.'

'Children,' she repeated without inflection.

'Don't you want a family?'

Darina thought about children. What sort of a mother would she make? She thought of dear little babies with William's eyes, then of horrible small children who wouldn't eat their greens. Of difficult teenagers who exploited the generation gap. She looked once again round the stylish room.

'I suppose running a hotel, creating the right atmosphere for people to feel happy and comfortable, feeding them, looking after them, trying to understand their needs, is somewhat like being a wife and mother.'

'And I bet the customers can be as difficult as any child, and as ungrateful. You can't seriously see a hotel as a substitute for the real thing?'

She felt uncomfortable before the intensity in his eyes, an intensity he'd managed to keep out of his voice.

'William, I'm not ready to settle down. I can't imagine loving anyone else but you but if I don't have a go at achieving my ambitions, however trifling they may seem to you, I'll only regret it later.'

'You'll regret marrying me?'

'That's not what I mean, but yes, I suppose it could come to that. I've seen it happen with friends.' She leaned forward urgently. 'Don't you see, now is my chance. There'll be time for us later. I'm only twenty-eight, there's no hurry for babies. But if I don't try and get my hotel now, it'll be too late. The competition is getting worse and the capital investment needed greater. Look at what new hotels are offering now: health clubs, swimming pools, superb surroundings. It may already be too late for people like me but I've got to try, don't you see?'

He said nothing.

'Can't we go on as we are?' she pleaded.

'You want to go on having an affair, you mean, but you don't want to marry me?'

'Isn't that the modern way?' She tried to lighten her tone.

'I suppose I'm not as modern as I thought. The cave man

14

appears to be only slightly below the permissive society surface.' He pushed away his plate, called over the waitress and ordered coffee.

'How's Inspector Grant?' Darina deliberately changed the subject. Her choice of a new topic was not happy. Gloom gathered ever more deeply on William's face.

'Full of enthusiasm for the new recruit to our team.'

'No use?'

'It's a girl.'

'You male chauvinist pig!' Darina was genuinely startled.

'No, you don't understand. I'm not against women, really I'm not. It's just we've had such a good team until now, chaps together; a woman means a completely different atmosphere.'

Darina looked at her companion. She'd known he had a solid core of conservatism but she hadn't realised it took quite this form.

'What's she like, this new recruit?'

'Only met her this morning. Quiet, seems competent, no raving beauty but nice looking.'

'Cheer up. If Grant is enthusiastic about welcoming a woman, she'll prove a worthy member of your team. I'd have bet my last bottle of hazelnut oil your excellent Inspector was a fully fledged member of the MCP club.'

William grinned suddenly, back to the man she loved. 'How perceptive you are. Look, let's forget about her. What I wanted to tell you about this place was . . . ' but at that moment the waitress came over to tell him he was wanted on the telephone.

Darina sipped her coffee and waited for him to return, wondering how her refusal of his proposal was going to affect their relationship. Why couldn't he have left things as they were?

It was only a few weeks since she had finally acknowledged the depth of the attraction between them. Then William had swept her off to a holiday in the Lake District, to the luxury and perfect food of the Miller Howe Hotel. No honeymoon could have been more enjoyable. The beauty of the landscape, almost bare of tourists in November, had matched their mood. Together they had scrambled up and down fells unchanged since Roman times, explored villages built of dark, rain-washed stone, read the Lakeland poets, debated wide-ranging topics, eaten far too much food and drunk far too much wine but without suffering adverse effects. And Darina had discovered sensual pleasures beyond those of the table.

On the second night of their stay they sat drinking wine in the lounge before dinner. They had spent the morning walking, had had a pub lunch and returned in the early afternoon, heading without discussion to their room overlooking Lake Windermere, a sparkling blue under a cloudless sky that morning but since then lost in veils of cloud and rain. Now, sipping the Australian Chardonnay, its golden buttery flavour chilled but not deadened, Darina revelled in the unaccustomed awareness of her body, at one and the same time drugged and alive, like a collection of naked electric wires clothed in velvet.

She was aware of every breath the man beside her drew. His left hand lay along the arm of his chair. She looked at the long, bony fingers, nails flat and ridged, neatly trimmed and edged with a border of chalky white. She could remember with intellectual precision their touch on her naked body, just as she could remember the clouded gaze of his dark flecked eyes as the fingers traced the outline of breasts and hips, just as she knew by the altered rhythm of his breathing that his thoughts had paralleled hers. She let the knowledge travel along those so recently awakened nerves, raised her glass, looked straight at him and with a confident delight she had never known before silently toasted all they had enjoyed that day and would enjoy in the days to come. He had returned the toast, they'd laughed, then talked of something quite mundane, hugging to themselves their knowledge of future delights, not like a miser hoarding treasure, more as a music lover might put away a greatly enjoyed record for a period of quiet before playing another piece by the same composer.

It was true what she had said, she couldn't imagine loving anyone else but William. He was friend and companion as well as lover; someone she thought she would be happy to grow old with. But not yet. So much had happened since they met, her life had changed so much. Then she had been running her own catering business, constantly worried about cash flows and finding new customers. Now she had independent means, the opportunity to fulfil a long-held ambition.

And there was something else. During the time she had known

16

Detective Sergeant William Pigram she had solved two murder cases. Generous though he had finally been both times, Darina knew he would have preferred her not to have involved herself in what he, no doubt quite properly, considered his business.

It had not exactly been her choice. On the first occasion she had been fighting to prove her innocence. The second was more debatable, she had considered it a matter of loyalties but recognised she had enjoyed the mental exercise, and had found it possible to achieve the detachment necessary to sift and assess the details that led to the solution of murder.

Darina gave herself a small mental shake. It was unlikely she would be connected again with a murder enquiry. But what would happen when William was? Could she contain her natural curiosity, avoid asking questions that might seem to him as though she was trying to get involved, even, heaven forbid, take over?

William obviously saw her as a wife and mother, not as amateur detective or even hotel proprietor, whatever he might claim to the contrary. And she was not prepared to settle down, build a nest, raise fledglings. Darina felt her ambitions rising like yeast in well-kneaded dough. She was like an athlete who had trained to run a particular race with a starting pistol about to be fired. Every muscle was ready, quivering with anticipation. She had so many ideas, knew exactly what she wanted to achieve. It just took the right property.

Was the Hotel Morgan the right property? And what exactly were William's motives in bringing her here? Darina gave the dining room a final glance. If this was the standard of their renovations, she could understand why they were looking for more capital. Almost she had made up her mind. If only the food had not been quite so dire, so pretentious.

'I've got to go.' The tall detective was back at the table, giving the bill that had been delivered in his absence a cursory glance and pulling out money. 'They've found a body and it looks like murder.'

Chapter Two

William left in a flurry of coat collection and hasty goodbyes. 'Have a word with Ulla, then ask Alex to take you home,' he shouted as he dashed for his car. 'Apologise for me, will you?'

Darina gave a last little wave at the sprayed gravel thrown up by his accelerating wheels and wondered when she would see him again. If he was going to get involved in a murder investigation, it was unlikely to be soon.

She turned her back on his departing car and took a good look at the Hotel Morgan.

A Victorian gothic façade, its long windows set in square bays jutting out from either side of an ornate porch, appeared to have been built on to an older building. Tudor chimneys rose from a jumble of lower pitched roofs behind the steeply gabled front. The grey stone was bare, no cover of creeper softened its severity. It absorbed the winter sun and gave nothing back.

Darina took a closer look at the building. The roof seemed sound enough but a couple of drainpipes were badly rusting and the pointing needed attention. And was it her imagination or did the porch lean slightly to one side? The gravel sweep in front of the house was neat enough but around a shaggy lawn loomed overgrown shrub beds. Broken branches hung from a few trees, probably victims of the latest set of strong winds. It was a setting for Sleeping Beauty but without the charm.

She gave a shiver as a chill wind blew and walked quickly back inside. The hotel's hall failed to offer a cheerful welcome. Dark panelling was gloomily lit and the furnishings lacked any sense of style. A table with barley twist legs had been set inside the entrance and offered a selection of tourist pamphlets. Several modern armchairs upholstered in uncut moquette with wooden

18

arms were anchored uneasily on a sea of flagstoned floor. A log smouldered sulkily at the back of a huge stone fireplace, doing little to raise the ambient temperature from what could only be classed as miserably cold. A reception cubby hole of stained plywood had been added to one corner. There was no sign of any receptionist.

The one redeeming feature of the place was a stunning arrangement of dried flowers on a centrally placed round table. An antique Chinese bowl held a selection of blues and creams, the stiff stems softened by tumbling additions of old man's beard, the whole arranged with delicacy and skill.

Darina stood admiring it and wondering where to find the owners of this unpromising establishment. Then she heard voices. Or, rather, one, female and extremely cross.

'And don't think you can stand me up again and get away with it! And if you do, you can at least apologise. I waited all yesterday for you to ring. And this morning.'

From a door at the back of the hall had emerged a girl pulling on a brown suede jacket, tossing her remarks over her shoulder as she walked across the hall. Her most remarkable feature was a mane of hair the colour of autumn leaves. It curled strongly, alive and glowing. The face it framed with such vigour was neat with cat-shaped, amber eyes and a sulky mouth. Her small frame had something of a cat's sinuousness, small and supple. Discontent dragged at her features, turning what might have been a very pretty girl into one that was less than attractive.

She turned as she reached the door, gave Darina an incurious glance and smiled at the man she'd been castigating. All at once the promise of her looks was fulfilled. 'What about tonight?' she said sweetly, irresistibly.

The man seemed unimpressed.

'I'll give you a ring later, Olivia. I can't promise anything, we could be busy.'

The small, pouty mouth lost its brief sweetness. 'Never tell me you've actually got guests. Well, don't think I shall sit around waiting for you again.' The heavy door banged with the force of her departure.

The man hardly glanced at her departing back as he came towards Darina. 'Can I help?'

She looked into eyes the blue of a sunlit sky reflected in ice and understood the girl's pique. He was about her own age, tall, with a rangy, spare body carelessly dressed in jeans and a sweat shirt. Pale blond hair flopped over a broad brow above the amazing eyes deep set under eyebrows so fair they looked non-existent. His eyelashes matched. Was it that that gave the air of someone looking at far horizons? Or was it just the fact he seemed uninterested in anything near at hand?

'I'm looking for the owner, or owners: Tony and Ulla Mason?'

He frowned. 'My father's dead. Ulla's around somewhere and I'm Alex Mason. I suppose I qualify as a part owner. What did you want?'

How unobliging of William to have disappeared before telling her this fact or what he had discussed with Ulla Mason, if indeed he had discussed anything.

As Darina tried to decide how to begin, a slight, fair woman, not much older than herself, came in the front door. 'What have you done to Olivia Brownsword, Alex? She drove past me as though a gale was behind her and wouldn't even wave.'

'She'll get over it. She thinks she has some sort of right to my time. There's someone here wants to see you.' He waved a negligent hand in Darina's direction and disappeared back into the nether regions of the hotel.

'Don't forget it's your duty tonight,' the woman called after him, then sighed deeply. 'Why that girl is so keen, I can't imagine, he treats her like dirt. Now, what can I do for you?' There was a slight lilt to her voice, a sing-song quality that suggested Scandinavia, as did the extreme fairness of her hair and skin.

'I am Darina Lisle. William Pigram brought me to lunch,' began Darina.

'Oh, William, of course. I'm so sorry I wasn't here, I had to do some shopping and it all took longer than I expected. For a Monday morning Yeovil had so many people. Did you have a good meal?' The question was eagerly put.

Darina hesitated.

'We have started our new menu this week. Chef created the recipes specially. We are hoping for lots of Christmas business, people must be so tired of turkey. Ah, Mr Nicholls, how nice to

20

see you. And how good of you to try us so soon. I do hope you enjoyed your lunch?'

The single diner who had eaten with such concentration halted on the edge of the hall as Ulla Mason moved forward to greet him. He took her hand and stood looking like a Father Christmas who realises he has forgotten his sack of presents. 'My dear Mrs Mason, I'm sorry but it won't do. I can't possibly give you a write-up in the *Western Chronicle*, you would never have any more business.' He patted the hand he still held. 'Get another chef and let me know when everything's sorted out. Then I'll try again.' He collected a coat from the old-fashioned stand in one corner of the hall and disappeared through the front door.

Ulla Mason gazed after him, shock freezing her expression. Then she turned to Darina. 'What does he mean? Lunch can't have been that bad.'

'I'm afraid it was.'

From the direction of the dining room came the two business men, roaring with laughter. The proprietor smiled at them nervously.

'God, Ulla,' said the large man with the growth behind his ear. 'What have you done to the food? What's wrong with turkey? We expect this overdressed crap at the Manor Park, though there I have to say you can eat it, but you used to be able to get chips and a decent pudding here. Not even a mince pie and we're into December.'

'I'm so sorry, we've a new chef and are trying a new menu. Come back next week and we'll see what we can do. The meal will be on us, of course.'

'Now, no call for that, the steak was fine.' The large man patted his capacious paunch. 'Stand us a drink next time we're in and no hard feelings. Come on, Derek, time we both got back.'

Ulla Mason watched them leave the hotel. Darina thought she was about to burst into tears.

'Two of the most influential County Councillors; Derek's Chair-. man of the Planning Committee, heaven knows if they'll ever be back. Tony would have known how to handle them, he had them eating out of his hand. Oh well, it doesn't look as though we'll be applying for any planning permission in the near future anyway.' The proprietor put a hand to her brow. 'But I don't understand.

You must tell me what's happened, William says you know so much about food.'

Slipping her hand through Darina's arm, she took her through the door at the back of the hall and into a small office off a dark corridor. A dirty window gave out on to a scruffy courtyard but failed to let in much daylight. It was left to a green-shaded central light to provide illumination of a slightly higher quality than that in the hall. The room was crowded with equipment and paper. A computer and copier occupied one corner, a large desk covered with files and leaflets another. Behind the desk sat Alex, studying a large atlas.

Ulla looked at him with exasperation, 'Have you checked the bar for this evening?'

He didn't look up. 'Plenty of time for that. We're unlikely to be rushed off our feet. The only booking we've got is that table for four.'

Ulla indicated a small easy chair. 'Please, sit.' She rubbed her hands. 'Isn't it cold? Perhaps we could have the fire on.' She bent and switched on one bar of a small electric fire. 'This is Darina Lisle, Alex. She could be interested in becoming a partner.'

The piercing eyes lifted their gaze from the atlas and looked across. 'Sell up, Ulla, get rid of the whole bloody incubus. You're fighting a losing battle.' The young man stood up and tucked the book under his arm. 'You've had a good offer, take it.' He strolled to the door.

'You know I won't do that, Alex, though sometimes I'm tempted. It would at least mean I'd never have to see you again.'

He turned in the doorway, 'Temper, temper! Be careful or I could disappear right now and then what would you do, mother dear?' The last words were given an ironic twist, then the door was closed carefully behind him.

Ulla made a noise somewhere between a screech and a growl and banged her head with clenched fists.

'That Alex, I could strangle him sometimes. Why is it that some people know just how to drive you to screaming point?'

It was a question that required no answer. Darina watched her seat herself in the chair Alex had vacated.

Ulla couldn't be more than thirty at the most. A few lines

were starting to etch themselves into the fine skin but the figure was in great shape, a knitted dress and jacket making the most of swelling breasts. The hips were slight and boyish. That combination of provocative sexuality and androgynous innocence must be lethally attractive to men, especially when matched with a face as sweet as a fairy princess's and hair with natural highlights so fair as to be almost white amongst shades of honey gold and umber.

'I take it Alex is your stepson?'

Ulla nodded. 'He isn't really a hotelier; after Tony died he came to help out. But don't let's talk about Alex, he always makes me so mad. Tell me what happened with lunch. I thought the new menu was going to be such a success.'

'Have you had your chef long?'

'Ken Farthing started a couple of weeks ago. I was so pleased, he seemed so good. Our previous menu was very straight forward, steak, chops, chicken, that sort of thing, all with chips, and a sweet trolley. He coped with that fine but I'd hired him to transform the food, bring it up to the standard of our new dining room. When he said he could create a new menu, stylish, top class, I said go ahead.'

'You didn't try the dishes first?'

Ulla looked crestfallen. 'I didn't think it necessary, I thought he knew his job. It all *sounded* delicious. What went wrong?'

'I'm afraid every dish was misconceived.' Darina briefly outlined their disastrous meal.

Ulla looked more and more miserable. 'What am I going to do? We can't go back to what we were serving before, it doesn't match the dining room.'

'I think you'd better have a word with your chef.'

She rose. 'Will you come with me? You're such an expert, I don't want him to confuse me.'

Darina reluctantly followed the proprietor along the badly painted corridor to the kitchen, passing odd nooks and crannies stuffed with boxes of loo paper and cartons of breakfast cereal. She wondered just what Ulla's qualifications for running a hotel were. Alex's advice that the place should be sold seemed sound. And just why she herself had agreed to act as back-up at what would no doubt be an unpleasant confrontation, Darina found it difficult to decide. There was something about Ulla, a helpless quality, that brought out protective instincts. It must be a priceless asset in business. Darina sighed. She had long ago recognised that she never brought out a protective instinct in anyone. Capability was her aura. Even William, who at least topped her nearly six foot by several inches, hardly treated her as 'a little woman'. But then, that was the last thing she wanted, wasn't it?

The kitchen was as radically different from the rest of the hotel as the dining room. A powerhouse of stainless steel, brand new ovens and gleaming tiles, it was having its floor wiped by a small girl dressed in grubby whites. A massive figure in equally grubby whites crowned by a tall chef's hat was making notes on the back of an old envelope with a blunt pencil.

'Chef!' Ulla's voice made a brave bid for authority.

'Yes?' Ken Farthing raised his head, revealing a face that seemed once to have tangled with the business end of a lorry. Flattened nose and blunted chin, pock-marked skin and small eyes added up to a sight better not confronted on a dark night – or in a kitchen well equipped with razor-sharp knives and a couple of cleavers to hand. Darina eyed their proximity with unaccustomed nervousness. It wasn't, she decided, so much the way he looked as the way he managed to invest that one word with an indefinable air of menace, as the piggy eyes looked first at Ulla Mason and then at her.

Ulla glanced at the minion cleaning the floor, then back at the chef. 'I would like a word with you in the office.' Without waiting for a response, she led the way back to the room they had just left.

Good psychology, thought Darina, get him off his territory, not to mention away from those knives. She knew many a story of chefs running berserk in their kitchens; until now, she had disbelieved most of them.

Ulla sat herself behind the desk. Darina stood to one side, watching the huge figure advance through the door.

'Chef, I want a word about lunch.'

Astonishingly, a broad, beaming smile split the giant's battered face. 'You tasted it? Fantastic, wasn't it?'

'Well, actually, no. I have had several complaints.'

The smile faded a little then composure was recovered. 'Pah, most of these people know nothing about food. They can't appreciate my cooking.'

24

Ulla looked helplessly towards Darina. 'But Miss Lisle here does know about food and I'm afraid she didn't like it either.'

The big head swung round to confront this new threat. 'You didn't like my cooking?'

Diplomacy struggled with honesty. With Darina it wasn't much of a struggle. 'The flavours were appalling.'

Shoulders that a self-respecting ox could have been proud of were squared. 'Appalling!' The word could have been heard several counties away.

Darina gathered courage. Only blunt talking was any use in this situation. 'To use dried tarragon with the cream cheese was inept and the cheese itself was unsuitable for that dish, the avocado and mango needed dressing, the sauce for the fish was bitter and had the consistency of wallpaper paste and what you did to the pastry for the dessert I can't imagine. But the fish itself was beautifully cooked,' she added hastily.

The tiny eyes surveyed her incredulously, then the body swelled alarmingly. A huge fist was raised. Darina flinched but stood her ground, ready to ward off the threatened blow, then watched it come pounding down on the desk instead.

'You know nothing about food,' he roared. 'Nobody knows anything about food. I create dishes, new dishes. I don't do what everyone else does, my food is original. Just because I don't have the name, you all think it's no good. You don't deserve success,' he shouted at Ulla. She clutched at the arms of her chair but said nothing.

The chef continued to look threateningly at her. A silence grew in the office. First one to talk loses, thought Darina, watching the anger gradually leak out of the large figure. His forehead creased in a frown as Ulla steadily returned his gaze.

'If you don't like what I did today, maybe I can do something else tomorrow? There's the grouse with pomegranate, that's got to be a winner.' But his confidence had been shaken, there was an air of uncertainty about him now.

Ulla glanced at Darina, who gave a tiny shake of her head. Under strict supervision this chef manqué might just be able to produce edible haute cuisine. On his own only disaster loomed.

'I'm sorry,' the Hotel Morgan's proprietor said, 'I need a competent creative chef and today shows you are not suited.'

25

She reached behind her and pulled a wages book off a shelf. 'I give you two weeks' wages and you leave now.' She opened the book with a snap.

A huge hand pushed the chef's hat askew and scratched at his head. Ken Farthing seemed bewildered. 'I can't stay?'

Ulla looked up from her calculations. The balance of power in the room had shifted. 'It's best you go now. You must find another job. Get your things together and I will bring you your money.'

The chef gave her another glance but Darina could see he had accepted the inevitable and a moment later he left the room. She was a little surprised he had given up so easily. One moment he had seemed angry enough to have smitten either of them to the ground, crushed like carcasses for the stock pot, the next he was like a child pleading with authority to be allowed a second chance.

Ulla opened a small safe, extracted a cash box, filled the wages envelope, sealed it, replaced the box in the safe and relocked it. She looked at Darina. 'Come with me to the kitchen?'

The tall girl nodded and followed her back along the passage.

In the kitchen, the chef had removed his whites and was dressed in a thick sweater and jeans. He seemed smaller and not in the least threatening. Without the chef's hat his hair was thinning and greasy. He took the envelope Ulla offered and turned it over in his big hands then raised his gaze and looked straight at Darina. 'It was no good, the food, really no good?'

She hardened her heart. 'No. Stick to plain cooking, you seem able to handle that.'

'That's what they all say.'

Ulla held out her hand. 'Goodbye, Chef, good luck.'

He wiped his hands on the back of his jeans and shook hers. Ulla blinked as he pumped her arm up and down, then massaged her hand as soon as he had released it. She stood and watched as he thrust the envelope in his pocket, picked up a hold-all and disappeared out of the back door.

'That's that,' she said. 'I'm glad he gave no trouble. For a moment I thought he was going to attack us. Now what am I going to do? No chef and Christmas coming up. Who is going to cook the food?'

Chapter Three

Cold crisped the edges of the afternoon as William drove up to the layby. Sunlight slanted across the scene low and bright but long shadows warned of dusk's approach.

At the top of a steep hill a slip of shrubby land bordered a half-moon shaped parking area on the busy A37 that runs from Yeovil to Bristol. Behind the parking space was a thick hedge and then fields. A number of police vehicles were lined up on the main road, the parking area itself having been closed off with white tape, its blue flashes adding a note of seaside gaiety.

William parked his car behind the last of the vehicles. As he got out a constable approached.

'Sorry, sir, you can't park here . . . Oh, Sergeant Pigram, I didn't recognise you for a moment, you've changed your car.' He walked up to it and stood admiring the classic lines of the 1950s Bentley. 'What happened to the Chevvy?'

'Big end went. Spares are too much of a liability in this country.'

'Pity, that was a real road-eater, that one.'

'This has a fair turn of speed and it's very comfortable. Lovely to drive, you must have a go one of these days. Now, what have we here?'

They left the car, William giving a little pat to its bonnet, and went together towards the layby.

'Young woman found the body, sir, a couple of hours ago. She was giving her dog a run in that field.' He pointed to a sweep of tussocky green beyond a gate in the hedge. 'The dog wouldn't leave something in the ditch so she went to investigate. Got quite a shock. Then she went down to the house at the bottom of the hill,' he pointed down the road, 'and rang us. I had a look, then called in your lot.'

'Where is she now?'

'Detective Constable James took a statement, then she said the woman could continue her journey. She was travelling down to Devon.'

'Wasn't Inspector Grant here?'

'No, sir. He arrived later.'

'Of course, he had some appointment this morning. I wish the witness had been kept till he or I arrived.'

'Young lady was in a hurry sir.'

'I take it Constable James has an address for her? Good.'

They had reached the layby. 'Local doc's been and pronounced the victim dead,' volunteered the constable, marking down William's arrival on his clipboard. 'They're waiting for the pathologist now.'

Through the leafless hedge, William could see his inspector and Detective Constable James scrutinising the ditch. Following a taped route marked out along the thick grass bordering a more obvious path, William went to join them and got his first glimpse of the body.

It lay amongst twigs, roots and dead leaves. The whippy little branches at the bottom of the hedge had already rearranged themselves over the sprawled limbs. Automatically, William noted spring's buds swelling along the branches' slender length. Nature renewing itself, drawing life from the vegetation rotting round the roots.

'Looks as though Johnny Murderer dumped it there.' That was Grant. William's immediate superior was as dapper as ever, his trench coat immaculate, a flash of Argyle sock catching the eye as he bent forward to look more closely.

' "Johnny Murderer", sir? You're assuming it's a man?' The light voice belonged to Detective Constable James. William sighed inwardly. How lucky could she get, a murder on the first morning she joins the team and she gets to be first on the scene. If he hadn't arranged to take Darina to lunch, he'd have been in the office when the call came through. He would have been able to interview that woman while the discovery was fresh in her mind. Now by the time he managed to get down to Devon to speak to her, she'd have told the story to half the county, the details undergoing a slight sea change each time she repeated them.

Constable Pat James's neat brown head turned and saw William approaching. She gave him a little welcoming smile, calmly self-possessed in the presence of death. He remembered the revolt of his stomach on the scene of his first murder and fiercely resented that self-possession. Then he reminded himself he had no way of knowing whether this was in fact her first murder victim.

Pat James had been introduced that morning by Grant. She had stood just inside his small office, smiling in that same quiet way, dressed in a brown skirt and blouse with some sort of jerkin on top. She had advanced with outstretched hand before he had had time to rise from his desk and said, 'I'm delighted to be working with you. I have joined a first-class team and I hope I can fit in.' Her voice, classless with a touch of Somerset, had sounded totally confident and William found himself shaking her hand without enthusiasm as Grant said heartily, 'No doubt of that. I'm off for the morning so I'll leave you with Bill here to go over the current case list. He's got some arrangement at lunchtime but I hope to be back around then so you and I can slip across to the local for a bite to eat.'

They had spent the morning working through outstanding cases, Pat James slipping in the odd pertinent remark that demonstrated her ability to grasp significant detail and showed that very little escaped the attention of her mink brown eyes. These attributes failed to endear her to William.

'Sergeant Pigram, sir,' she said now.

'About time!' Grant turned and beckoned the younger man forward. 'What do you make of this?'

William advanced to the edge of the ditch and crouched down on his haunches, steeling himself for the inspection that had to be made; familiarity with death removed none of the flinching of his stomach and soul that came whenever he was brought face to face with the final enemy.

She could have been pretty before she met whatever fate had brought her to this place. A wealth of fair hair was tangled with dried leaves and twigs, the legs that splayed out from under a short, pert skirt, rucked up on one side, were long and shapely and ended in boots that could have been borrowed from Little Red Riding Hood. Her anorak was red too, red with white stripes. And red streaked the swollen face as though blood had run down inside her skin like rain down a windowpane. But her lips and ear – the head was turned to one side so that only the right was visible – were bluish purple, and there was pinpoint haemorrhaging in the wide open eyes.

William swallowed hard. He felt the need to make some remark. 'She's wearing stockings, not tights.'

'Do you feel that is significant?' The inspector's voice was dry.

The act of speaking had helped settle his stomach and bring back his wits. 'It's a fact, sir.'

'True, we shall keep it in mind.' Grant was at his most sardonic. 'Anything else occur to you, Bill?'

'She would seem to have been strangled, clear signs of cyanosis and the throat is badly bruised. And scratched. That could have happened whilst the victim tried to dislodge the strangler's hands. No overt signs of rape, the clothes aren't torn and I can't see any bruising on the thighs.' He paused. There was something else pushing at the boundaries of his consciousness but he couldn't quite grasp at what it was.

A quiet voice broke into the silence. 'I can't see a handbag.'

'Right, good point,' said Grant. 'She could, of course, be lying on it.'

So that was the incongruity. Few girls are seen without some sort of tote or handbag. It could easily have been thrown in the ditch underneath the victim but William wished he had articulated the missing factor before Pat James.

The detectives glanced about them as though expecting to find the bag hanging from a branch. Grant called over a uniformed officer and asked him to tell the searchers a handbag could be missing. Then he said, 'I wonder how long the body could lie here without being noticed. The layby is used quite frequently by lorry drivers and others. If that dog hadn't discovered the corpse, no doubt some driver taken short would have. There's been no real attempt at concealment. Look at all the rotting vegetation at the bottom of the ditch; it would have been quite easy to have more or less covered the girl.'

'Death probably occurred at night and it was as much as the murderer could do to find the ditch,' said William.

'Possibility they came in here for a bit of nooky and matters got out of hand?' suggested Grant.

'In the cold snap we've been having lately? I think it more likely the murder took place in a car or lorry. Perhaps the girl was a hitch-hiker and was assaulted by the driver – the fact that obvious signs of rape are absent doesn't mean one didn't take place.'

'So,' said Grant, 'we have a murder by strangulation. On the evidence of the victim's stockings, Sergeant Pigram considers she was raped then killed, probably in a vehicle parked in the area behind the hedge. The murderer then brought the body through that gate and dumped it in the ditch, got back in his vehicle and drove away. Is that your theory?'

William flushed. 'I did not mean to suggest that was the only scenario, sir.' He was glad Darina wasn't present. He could guess exactly what her opinion would be of men who considered stockings an open invitation to rape. He glanced at Constable James, half expecting her to make some comment, but she seemed too busy making entries in her notebook to stand up for a girl's right to choose her wardrobe without being stereotyped.

For a brief moment William's mind left the murdered girl and went back to lunch with Darina. He'd handled things badly there. He hadn't meant to propose, not yet, he knew it was too soon. But he could see her getting involved in a life that was not going to offer much room for him. So he'd plunged in and, in some way he didn't understand, he knew he'd disappointed her. He brought his mind back to the matter on hand.

'How heavy would you say the victim was, Constable James?' Grant was asking.

'Nine stone?'

'You agree with that, Bill?'

'She looks well built but not at all overweight; perhaps a little less.'

'A not inconsiderable weight to lug about in the dark. Do you think he had local knowledge?'

Pat James looked at William. He felt oddly pleased at this sign of deference.

'Not necessarily, sir. The layby is well marked, the gate would have shown up in the headlights as the vehicle drew in, a hedge is usually accompanied by a ditch and even if there wasn't one, there would still have been a certain amount of concealment for

31

the body. It could well have been a driver on his way through the county.'

'But not using the motorway?'

'He could have started from Bath or Bristol, or perhaps came from the centre of Gloucestershire and chose the more direct route intending to pick up the M5 at Taunton.'

'And you think the girl was a hitch-hiker?'

'Seems likely, sir. The dangers never seem to get through to these girls.'

'Or it could as easily have been a local driver out for an evening with a girlfriend. He takes advantage of a convenient place to stop for a few words, then gets into a quarrel that grows out of control.'

'We may know more when we find out who she is. I hope her handbag is somewhere near or that someone misses her soon. We need to start tracking her movements quickly.'

'As you say, sergeant.' Grant's voice was dry. 'Ah, make way for the SOCO boys.'

The three detectives stood back from the ditch as the scene of crime officers began to video the dead girl and commence their forensic examination of the body and its vicinity.

The scene filled with more and more officers. As the last of the daylight slipped away, the area round the body was lit with arc lamps and a plastic tent offered protection from the rain that began to lash down – protection intended for the corpse and its secrets rather than the painstaking searchers after evidence.

The Home Office pathologist arrived and conducted the second medical inspection of the body.

Finally the dead girl was removed from the ditch, zipped into a bag and sent to the mortuary to await the autopsy.

'Anything you can tell me?' asked Grant as the pathologist blew on his hands to warm them.

'As you no doubt saw for yourselves, she was strangled. Both hands were used and considerable force. Unlikely, I would say, to have been a woman but not impossible. With this cold it's difficult to say how long she's been dead, but I would estimate at least twenty-four hours and probably not more than thirty-six. Intercourse would seem to have taken place shortly before death.'

The listening police officers drew in a collective breath.

'Was it forced?' asked Grant.

'Rape, you mean? Unlikely. There are no signs intercourse was opposed. At this stage I can't confirm penetration occurred but there are semen stains on the upper thighs and the victim is not wearing panties.'

'Aaah,' Grant let out a sigh. 'Now that does seem significant.' He watched as the body was removed from the scene, then turned to the forensic team once more at work in the ditch. 'Any sign of a handbag or panties?'

'No, sir, there doesn't seem to be anything here other than old paper bags and the usual odd bits of rubbish.'

'So now we've got two items to look for, the handbag and a pair of pants. Assuming, of course, that she wore them.'

'In this cold, sir, with that short skirt and stockings? She'd freeze without them.' Pat James was emphatic.

Chapter Four

Ulla Mason took Darina on a tour of the hotel.

'One of the things that attracted Tony was the layout of the ground floor. A nice large reception hall with the dining room off one way and this lounge and the library leading off the other.' She led the way into a sizeable room on the opposite side of the hall from the dining room. The last rays of the winter sun highlighted the same style of shabby armchair that furnished the hall; small, cheaply veneered tables were stained with the marks of glass rings and hot teapots. A fire smouldered in a grate swamped by its handsome marble surround and a couple of huge, old-fashioned radiators burbled and gurgled a song of warmth without the room achieving an acceptable temperature. A couple of attractive dried flower arrangements set on pedestals stood on either side of the fireplace but the only other decorative feature was a series of small flower pictures that tried and failed to break up the expanse of faded flock wallpaper.

Darina looked at the ancient squabs lining the deep window seats and thought their tattered old gold damask an odd contrast to the bright blue and orange small floral print on the skimpy curtains that hung incongruously at the sides of the square bay windows.

'Tony had such plans for this room. It looks dreadful now, of course, you can see that, but he said it had such potential. It was to be our next project after the dining room. The previous owner hung those curtains, they are at least fairly new.'

'What sort of place was it before you and your husband acquired it?'

'A residential hotel. Full of old people. Well, not full, that was part of the trouble. The Morgans bought it a few years ago, it was on its last legs as a guest house. They thought they were going to do tremendous business providing a home for retired folk. I think they just about had enough residents to make it a going concern when Mrs Morgan ran off with the local vet. Morgan couldn't manage on his own and couldn't afford to hire experienced staff so put the place up for sale.'

'What did you do with the residents?' Darina followed Mrs Mason out of the lounge and across a wide corridor into the library. Only a couple of bookshelved alcoves qualified it for its title. Once again a handsome marble fireplace housed a small fire, its output supplementing the efforts of the radiators to warm the overlarge room. A huge bay window offered a backdrop to another dried flower arrangement, its effect considerably lessened by the same floral curtains as had graced the lounge. The rest of the furnishings consisted of a double rank of more wooden-armed chairs arranged round a large television set.

Ulla Mason went and removed a newly added log from the fire and gave the remaining fuel a good poke. 'I've spoken to you before about adding unnecessary wood to the fire, Mr Prendergast,' she said, giving an irritated flick with the hearth brush to the tiled fire surround, now ash-strewn.

At a desk at one side of the room, conveniently placed next to the radiator, sat the podgy man Darina had noticed at lunch. The desk was arranged with neat piles of papers and a small portable typewriter. On the floor stood an open briefcase. Mr Prendergast rose and came across to the fire. 'Let me, Mrs Mason.' In a trice he had removed the brush from her grasp and finished the job. 'I do apologise, it just seemed such a cold day.'

'You look as though you're working hard,' said Darina as Ulla failed to respond to the man's friendliness.

'Just trying to get some old papers into a semblance of order. It has been suggested I might try my hand at writing a book, an account of my days at the Foreign Office, you know.'

'Aren't you bound by the Secret Act, or whatever it's called?'

'My book would be nothing anyone could object to, I assure you, unlike some others. Not many seem to pay much attention to loyalty, discretion and other old-fashioned virtues these days. I have known so many interesting politicians, watched world events from the sidelines, as you might say. And now it appears a publisher feels others could be interested in my little experiences.'

'How interesting,' murmured Darina. 'Did you enjoy your lunch?'

He looked at her more closely. 'Of course, you were lunching too, with that tall young man. I thought to myself what a well-matched couple, such an attractive young lady and such a handsome escort. I hope I do not presume?' Darina muttered something about good friends. 'And I do hope your lunch was as good as mine. Your new chef,' he turned to the hotel proprietor, 'excelled himself today. The shepherd's pie brought back memories of the one my dear mother's housekeeper always provided on a Monday. Such a nice follow-up to that splendid roast we had yesterday. I look forward to my meals with increasing pleasure these days.'

'I am afraid I have to tell you that Chef left this afternoon.' There was unmistakable relish in the way Ulla Mason produced this news.

'Oh?' Mr Prendergast stood waiting but no further information was forthcoming. He gave a small inclination of his balding head and went back to his chair, switching on an ancient desk light as he resumed his seat. The bulb promptly flickered and died. Mr Prendergast gave an exclamation of annoyance.

'I'll get Alex to find a replacement,' said Ulla and whisked out of the room, followed by Darina. Back in the hall she shouted but no one came. After waiting a couple of minutes, tapping an impatient toe, she opened a door in the panelling under an alcove furnished with a cracked willow-pattern plate, found a box of lightbulbs, removed one and led the way back into the library. Here they found the desk lamp once again alight.

'I borrowed the bulb from the standard lamp,' Mr Prendergast murmured apologetically. 'I thought it might take Alex a little time to turn his attention to this insignificant task.'

In silence Ulla placed her new bulb into the plundered light socket, then switched it on, leaving the parchment shade directing a pool of light on to the TV set at the far end of the room.

Outside the library once more, she turned to the left and led Darina up a pretty staircase that swept down from the floor above. Its effect was somewhat marred by a lift that had been inserted in its curve.

'Morgan installed that. He said he thought it was necessary for his clientele. Tony intended to remove it but it really is useful for the baggage.'

'If it was one of those lovely open ironwork lifts, it would look decorative as well,' commented Darina, following her guide up the stairs.

'I can't imagine what they would cost.' Ulla paused by a long window. 'This is quite nice stained glass, the sun shows it up best in the morning.'

Darina had been waiting for some word of explanation on the barely concealed animosity shown towards the podgy guest. With none forthcoming, she had to ask, 'Who is Mr Prendergast?'

'George Prendergast is the last of those residents you asked about earlier. We had no trouble with most of them. As soon as we put the rates up, they made other arrangements. George Prendergast just smiled in that infuriating way he has and paid up. I can't think why he wants to stay and he's nothing but a nuisance. His pension rates even now barely cover the expense and trouble of feeding him, he's always cluttering up the library with his papers, or the lounge with his tapestry. We got quite busy this summer and Tony persuaded him to move over to the stable block. We thought winter would persuade him to move on; the heating there is night storage and by the end of the day it's quite inadequate. But, no, he either has an electric stove producing the most unhealthy fug at our expense or he's over here.'

If Mr Prendergast found the temperature in the main hotel more comfortable than his stable room, that must indeed be inadequate.

Ulla marched into the first bedroom at the top of the stairs. 'This should be our best room. As you can see, it needs a real doing over.'

It was handsomely-sized with a bay window looking out over the front. A bathroom had been inserted into one corner, making the room a somewhat awkward L shape. The same bright blue and orange floral curtains hung at the windows; the furniture was heavy and old fashioned without achieving antique status. The bathroom had a wealth of institutional white tiles and looked as though it

37

had been done several years ago on the cheap. The other rooms on the first floor were much the same. But out of all the windows were views of the rolling green Somerset countryside, a pastoral paradise of peaceful fields, hedges and trees. There was a stream bordered by willows and the horizon was ringed by gentle hills. The small village that lay close by managed to tuck most of itself out of sight and it was hard to realise a busy main road was not far away.

On the second floor were attractive sloping ceilings and dormer windows with the same entrancing views. These rooms had all been painted white, in nice contrast to the faded regency stripes and flock wallpapers of the larger rooms on the floor below. And instead of the floral curtaining there was linen in singing shades, tied back with toning ropes and tassels. The bathrooms, equipped with superior modern plumbing, had been cunningly fitted into odd spaces and small rooms, leaving the bedrooms nicely proportioned.

'These rooms were a real warren and hadn't been used for years. They were our first project after fixing the roof. We needed the extra space; you can't run a viable hotel of the sort we planned with only ten rooms. Now there are seventeen, plus a couple in the stable block if we are really pushed. At the moment it looks unlikely they will be needed until next summer. But the way business is going I doubt if we'll still be here then.'

'Do you handle receptions, conferences, that sort of thing?' Darina's mind was busily exploring the possibilities offered by the Hotel Morgan.

'Tony had lots of plans for that side. There's a large hall dating from Elizabethan times on the dining room side of the hotel. They think it was part of a small abbey originally, and the house was built on to it, starting after the time when all the religious houses were split up – isn't there a name for it?'

'The Dissolution?'

'Yes, that's it. I find your English history very confusing. Well, the house was added and added to at different times. The present front is mainly Victorian but the back, where you no doubt noticed that the rooms are so much smaller, is apparently much earlier. Anyway, the old hall could be wonderful; it could hold two or three hundred people for a wedding reception or could be used for a large dinner dance. So many possibilities, but it will cost such a lot before we can use it. There's no heating and the roof is unsafe.'

They had worked their way back down a narrow staircase leading from the second floor to the regions behind the reception hall. Ulla flung open a few store room doors, describing how her husband had planned for a laundry, ironing room, china and glass store and other facilities. Then she looked at her watch.

'It's time we had a cup of tea and I had better have a word with Tracey about dinner tonight.'

They went into the sparkling kitchen. Now that Darina had seen the rest of the hotel, she could understand what a transformation had been achieved here. All the equipment was of the most modern, the layout was carefully planned, the walls and floor were both tiled for maximum ease of hygiene. Ulla showed Darina the cold store, the dry goods store, the large, walk-in refrigerator. The basic stores were at a low level, though the amount of fresh food seemed extraordinarily high, given the apparent lack of restaurant clientele.

'Where's that girl?' Ulla went into a small room equipped for pastry-making that led off the main kitchen, then into another room furnished with a plain table and chairs plus a padlocked wine store. There was no Tracey.

They returned to the kitchen. On one of the far walls was a blackboard bearing the message, 'Dinner, Monday, 4 covers'. Underneath was scribbled, 'Tracey off'.

'Oh, my God,' said Ulla. 'I had completely forgotten. Why didn't she say something? She was here when Chef left. If only we didn't need staff – they never think for themselves.' She giggled suddenly. 'Tony had a friend who always said running a hotel would be wonderful if it wasn't for the staff and the guests.' Then she grew sober again. 'A couple called Chamberlain have booked in for tonight to see if they want to stay over Christmas and they have invited two local friends to join them for dinner. It's so important it goes well. If the Chamberlains come, we could make a reasonable profit over the holiday season. It's always the last few bookings that are the icing on the cake.'

'What are your advance bookings like?'

'Let's have a cup of tea and I'll tell you about the business.'

39

Ulla filled a teapot, put it on a tray with two cups of the Villeroy and Bosch china the hotel used and led the way back into the office.

Alex was once again behind the desk, still in sweatshirt and jeans, pouring over a travel brochure.

Ulla banged down the tray, causing hot liquid to spurt out of the teapot over some letters on the desk. The blond man snatched them up angrily, using his sleeve to wipe them clean.

'Why can't you watch what you're doing? These confirmations will have to be retyped now; that can be your job.'

Ulla's mood underwent a dramatic change. 'Confirmations? You mean we have more bookings? Why didn't you say?'

'Hang about.' He held the letters out of her reach. 'Let them dry first. They're only for the odd night in January.'

Her face fell. 'January? But we were going to close then.'

'Can we afford to? I thought originally it was because more work was going to be done. You know that's off now. I assumed that you'd want any business going. Unless, that is,' his voice changed, 'you've decided to sell, after all. Have you?'

'I have *not* decided to sell, as you well know. Alex, why aren't you seeing to the bar? And it's time to do something to the hall fire. You know the Chamberlains are arriving soon. If it isn't welcoming, we have no hope of their spending Christmas here.'

'Where else are they going to go? How many other hotels still have vacancies three weeks before the season of glad tidings bursts upon us like a wet paper bag?' But he slowly unwound his length from the chair and ambled to the door. 'Don't worry, they'll book all right.' There was an unexpected softening to his tone.

Ulla gazed after his disappearing back. 'Oh, I could strangle that Alex.' She lay back in her chair and closed her eyes. 'I'm so tired, sometimes I think the best thing might be to sell the hotel, after all.'

Darina said nothing.

A moment later Ulla galvanised herself into life, started pouring tea and said, 'But I won't! This hotel was Tony's dream, I can't abandon it. And, anyway, what would I do, where would I go? By the time all the debts are paid off, there won't be much money left, whatever Alex thinks.'

40

Over the tea Darina gradually put together the story of Ulla Mason and the Hotel Morgan.

She had met Tony Mason, Alex's father, whilst running a flower shop in the big London hotel he was managing. His wife had recently died of cancer. 'My fiancé had also died the same way, it made a bond between us. I came over from Norway first as an au pair, then I wanted to stay and train as a florist. My family thought I would return and run a shop in Oslo but I knew I would never go back. The winters are so dark and so long. It is very beautiful but the people are not like here, they don't take life easy and I like to be gay, to enjoy myself. Michael, my fiancé, was such fun, everything was a joke to him, even his death.' Ulla gazed at the electric fire for a moment. 'Tony was something the same. He was sad when we first met because Trudy his wife had died. We understood one another's sadness and we knew that, one day, we would laugh together.'

Ulla smiled at Darina, the fine lines at the corners of her eyes crinkling, the light blue eyes suddenly dancing with delight. 'Oh, he was such fun, I wish you could have met him. Always a joke, always wanting to make life happier for everyone. That's why he was so good at hotels. Everyone liked to come and stay with him, they were all friends.'

For a few years after Ulla and Tony Mason married, he had continued to manage the London hotel where they met. Ulla had started a small business providing dried flower arrangements for London hotels and offices. 'Then Tony said if we didn't try to get our own hotel, we would miss out, we would be too old. So we sold our Kensington flat and my business and bought this. But I think it was already too late.' The gaiety faded out of her face again.

Reading between the words as Ulla described their struggle to update the archaic hotel they'd acquired, Darina decided Tony's fatal heart attack had been brought on by stress and overwork.

'Why didn't you find a place that didn't need so much doing to it?'

'We couldn't have afforded it,' said Ulla simply. 'As it is, we now have a huge mortgage and a bank overdraft. In January we should be repointing the outside, installing a new central heating system and doing the first-floor bedrooms, Tony had all the plans drawn up, but the bank won't lend me any more money. They say that the building value has declined and with Tony gone it's not a good investment. And I know the bookings have gone off, it's not just the time of the year. I don't have his knack for marketing, I don't know where to go from here. And if it weren't for Alex, I wouldn't be able to manage to hold on at all.'

Alex, who apparently wanted Ulla to sell the hotel. Why work in it in that case?

'When Tony died he'd just returned from travelling round America and he said he'd help me to sort everything out. I didn't realise to start with that he meant so I could sell up. But I won't sell up. I won't!' Ulla beat on the arms of her chair, her hands in little fists, knuckles whitened.

'So you're looking for a partner?' Darina spoke slowly, her mind racing.

'Yes, it seems the answer to everything. Someone who can bring some capital in, help to run the hotel, with ideas and preferably experience.' Ulla's eager voice slowed over the last words.

'I have no hotel experience at all.'

'But you know food. William said you are a great cook and have run a catering company.'

'Yes and worked in a restaurant. That side of things I know quite well. But hotel marketing and organisation is, I'm afraid, something I know I'm going to have to learn.'

'Couldn't we learn that together? If we had more capital, I'm sure we could finish turning this place into a wonderful hotel. I'll show you Tony's plans.'

'I can see the potential,' Darina said half an hour later. 'And it's got a lot of the attributes I was looking for in a hotel. Good country location, good communications nearby. Lots of potential space for expansion. Bigger than I was thinking of but that was on the basis I was on my own.'

'I'm sure we could work well together.' Ulla was perched on the edge of the desk, now covered with plans for bedroom renovations, the rebuilding of the stable block and the restoration of the old hall.

Darina thought that they probably could. In the hours they'd spent together since lunch, she had warmed towards the volatile Scandinavian. Ulla was very different from herself, she veered between excitement and despair. But she was dedicated to the hotel, had ideas, a sense of style and wanted someone to help take decisions. Darina thought they would agree on most major matters.

'Look,' she said finally, 'I can't commit myself at this stage. I haven't sold my Chelsea house and until then I have no money to invest. What I will do, if it sounds sensible to you, is come and work here for a couple of months and see how things go.'

'Oh, that's wonderful.' Ulla leant forward, her eyes shining.

'Just a minute. There would be certain conditions. The first is that I do not do the cooking. I am trying to get away from constantly producing food, I want to broaden my experience and I'm certainly not going to learn whether I can manage a hotel if I'm confined to the kitchen. I will, if you are really stuck, produce this evening's meal but tomorrow we find another chef. The other condition is that I get paid. It needn't be very much, say a receptionist's wage. This place needs more staff and if the business can't afford an extra person, there is no point in it continuing.'

'I have had no wage for months,' said Ulla. 'I don't know when I last bought something new to wear.' She looked at Darina's chic suit.

The tall girl glanced guiltily down at the soft, expensive material. She had been slightly shocked at how much she had enjoyed spending some of the money she had inherited, buying clothes that had been beyond her purse before. Now she felt like a chicken masquerading in a pheasant's finery.

'I'm used to making do with little money,' she said quickly. 'And if I come in as a partner, I would not be expecting quick returns. But if I didn't think the hotel could be made to pay eventually, I wouldn't consider investing in it.'

Ulla acknowledged that was fair. 'Would you want to live in?' she asked. 'You could have a room in the stable block?'

Darina thought for a moment. 'I'm staying with my mother at the moment. She doesn't live far away but, yes, I think it would be better.' Then she remembered. 'My mother – she's expecting me back for dinner. Not only that, I agreed to cook it. I'd better give her a ring.'

Ulla dragged forward the telephone. 'Ring now, tell her to forget about you for the next two months!'

43

Chapter Five

'Going to work in an hotel? Now? Before Christmas? Indeed, if I have heard correctly, all over Christmas? I can't believe you can be so selfish!'

Darina winced.

'You know we had such plans. You never think of me, it's always your career. What am I going to do, left here all on my own?'

The picture of the Hon. Ann Lisle as a lonely widow bereft of all company and consolation over the festive season was not one that stood up under close examination. A large circle of friends was available for drinks parties, little bridge suppers, outings and other diversions. And invitations by the dozen cluttered the mantelpiece. No, what Mrs Lisle was going to miss was her daughter's ability to produce mouth-watering morsels to feed her army of acquaintances.

The small figure twitched fretfully at her lace bedjacket, then smoothed the satin cover of her bed, her eyes refusing to look at her daughter. Instead their gaze roamed over the bedroom, furnished with treasured antiques, trimmed with porcelain and glazed chintz. Abandoned on the bedcover was the bestseller she had been reading when Darina had finally arrived home and broken the news of her new venture.

The restless gaze came to a stop on a still life above a small bow-fronted chest. The sulky face, greasily enriched with night cream, underwent a rapid transformation.

'I have the most wonderful idea,' Darina's mother leaned forward confidentially. 'Didn't you say this hotel is having some sort of house party over Christmas?'

'A Christmas Holiday is what it's been billed as.'

'Well, I shall join it.' Ann Lisle lay back on the pillow in triumph.

Her daughter gazed at her in consternation. 'Mother, you'll hate it.'

'Why? Will the other guests coming hate it?'

'No. Well, we hope not. But it's not your sort of thing. I have no idea who they are but I shall be very surprised if they are the kind of people you will enjoy meeting.'

'What an extraordinary remark. You know I enjoy meeting everyone.'

It was true that Mrs Lisle was never at a loss for conversation, whoever she met.

Darina thought about the Chamberlains who had arrived that night for an experimental stay. Sober, middle-class citizens with tight mouths. Would they be typical of the other guests who had booked for Christmas?

'And aren't you going to provide entertainment of some sort?'

'Of course. Carol singers, dancing, games,' Darina improvised wildly. The brochure advertising the holiday had spoken of 'An Old-Fashioned Christmas in an old-fashioned hotel furnished with every modern convenience' but what it all added up to she had no real idea. She would have to discuss that with Ulla tomorrow.

'It sounds wonderful. And such fun to see my clever daughter in action.'

'Mother, it's not a five-star hotel, not even three star. I don't think you'll find it very comfortable.'

'Do the bedrooms have private bathrooms? And presumably it's got central heating.' It wasn't even a question.

Darina seized the slim chance. 'Most inefficient, the temperature hardly rises above freezing.'

'Sheer exaggeration, darling, it has to be. But you are right to warn me, I shall take plenty of warm clothes. You have got room, haven't you?'

Darina toyed briefly with the possibility of claiming the hotel was booked out. One phone call tomorrow morning would explode the myth. And call she certainly would. Darina knew her mother. Once her mind was set on something, nothing must be allowed to stand in the way of its achievement.

Now a refinement to her initial idea had presented itself.

45

'I shall call Gerry Stocks in the morning and see if he would like to accompany me.'

There was little possibility he would refuse. A widower of some nine months' standing, General Sir Gerald Stocks had appointed himself chief escort to Ann Lisle and the man to turn to in any crisis; a failed butcher's delivery, a plug to be rewired, a fourth for bridge, in all such situations the General could be relied upon to turn potential disaster into a victory for the unruffled life. He could even possibly prove an asset at a Christmas hotel party. He would at any rate provide a buffer between her mother and the more disastrous of the other guests. It was an idea Darina could approve of and she said so.

'That's all settled then. There, I am quite looking forward to Christmas again. Lots of new people to meet, lovely food to eat, it's going to be such an exciting experience.' She smiled happily at her daughter.

Darina bent and lightly kissed the cheek still sticky with night cream. 'It will be great fun to have you there, Mother.' One learned that these little white lies cost nothing and smoothed the path of your relationship with a mother who had little understanding of her daughter's life.

The daughter went to bed concluding that the addition of Mrs Lisle to the proposed Christmas party might, in fact, be no bad thing. And it would anyway save the said daughter feeling guilty about not cooking her mother's Christmas turkey. She then fell to wondering where she could find a new chef for the Hotel Morgan. She was determined not to end up doing the cooking herself, though that night's meal had not presented great problems.

The departed chef, Ken Farthing, had planned to offer a choice of three different starters, six main courses and five desserts. Darina studied his projected menu with dismay. Apart from the stomach-turning thought of what Ken's creative approach would have produced for dishes such as salmon goujons with orange and kiwi fruit, red mullet with a vermouth sabayon sauce, roast guinea fowl with madeira and chicken livers, tornedos on lentils with smoked bacon, an exotic sorbet with fruits or a parfait of two chocolates with raspberry coulis, the expense of the ingredients and their diversity and quantity when all the hotel was expecting to feed was a table for four promised a quick route to bankruptcy.

'Ken said we would build up custom and word would never spread if we didn't offer a choice and we should be prepared for last-minute arrivals,' explained Ulla when Darina tackled her. 'And of course there's always George Prendergast to be fed.'

'But I understand he isn't offered the menu. What does he usually get?'

'Anything that's cheap and convenient. Ken called it pub food. But George certainly seems to have been enjoying it, which wasn't what we intended at all, he's such a nuisance!'

Investigating the stores once more, Darina decided a pork chop must have been meant for the unloved Mr Prendergast. There was also a bowl of surprisingly good stock and some bunches of fresh watercress.

Darina gave the permanent resident potato and watercress soup, pork chop cooked with apple and cider, and pancakes with orange. For the Chamberlains she offered a choice of the soup (with added cream) or escalope of salmon with hazelnut oil and coriander accompanied by a salade frisée; for the main course she offered guinea fowl with madeira and mushrooms, grilled mullet or a straight tornedos with braised shallots (she discounted the lentils as both passé haute cuisine and unlikely to attract the Hotel Morgan's present clientele); and for desert crepes with mango ice cream (there was a superb ice cream machine amongst the kitchen's equipment) or exotic fruit salad. Both Prendergast and the Chamberlains got the same vegetables: small potatoes rosti and a plate of baby legumes cooked to tenderness. Whatever she felt about vegetables being at their best slightly crisp, Darina knew from her catering experience that a country clientele generally preferred them cooked a little longer.

During brief intervals between cooking and plating the meal, Darina noted the stores of fresh ingredients and made plans for their best use over the next few days. Half the meat she carefully wrapped in foil and deep froze. There was no point in it going off before paying guests were available for its consumption and a few days or so in the freezer would not make an appreciable difference to these consumers.

'The Chamberlains are so happy,' said a delighted Ulla as

Darina reported to her after the kitchen had been cleared up. 'They told me it was their most enjoyable meal for months. And they said the room was comfortable. I think we can count on them for Christmas. Such a relief.'

She put down the pen she had been using to sign letters and stretched, yawning. She looked tired.

'Are you off home now?'

'Ah,' said Darina, 'I'm afraid I don't have a car. William drove me here for lunch. When he was called away, he mentioned Alex might be able to give me a lift back. But perhaps I could call for a taxi?'

'Nonsense, Alex will be delighted. He hasn't done much else this evening except talk to that Olivia.'

'The girl who was so cross with him this afternoon?'

Ulla did not look amused. 'How she can run after him like that, I do not understand. She walks in after dinner, dressed like a brass monkey' – Scandanavian scrambling had been at work there but Darina failed to identify the starting point – 'and says as he is obviously overworked, she has come to cheer him up. Then proceeds to monopolise him. The Chamberlains had to ask three times for their brandy. They were not amused, I can tell you. It's not even as though he is really interested in her. And I don't expect she will pay for the champagne she ordered.' Ulla was now angry as well as tired. 'I will go and tell him he has to take you home now.'

Ulla Mason left the office and Darina followed. In the main hall the Chamberlains and their guests were gathered round a fire that was now burning brightly. Darina wondered if it had been Mr Chamberlain who had heaped on the logs; he looked the sort of man likely to take matters into his own hands if things were not as he liked them.

Alex and Olivia were in the bar opposite the dining room. The girl sat on one of the bar stools, her legs crossed, the short skirt showing a length of shapely thigh. The skirt belonged to an extremely smart russet dress, the colour complementing the tumbling glory of her hair. But the fingernails on the hand holding a champagne flute were badly chewed and the discontented drag to her mouth was back as Ulla issued her diktat.

'What do you mean, you have to drive the cook home?

Surely he or she ought to find their own way? First you stand me up, then you can't be bothered to talk to me for more than five minutes.'

'Olivia, you have been here two hours, I have done nothing but talk to you and it is now time for you to go home.'

Darina noticed Ulla had placed herself between the girl and the object of her affections and now gave a smile of grim satisfaction.

Alex seemed in no way discomposed, either by the chauffeuring request or Olivia's petulance. He smiled with easy charm at Darina. 'Ready to go? Right, we'll be off then. Won't be long, Ulla.'

He ushered her out of the room quickly and smoothly, through the front door and into a somewhat battered Volvo station wagon.

'Do I gather you are coming to Ulla's rescue?' he asked as he put the car into gear.

'Not quite that. It depends what I think the prospects are and if I can sell my Chelsea house. Do I gather you would rather she sold up than try to carry on?'

'I? I have nothing to say in the matter. It is purely up to Ulla.'

'I rather got the impression you were a partner in the business.'

'Only in so far as I get half the proceeds if she sells and half any profits if she doesn't. As profits seem as far away as Antarctica, I would rather she sold.'

'But if the hotel could produce good profits?'

'Pie in the sky, my dear Miss Lisle. Ulla has no experience of hotel work beyond what she has learned at the Hotel Morgan. The place is saddled with debts, there is no money to do what you must have seen are urgently needed renovations and a marketing genius is required to bring in the necessary clientele to make it pay.'

'Yet I gathered you had a good summer?'

'A few swallows only. And that was when my father was alive. He was a brilliant hotelier, he knew exactly where he was going, the bank had confidence in him. I had confidence in him. You must realise I have been more or less brought up in hotels, I know something about how they should be run. Ulla has no talent for it at all. She thinks if you put some pretty flower arrangements around, talk nicely to the guests and staff, everything will happen.'

'And how much help have you been? How much of your vast experience have you made available?'

'I said I knew how hotels were run, I did not say I was a hotelier. As a manager I would be even more of a disaster than Ulla; I would alienate the clients and drive the staff to distraction. It's as much as I can do to be civil to them half the time.'

'Have you tried to give Ulla advice?'

'Look,' Alex drew into a convenient layby, switched off the ignition and turned to face Darina. 'If you are going to be around for any time you had better know the score. Ulla is my stepmother. I can't stand her. I've hung around after my father's death to protect my interest in the place and because I have nowhere else to go at the moment. My main concern is to see it sold for the best price possible.'

'But wouldn't the best price come if the hotel is well run? Are you perhaps afraid she might manage to keep the hotel running despite your dire predictions?'

'Ulla might just manage to keep a brothel running, never a hotel, not even a third-class one.'

Darina was silenced by his animosity.

Alex restarted the car. 'Don't misunderstand me, I've nothing against you. I'm merely issuing a warning against throwing your money down the drain.'

'You don't think I can succeed where Ulla is failing?'

'To be frank, no. You have no more experience than she. Certainly you can cook, the meal this evening was brilliant, but much more is required from a hotelier than knowing about food.'

'It could be said to be a start, though?'

The car drew up in front of Darina's old family home, a pretty Georgian house on the outskirts of a small village. The porch light was on and shone into the interior of the car, illuminating Alex's face.

He looked at her for a moment, then gave her a smile free of all animosity. 'It certainly could be said that without it you wouldn't stand any chance. I can understand how you have managed to captivate Pigram, you are something rather special. How is it I haven't met you around here before? I thought I knew all the attractive local girls?'

50

I bet you do, thought Darina. 'I live in London. I haven't spent much time down here in the last few years.'

'I could almost hope you do decide to work with Ulla.'

He got out of the car, opened her door and watched whilst she found her house key.

'Thank you for the lift. Can I offer you a drink, coffee perhaps?'

'An enticing invitation but I had better be getting back. It's my turn to lock up tonight.'

He vanished down the drive leaving Darina to open the front door deep in thought, then realise, with a slight shock, how late it was. The Hotel Morgan was a good half hour's drive away and it would be well after midnight by the time Alex got back.

She went upstairs to face her mother and apologise for her non-appearance that evening.

Chapter Six

It was early morning by the time the police team reassembled at the mortuary. The smell of formalin underlain with some other even less pleasant smell permeated the post mortem room. On a metal table lay the body of the girl with long blonde hair and shapely legs.

Every item of clothing had been removed piece by piece, the body photographed at each stage. Scrapings from under the nails had been taken and marked for later examination. The body itself had been minutely examined and swabs taken from internal areas. It had been washed and cleaned and now lay naked under the pitiless lights.

Even under these conditions, the dead girl exuded a certain sexuality. The wealth of richly blonde hair had been tidied out of the way into a green mob cap, but the breasts were high, full and firm above a trim waist and gently rounded stomach. The lower body with its excellent legs displayed sweetly swelling hips and tight little buttocks. The poor swollen face topping this ripe maidenhood was an aberration the three policemen watching the pathologist and his assistant preferred not to consider.

Except they were there to consider everything. To listen to the running commentary by the pathologist as he went through the detailed routine of his task, each word being recorded as he spoke.

'Right, lads – and lady, I forgot you now had a female member of staff, Dick.' The pathologist turned to the inspector, relaxing his attention from his work for an instant.

Grant grunted. Beside him, Pat James raised a faint smile on her pale face. It was the early hours of the morning and they had been working non stop except for a brief break over hot tea in the mortuary office before the autopsy started.

'We're nearly there, merely the internal examination to go now. What you might call the fun bit.' The pathologist had a somewhat ghoulish sense of humour.

William stood quite still. He had attended a number of autopsies but familiarity hadn't dulled the sharp anxiety he felt each time the knife hung momentarily poised while the surgeon assessed the line it would take from neck to pubis. The fact that he had never yet fainted or brought up the contents of his stomach as those of the corpse were revealed, never reassured him it would not happen this time. He envied the self-possession of Detective Constable Pat James, the neat brown head still beautifully poised above relaxed shoulders.

Inspector Grant shifted impatiently from one foot to another. 'Are you deciding what you're going to have for breakfast or going through your ABC of cuts? Can you not get on with it?'

'A little testy, aren't we? You can't hurry these things, the sensitivity of an artist is required here as well as the techniques of a surgeon.'

With an inward sigh, William saw the knife make a swift and sure slice straight down the body.

There was a little groan and Pat James slipped quietly to the floor.

Grant gave a tetchy click of his tongue. 'Help her out, Bill.'

William stooped, put one of the unconscious girl's unresisting arms around his shoulders and hauled the collapsed officer to her feet. She was so small compared with his six foot three inches, that he was forced to bend awkwardly. It seemed easiest to scoop her up bodily and carry her out to the anteroom, where he placed her on a chair.

Pat James groaned slightly and opened her eyes, her eyelids fluttering nervously, her gaze slipping round William to search beyond him.

'It's all right, you're not in the PM room.' He fetched a glass of water and held it for her to drink. 'Feeling any better?'

'Oh what a fool you must think me! It's just that I've never seen a body cut like that before.'

'But you seemed so self-possessed, and you never flinched when we were looking at her in the ditch.'

'That was different. Here, that knife, the way it cut into

her . . . ' she swallowed hastily and then sipped more water, taking the glass into her own hand.

William stood watching her for a moment. Her extreme pallor was gradually becoming suffused with a warmer colour. She closed her eyes and held her head back, breathing deeply and slowly. She looked very small and rather vulnerable.

Her eyes opened again. 'Thank you, I'm much better now.'

'Would you like to go back to the office?'

'No, I think I would like to try again. It can't be much worse.'

'It can, you know. He has to . . . well, he has to remove certain portions of her insides.' William could not bring himself to be any more graphic.

'I think I can take it now.'

Dubiously he followed her back into the post mortem room, where the mortuary attendant had lined up near the sink the contents of the chest and abdominal cavities.

The pathologist had already commenced his examination. 'Well, well, now here we have something,' he said, turning his head to look at Grant and interrupting his clinical recitation. 'She was pregnant, at first glance about three months.'

Pat James clamped her hand to her mouth and stumbled out.

'For God's sake, Bill!' Grant exclaimed exasperatedly. 'Keep her out of here. Go back to the office and start planning the house-to-house and other enquiries. The Chief Inspector should have organised a team to carry them out and we may as well be ready to set it all in motion at the start of the business day. And check Missing Persons as soon as they open, we need to put a name to, to . . . ' he gestured towards the gaping body.

Torn between relief and reluctance, William left the pathologist to the remainder of his task. Whilst he waited for Constable James to emerge from the ladies, his mind hummed with possible implications of the fact so recently revealed. Suddenly the hitch-hiker theory had lost some of its attractions. The sooner enquiries were started, the sooner more detail would emerge. And it was detail that was needed to start filling in the murderous picture. Murder now of not one but two persons.

Pat James returned to the mortuary office. She was even paler but quite composed. Only William noted that the top button of her demure blouse was now undone.

'I apologise, you were quite right. I should never have gone back in. What shall I do? I'll never be able to attend autopsies.'

'Yes, you will. I can name you any number of young men who behaved exactly the way you did at their first PM and now scarcely blink an eye.'

'Did you?'

William looked shamefaced. 'Sorry, I just about managed to hold on to both my composure and my breakfast. Come on, we're to return to the office.' He opened the door for her.

Constable James squared her shoulders and picked up her coat. Feeling for her car keys, she left the mortuary, followed by William Pigram.

Chapter Seven

'Darina, it's your mother on the telephone.'

Darina sighed deeply. She was involved in going through the Christmas programme with Ulla and they had suffered one interruption after another. An electricity failure had brought panic to the kitchen, where the young assistant was preparing lunch for George Prendergast and the staff, complaints from the housemaid vacuum cleaning the main rooms and curses from Alex who was trying to operate the copier. Sales reps had tried to arrange meetings to sell equipment the Hotel Morgan couldn't afford and didn't want and a local printer wanted to persuade them into trying his services. A representative of the meat wholesaler they used had called to run through some new cuts and incidentally, in passing, mention the price rises that would be effective in the New Year.

'If they had any sense, they'd call in the afternoon. Mornings are always busy in hotels,' said Alex, giving the inactive copier a disgruntled thump with his fist.

'Busy with what?' asked Darina, drawing out a plan of timings on a large piece of accounting paper and thinking that reps with any sense made full use of their day and probably reserved the afternoons for hotels likely to give useful orders.

'Making out accounts, dealing with departing clients, sorting out new bookings, all that sort of thing.'

'How much of that have we had to do today?'

'I told you the place was a business disaster. No wonder the locals call it Hotel Morgue.'

'They do?' Darina was diverted.

'Apparently started when Morgan bought the place. He used

to ask his mates round for drinks at the weekends to try and liven up the place.'

'Terrible rowdy bunch they were, kept on coming after we took over,' broke in Ulla. 'Not the sort of clientele we wanted.'

'As they quickly realised. I can just see Dad freezing them out without an inhospitable word. What had started as a joke name, because of the generally morgue-like décor, became a term of revenge.'

'If your father had lived, they would have laughed behind their faces.'

'On the other side of their faces, you Scandinavian dodo.' Alex flashed Ulla a genuinely amused smile, the cold, bitter man suddenly disappearing. What might have been a response flashed in Ulla's eyes, then the telephone rang.

Darina took the receiver. 'Hello, Mother, what can I do for you?'

'Darling, I've just had such a bright idea; I've rung my old friend Adam Tennant, you do remember him, don't you?'

'The name rings a faint bell.'

'He's been to drinks here, you must have met him. Well, he's agreed to spend some time talking to you and showing you around.'

'Around what, Mother?'

'You might sound a little more pleased, darling. It's not something he'd do for everybody.'

'If I knew what it was he was going to do for me, I might be able to respond with suitable enthusiasm.'

'You should learn to curb that tendency to sarcasm, darling, it won't get you anywhere. Men hate it.'

Darina sighed and tried a new tack. 'I really am grateful, Mother, I just want to know where I'm to go and when.'

'To the Manor Park Hotel, of course. And at noon today. Play your cards right and you will probably get lunch. Lunch at Manor Park is an experience. I only wish he had suggested I came too. What a pity I didn't think of it sooner, I'm sure I could have helped enormously, I'm so good at noticing things.'

Light dawned on Darina. 'Thank you, Mother, I think that's an excellent idea, I really am grateful. I'll let you know exactly how it goes.'

Five minutes later she replaced the telephone receiver, not quite able to ignore the stream of advice and exhortations that she had finally managed to stem.

'Apparently Adam Tennant of the Manor Park Hotel has agreed to show me around,' she announced to Ulla and Alex, busy once more with his copying, the electricity having been restored whilst Darina had been on the telephone.

'Well,' he said to Ulla, 'are you to have your nose put out of joint by our Valkyrie?'

'Don't be ridiculous, Alex.' But did a slight flush, so slight it was no more than a rosy hint, just blush her cheeks?

'You can't deny he's been making eyes at you ever since my father died. And probably before, I shouldn't wonder.'

'You know nothing about it. He has been very helpful. After all, he's the one who made that offer you are always on at me to accept.'

The telephone rang again. And again it was for Darina. This time she replaced the receiver after the call with a triumphant flourish.

'We've got another chef!' she announced.

'Wonderful! Who is it?' asked Ulla.

'A friend of mine I trained with. You know I made all those calls yesterday? Someone told me Sally Griffiths had just returned to this country after a period in France working in a three-star kitchen. I left a message on her answering machine and that was her on the phone. She's desperate for a job, I don't think she got paid over there, it was one of those training positions, and she's agreed to work here for the next two months. As you no doubt heard, I told her what a great opportunity it could be. She's going to come down tomorrow and look us over and discuss money. You'll have to tell me what you were paying Ken Farthing, we may have to go a bit higher but a reliable chef is absolutely essential.' She spoke with brisk finality.

Ulla looked slightly shell shocked.

'Is there somewhere for her to sleep?'

'We have a few rooms in the stable block, you'd better come over and see. As a rule we try to get staff who don't have to live in so there is no special accommodation.'

The stable block was to one side of the hotel, behind the

58

medieval hall. Like the main building, it needed renovating. Tiles were missing from the roof, gutters sprouted vegetation, the window frames showed signs of dry rot and there was a general air of desolation that was added to by dead plants in two large tubs placed either side of the main entrance, under a small clock tower. The clock showed half past four. The time was eleven a.m.

Ulla took Darina inside and showed her the accommodation that had been made out of the converted stable block. The work had been done some time ago and very cheaply. The dividing walls of the bedrooms were thin; Darina could hear George Prendergast's music system playing Mozart's Clarinet Quintet from two rooms away. The en suite shower rooms were basic but adequate; the décor of the bedrooms best forgotten. Darina bounced on a couple of the beds and found they were reasonable.

Then Ulla showed her the small flat made out of what had been the groom's accommodation on the first floor, right under the clock tower. 'This is where Tony and I made our home,' she said, leading the way into a tiny hall at the top of a steep staircase. The rooms had been recently painted and were sparsely but stylishly furnished. There was a small living room, a bedroom of the same size, a bathroom and a tiny kitchen. 'It was good to get away from hotel food sometimes. Tony loved my Norwegian specialties, the gravad lax everyone seems to do nowadays, Får i Kål, a lamb and cabbage stew, and my fish soup. They were his favourites.' Ulla's eyes became suspiciously bright.

Darina turned away to study the galley-like area with not a pan to be seen. 'Is Alex any good as a cook?'

'Alex? I've never seen him with so much as a frying pan in his hand.'

'It's a pity the two of you don't get on better.'

Ulla blew her nose with delicate emphasis into a lace handkerchief. 'He's never given me a chance. As far as he was concerned, I'd taken Trudy's place, the fact that I didn't even know her, that she'd died before Tony met me, meant nothing. Nor that I was making his father happy. He'd made up his mind and that was that.'

'How old was he when you married his father?'

'About twenty-two, I suppose, it was seven years ago. He was just finishing university. Tony hoped he'd come into the hotel world but Alex immediately went abroad, bumbling around the Continent.' Was it 'bumming' she meant?

'When he did come back, there were always quarrels. Tony wanted him to settle down to something, a proper job. All right, maybe the hotel world was not what Alex wanted but there didn't seem to be anything else he wanted to do either. There would be some great bust-up with his father and Alex would disappear again for months and months. We just got a few postcards, always from somewhere further and further away.'

'Didn't the situation between you get better as time went on?'

'You've seen him. Alex never changes his mind. He never considers other people. Oh, sometimes he can be so charming, I can quite see what Olivia and all the other girls around here see in him. But if they knew what I do, if they'd seen how icy his eyes so often are, how cutting he can be. He breaks their hearts and they never seem to have realised he wasn't really interested in them. He's just a womanseizer. Now, you mustn't laugh at me, I know my English is terrible at times.'

Darina carefully straightened her face.

'Does he sleep over here as well?'

Ulla walked back to the top of the stairs and started down. 'He has the first room on this side.' She gestured to the left of the entrance hall. 'We gave all those rooms a lick of paint. Tony said we could hardly move George Prendergast over from the main hotel without doing something to make him comfortable. We were going to do the rooms on the other side as well, hoping to let some of them as an annexe but Tony died before we could get it all organised.'

There were six free bedrooms, two in reasonable decorative order.

'Fine,' said Darina. 'One for Sally and one for me.'

'You've decided to move in then?'

'It's a good half hour's drive from Mother's and I'd rather be on the spot, especially over Christmas and New Year. Did you have anything planned for that, by the way? All we've talked of so far is Christmas.'

'We've advertised a dinner-dance and have a small local group booked.'

Darina looked at her watch. 'Heavens, I shall have to dash. You couldn't give Adam Tennant a quick ring, could you, to say I am on my way but will be a few minutes late?'

Chapter Eight

Inspector Grant, William Pigram and Pat James sat surrounded by computer printouts of the reports from the house-to-house and other enquiries. They were assessing progress in the case of the murdered girl.

So far the CID team had found no way to identify the body. No handbag had been found at the layby, where the search had encompassed a wide area of surrounding countryside. None of the nearby houses could help at all. Nobody had reported a missing girl in her early twenties. There had been nothing in any of her pockets or on her clothes that could help identify her. But it was early days still, there could be many reasons why no one would miss her for several days.

'Run through the information we have to place the time of death for me,' instructed Grant.

Pat James wrinkled a small nose. William caught himself thinking how appealing it made her look. Was he a fool that he had changed his mind so completely about her joining the team? Or intelligent because he had admitted, at least to himself, that he had been wrong? Apart from her lapse in the PM room she had been level headed, hard working and perceptive. Now she was saying: 'The farmer who was spreading slurry on his field by the layby says nothing suspicious happened there on Sunday.'

'And what was he doing spreading slurry on a Sunday?' asked Grant. 'Doesn't he take time off like any normal man?'

William searched for and found the relevant report. 'He stated the weather had been frosty with rain threatening for the Monday, perfect conditions for spreading slurry, and he had to get on with it, Sunday or no Sunday.'

'A farmer's life is not much different from a police officer's.'

Grant reached for the report. 'Would he have noticed the body in the ditch if it had been there?'

'He doesn't think so. He was working parallel to the ditch and finished well short of it.'

'Still, he can't have been there much beyond half past four, it must have got dark around then. Ah, I see he says a car with a puncture pulled in about that time.'

The farmer had gone across to see if he could help but the wheel nuts were so firmly screwed into place it was impossible for either he or the driver to shift them. The farmer had said he was on his way home and offered to telephone a garage. The driver was a member of the AA and had given him his name and membership number.

A follow-up to the AA had confirmed the call had been received shortly after five o'clock and provided the car number. Later statements taken from the AA mechanic and the driver revealed the car had been at the layby until nearly eight o'clock in the evening. It had been a busy night, the service personnel were short staffed and it had been almost seven thirty by the time an AA van had pulled into the layby. According to the driver, no other vehicle had parked there during that time nor had he seen anyone on foot.

'Possible he'd drifted off to sleep at some stage, I suppose,' suggested William. 'It must have been a cold and tedious wait. Over two hours!'

'He says he walked up and down, listened to the radio and made notes by torchlight on some work he had to do next day.' Pat had the statement made by the driver.

'Where was he travelling from?' asked Grant.

'Been visiting his mother in Bristol and was on his way home to Yeovil. He's a sales rep, unmarried.'

'Conceivable the victim came along and he chatted her up?' offered Grant, looking at his two assistants.

'Unlikely he would either become intimate or murder her, knowing the AA could come along at any minute,' said William.

'So, it would seem the body was either in place at nine a.m. Sunday morning or was placed there after the rep and the AA man left on Sunday evening.' Grant made some notes on the pad in front of him.

63

'The pathologist feels it unlikely the body had been there for less than twenty-four hours when he examined it at around six o'clock Monday,' contributed Pat James.

'Saturday evening is a traditional time for dates,' said William.

'Dates,' repeated Grant. 'So, we think it likely now she was killed by someone she knew?'

'A boyfriend shocked at the news she was pregnant?' suggested Pat James.

'These days?' William was sceptical. 'Surely no one gets that worried. Abortion on demand, unmarried mothers more or less totally acceptable, half the time now it's the father trying to get some rights to the child.' How angry he'd be if someone tried to close him out of the life of his child. The words of the marriage service came to mind: 'ordained for the procreation of children'. 'Procreation' – what a stumbling word for a glorious act. 'If, though, the man was married, he might feel threatened. Or she could have been an opportunist trying to trap a lover into marriage or a girl pushing a reluctant boyfriend into facing up to his responsibilities.'

'Or a girl picked up by some pervert who knew nothing about the child. Until we get a lead on who she is, speculation is useless,' said Grant repressively. 'Bill, try Missing Persons again.'

William placed the call.

'Funny you should ring now, I was just about to contact you. We've had an enquiry that could relate to your Jane Doe.' Alan in Missing Persons had been seconded to the San Francisco police for a short while and liked to display his knowledge of American argot. William ignored the term, reached for a piece of paper and scribbled down the details.

He replaced the receiver and gave the note to Grant.

'Right,' said the inspector, scribbling out an Action for the team to pursue the lead. 'Off you go and interview this Shirley. The chances are her friend's just taken a few days' holiday, is alive and well and living in Blackpool, Weston or wherever it is the young hang out these days but then again this could be our lucky day.'

Both the junior officers stood, Pat James picking up the case file.

'Right you are, sir,' said William. 'I know where the place is, it shouldn't take us long.'

'Let it take as long as it needs,' was Grant's parting shot.

Chapter Nine

Darina drove up to the front entrance of the Manor Park Hotel with a flourish. It was the only way to arrive at the region's premier luxury establishment. She parked her aging Ford estate car between a Rolls Royce and a Mercedes, noted the preponderance of high-octane, high-expense marques sitting on the smoothly pressed tarmac, tucked her patent leather envelope of a handbag under her arm and walked with confident steps into the hotel.

She entered a world that orbited a different universe from the Hotel Morgan. All was light, warmth and glowing colour. No harsh notes, no loud noises, no vulgar display. Fresh flower arrangements perfumed the air, logs crackled and blazed invitingly in the marble fireplace at one end of the reception hall. Beautiful people beautifully dressed sat either side of the fire in plumply comfortable sofas, drinks conveniently placed on small tables. They were chatting quietly. A waitress in black skirt and white shirt carrying a small tray bearing two drinks moved silently through the hall to a lounge off to one side.

Darina stood in the doorway drinking it all in. She noted the absence of reception desk, the fact that the only printed matter around appeared to be a selection of the latest magazines, that the waitress on her way back from the lounge glanced across to the fireplace, allowing her attention to be caught if required. But the drinkers were happy. Then she noticed Darina.

'Can I help you?'

As Darina stepped into the main part of the hall, a quiet voice said, 'I'll deal with this, Jenny. The Davises have just gone into the library and need drinks.' The girl gave a smile and moved off towards the back of the hall through a wide arch.

The newcomer stood quietly in front of Darina. She wore the

sort of sober dark dress Darina associated with housekeepers. Middle aged, overweight and looking tired, her skin had an unhealthy pallor and her thin lips were forced together as though only that pressure kept her world from falling apart.

'I think Adam Tennant is expecting me. I'm Darina Lisle.'

The woman inclined her head. 'Will you take a seat and I will let him know you are here?' She ushered Darina into the lounge, then moved away with measured steps.

Instead of sitting down, Darina walked to the end of the long room and looked through the window that came to within a foot or so of the floor. Careful landscaping gave the garden a structure that was attractive even at this dead time of the year. Variegated evergreens, winter flowering shrubs, a couple of classical statues, created a graceful effect that pleased the eye, just as the lounge did with its groups of deeply upholstered armchairs and sofas, luxurious curtains, richly polished antique furniture and individually lit oil paintings of land and sea scapes.

'My dear Miss Lisle, how nice to meet you.'

Darina knew she had never met the man coming towards her before, she could not have forgotten his aquiline charm, nor the abundant hair gone prematurely white and smoothed back with glossy control. Dark brown eyes gleamed with good will and satisfaction, a slim body was encased in immaculate tailoring. But there was a dessicated quality to him, as though his vital juices were drying up, and he couldn't quite conceal the sharpness behind the *bonhomie* as he greeted her with outstretched hand.

'Mr Tennant, this is very kind of you.'

'Not at all, I'm delighted to be of help. Now, shall we have a drink and you can let me know exactly what you want?'

He clicked a finger and thumb and the smiling waitress reappeared to take their order. In a few minutes Darina was sitting in a quiet corner and supplied with Perrier water in a cut crystal glass, ice and lemon adding the right degree of chill and zest.

Her host clasped an equally large glass of whisky and soda. He adjusted one leg over the other, pinched the razor-sharp crease of his trouser and gave Darina another flashing smile. 'So you've decided to enter the hotel world?'

'I'm considering it.' In a few words she related her long-held desire to run her own hotel, the possibility that the Chelsea house she had inherited from a cousin could provide the necessary finance, the realisation that considerably more backing would be required for the sort of place she wanted, and the opportunity that the Hotel Morgan could maybe provide.

As she talked, Adam Tennant held her eyes with his, one foot, clad in its highly-polished shoe, gently swaying from side to side. When she explained the agreement she had reached with Ulla Mason, he smiled.

'Ah, the beautiful Ulla. What a tragedy Tony dying like that. She needs some support.' Darina was not sure he meant her support.

'So,' he took a deep swallow from his drink and adjusted his figure more comfortably in the chair. 'You want my advice as to how you can make the Hotel Morgan into a suitable rival for my hotel?'

'No . . . I mean, it could never aspire to your heights. I really wouldn't have come if that was my intention.' Darina was confused, she had not looked at the situation in that light.

Adam laughed. 'No, I don't suppose you would. When your mother rang, I wondered just what your intention was. A spy in the camp, an adventuress or just a stupid girl.' The final snap in his voice straightened Darina's backbone. She put down her drink and stood up.

'I'm sorry she troubled you. Thank you for the drink and for agreeing to see me but I won't take up any more of your time.'

'Sit down, please. You make me nervous standing there like some goddess about to cause lightning to strike. I didn't mean to upset you.'

Darina eyed him; he seemed all relaxed charm, to be laughing at her reaction. Slowly she lowered herself back into the chair, rapidly revising her initial opinion of Adam Tennant.

'Mother knows I have no experience of hotels. I think she feels if I see how a really great hotel is run I will get cold feet and back out.'

A raised eyebrow acknowledged the flattery. 'In that case I will take you on a complete tour. But first I hope you will lunch with me and I will tell you the history of this place. You say the Hotel Morgan could never be a rival but let me tell you that when I found the Manor Park, it made your Hotel Morgue look a luxury establishment.'

Darina looked around the room in astonishment.

'Yes, it's taken fifteen years of extremely hard work, great experience, considerable investment and, if I may say so, a certain genius to achieve what you see today.'

'I understand you've made Ulla an offer for her hotel?'

He smiled at her. 'That convinces you it's possible for the Hotel Morgan to be a serious rival, does it? Let me explain why, despite what I've just said, it never could be.'

He broke off to allow the waiter who had appeared to offer Darina a menu.

'Can I recommend Madame tries the escalope of venison with red wine and juniper jelly? It's our chef's speciality.'

Darina cast an envious eye over the enticing menu and agreed that the chef's dish of the day looked a good choice. She refused a starter and wine. Adam ordered a half bottle for himself and more mineral water for her. 'And I think Badoit with the meal, don't you? Perrier is a little *gazeuse* to drink with food.' The waiter disappeared as silently as he had appeared. 'Now, where were we? Ah yes, the Hotel Morgan. It lacks the first essential of a really top-class establishment. Do you know what that is?'

Darina thought for a moment, then shook her head.

'Location. You could say there are three essentials to make a real success of any place and they are: location, location and location. Take this place. We are within easy reach of both Bath and Bristol, cities with a highly active commercial life as well as tourist attractions. Rely solely on tourists and you have no trade outside the season. Rely on high-spending tourists and there are always hazards. The Libyan bombing in 1987 destroyed our summer trade, the Americans stayed away in droves. Then when the pound strengthened they also stayed away. Also there are hazards. With a strong commercial clientele you are cushioned. And for this you need to be near commercial centres. 'I'm afraid that your Hotel Morgan is too far away from a sufficiently large one.'

Darina considered location. 'I understand what you are saying. The Hotel Morgan has tourism, good communications by rail and road and a number of medium-sized towns nearby but it undoubtedly lacks the advantages you have here.'

'Apart from that vital factor, potentially the Hotel Morgan could be a most attractive hotel. All that's required is that a great deal of money be spent on it.'

'Is that what you would do if you bought it?'

Adam gave a graceful wave of his hand. 'I made the offer more out of a spirit of sympathy with Ulla in her plight rather than as a commercial venture. If she agreed to sell, I would probably put in a first-class manager for six months or so, build up the turn-over to make the place a more attractive proposition, then sell it on. The capital investment required to bring the place up to the standard of a hotel I would be happy to operate is out of proportion to the returns it could bring.'

'You are saying that I would be advised to look elsewhere for an investment? That the Hotel Morgan is unlikely to make money?'

'I think it requires very special expertise to make it pay attractively. However, if you are content with a run-of-the-mill operation, you could probably manage to scrape a living, at least cover your living expenses.'

'I would never be happy with a run-of-the-mill operation,' declared Darina.

Adam Tennant looked at her. 'No, I don't suppose you would.'

The waiter reappeared with the news that their table was ready.

As she followed the slim back of her host through the hall, Darina glanced again at the brilliantly blazing fire and stopped short. The people who had been sitting on the sofas when she arrived had left. Beside the fire now was a young woman perched uneasily on the edge of her seat, hands clutching a notebook and pencil, a look of deep anxiety on her face. Lounging easily opposite her, looking round him with interest, was William.

She had had one quick phone call from him since their lunch had been ended so abruptly. Murder cases, she knew, were all-involving but she had been hurt he hadn't found time for more.

His face lit up as he saw Darina. He rose swiftly and elegantly and came towards her. 'What a stroke of luck! Are you lunching here?'

'I'm fortunate enough to be the guest of the proprietor.' She introduced Adam Tennant, who shook the young man's hand with easy charm.

'Are you being looked after?'

'Yes, thanks. I'm afraid we're here on business.'

'Afraid?' Adam raised a questioning eyebrow.

'No one, in my experience, likes to have the police on the premises.'

'Ah! So you are the police. Darina's introduction was not quite complete.' She didn't like the way he glanced at her, felt he was being unfair. How was she to know why William was here? 'And what brings the guardians of the law to this establishment? I was not aware we had a problem.' The eyebrow climbed a little higher up the smooth forehead.

'One of your receptionists has reported that a member of staff may be missing.'

'Really? I had no idea.' The inference was that any such event should be known to him. 'Who is the receptionist? Ah, Shirley, was it you who rang the police?'

A young woman had emerged from the arch at the rear of the hall. She was dressed in a dark coat and skirt with a white blouse as dazzling as any an advertisement-conscious housewife could produce. Her looks were pleasant without being sensational. She blushed at Adam Tennant's pointed enquiry but said, 'It was just that Sharon hasn't been back since Saturday evening.'

'Why didn't you mention it to me?'

She blushed even deeper. 'I knew you had given her the week off, I thought it better not to trouble you.'

'But you have troubled me, you have brought the police to my hotel.'

'Why did you give her the week off, sir?'

William's manner had subtly altered and the young woman had risen from the sofa and was standing slightly behind him, pencil poised above her notebook.

'Oughtn't you to caution me before you start taking down my words?' It was difficult to tell whether Adam Tennant was serious or not.

'It is only an enquiry at the moment, sir, we don't know if Sharon Fry is indeed the girl we are seeking.'

'And why are you seeking her?'

'A body was found on Monday some ten or so miles from here, in a ditch on the A37. It is, at the moment, unidentified.

70

From Miss Harris's description, we think it possible it could be that of her friend, and your employee, Sharon Fry. Pat, have you got that photograph?'

His companion dug into a capacious bag and produced a glossy print. William held it so both the receptionist and Adam Tennant had a good view.

'Could that be Miss Fry?'

Adam Tennant looked at it without a muscle moving in his face but the receptionist gave a gasp and brought her hand to her mouth.

'Sharon doesn't look like that! Something's happened to her!'

'Please, Shirley, control yourself. Perhaps, Inspector Pigram, you could continue this interview, interrogation, whatever you care to call it, in some more private place.' It was not a suggestion.

'I shall be delighted, sir, and it's Sergeant, in fact. I don't want to interrupt your lunch,' this was said with a sidelong glance at Darina, 'but I would like to ask if you also recognise this photograph as being Miss Fry?'

The hotelier reluctantly took the print, glanced at it quickly and handed it back. 'It's difficult to say. Something very unpleasant seems to have happened to her. I suppose there could be a resemblance.'

'And why did you give her the week off?'

Adam Tennant's slight uneasiness intensified. 'My wife handles that side of the business, you should ask her.'

'If it is in fact Miss Fry, I shall have to ask not only her but also other members of your staff and you yourself a great many questions.' There was no hint of apology in William's voice now.

'If you must, I suppose you must. Shirley, take Sergeant Pigram and . . . ' he glanced towards the young woman taking notes. William took her gently by the arm and drew her forward.

'Detective Constable James. She is working with me on this case.'

'Right, take Sergeant Pigram and Detective,' he gave the word a slight emphasis, 'Constable James to my office. I won't be needing it for some time; after lunch I'm showing Miss Lisle round the hotel. Come, my dear.' With what Darina felt was unnecessary care, he placed a hand under her arm and gently shepherded her in the direction of the dining room. In view of the fact she topped the hotel proprietor by a couple of inches, she felt the gesture must look slightly ridiculous.

'Nice meeting you,' she said to William as she was steered away.

'I'll try and ring you tonight,' he called after her.

Her last glimpse of the tall detective was of him shepherding the female constable after Shirley in much the same manner as Adam Tennant had taken charge of herself.

The gesture told her more graphically than any words could have how his opinion of female CID officers had altered.

Chapter Ten

Pat James felt happier once they were on their way to the mortuary with Shirley Harris. A brief visit to a London Holiday Inn had done nothing to prepare her for the luxury of the Manor Park.

She had had the feeling of being in someone's private house, one that was much grander and more sophisticated than anywhere she could imagine herself visiting. She had been terrified she was going to mark that beautiful sofa by the fire in some way. That she would knock over one of those lovely tables.

It didn't help, either, to see how at home Sergeant Pigram was, as though this was the sort of place he came to all the time. Perhaps it was.

Bill Pigram was different from most of the policemen she had worked with up to now. It was difficult for Pat James to analyse that difference. It had something to do with the way he spoke, which was like the way the owner of a great house whose burglary she had once helped to investigate had spoken. It wasn't particularly lah-di-dah, rather a mixture of courtesy and natural authority. The owner had been someone high up in the Foreign Office, spent most of his time in London. Someone had told her Bill Pigram had also been in the Foreign Office once.

And the difference was also to do with his general behaviour, the way he wore his by no means out of the ordinary clothes that somehow looked special on him; the way he held doors open for her, helped her into a car, was so tactful when she made such a fool of herself in the post mortem room.

Pat James had no illusions as to the welcome she had had from the detective sergeant. Courteous and punctilious as he was, she knew as soon as she walked into his office with Inspector Grant that he resented her. She knew she was disturbing a previously well-knit team. She was prepared to fight for her right to be a member, display her abilities, show she was as well trained, had more than the average intelligence of and could work as hard as any of the men who might have been assigned to the CID team. She had passed her probationary period, done exceptionally well during her thirteen-week CID course; now she was on her first assignment as a fully fledged detective, determined to succeed.

She was totally unprepared for either the effect the easy charm of the tall, dark-haired policeman had on her or the unexpected way he suddenly changed his attitude and seemed to accept her. She had thought she would have to earn her stripes to be admitted as part of the team; instead it seemed to have taken her demoralisation to achieve it. She was not sure she liked that. But she reckoned she would have ample opportunity with this case to demonstrate her abilities. It was a stroke of luck, really, this body turning up now; it would give her a real chance to show what she could do.

It had been unfortunate, then, that they had had to wait so long at the Manor Park for the receptionist to be free to speak to them. The surroundings had definitely undermined her confidence.

Noting the way Bill Pigram had greeted that girl hadn't done anything to improve the situation either.

What a looker she was. Pat had always been pleased at her own diminutive size, noting the protective instincts it brought out in men. She liked the way they would fuss around her, be amazed she could do her job, handle herself with villains. She would hate to be large. It wasn't that one look at Darina Lisle changed her mind on that but it did make her realise a tall girl could be spectacularly attractive. She'd been wearing a blonde wool suit with a cream silk blouse that almost exactly matched the long hair caught back with a brown silk ribbon. Pat admired not only the cream hair – she'd always longed to be a blonde – but also the suit and the heavy chain that hung almost to her waist and looked as though it might be real gold, and the patent shoes and bag. Pat's mum, who was a hairdresser, had always told her a lady could be identified by good quality shoes and bag. 'It doesn't matter about the clothes, some of them look a fright, but the bag

74

and shoes are always good,' she'd said. But they cost such a lot of money, far more than Pat could afford. So she made do with the best Marks & Spencer could offer. She chose most of her clothes there, too, going for what she thought of as the 'classic' look. One glance at Darina told her how far she was from achieving it.

And one glance at Bill Pigram as he leaped to greet the girl told her they were more than casual acquaintances. As did the way the tall blonde's face lit up on seeing the policeman, suggesting to Pat that his interest was returned.

It was with an effort that she had brought her mind back to the matter in hand – and was rewarded by being able to observe the uneasiness with which the owner of the hotel seemed to treat the enquiries regarding Sharon Fry.

The interview with receptionist Shirley Harris had been short.

'We share a terraced cottage in the village, just outside the entrance to the drive, it's ever so convenient,' she'd explained once they'd seated themselves in the small but perfectly appointed office behind the main hall. Sergeant Pigram was behind the big desk, Shirley in front and Pat herself sat on a chair at the side, taking notes.

'Sharon and me met the day we both applied to work here. She wanted to be a receptionist too but Mr Tennant said he only had the one vacancy. But they wanted a waitress, so Sharon said she'd take that. I think she'd have done anything to work here. Well, you can see for yourself how lovely it is. And they're very good to the staff, as long as you do your job right. Mrs Tennant's a bit of a tartar, Sharon's always in trouble with her, but Mr Tennant's usually very nice.'

'What made you ring the police to report Sharon missing?' asked Bill Pigram, slipping in the question as Shirley paused for a brief moment to catch her breath.

'She hasn't been home since Saturday. I mean, I know she's stayed out nights before and she said she had a week's holiday and she wasn't sure what she was going to do with it, but I'm sure she'd have said if she was going away anywhere and you do hear such dreadful things these days.' Shirley's pleasant face screwed itself into an anxious grimace.

'Where did she go on Saturday?'

'She said she was meeting someone.'

'Do you know whom?'

'She didn't say. Sharon never does. Sometimes I think she doesn't know herself. She'll meet a chap in a bar, somewhere, anywhere, and if she likes him, that's that.'

'She didn't . . . doesn't' – Pat liked the way Sergeant Pigram changed the tense to the present; no use in upsetting Shirley Harris more than they had to at this point – 'have a regular boyfriend?'

Shirley paused for the first time and thought about her answer. 'Well,' she said doubtfully, 'I know there were several men she saw more or less regularly. She told me she thought she might be able to bring one of them up to scratch.'

'Up to scratch?'

'Get him to marry her!'

'She wanted to get married?'

'Doesn't every girl?' Shirley was amazed.

'Not these days,' Pat interjected.

Shirley turned and gave her an astonished look.

'Why ever not?'

'Some girls want a career, want to make their mark, not spend their time looking after a man and clearing up after children.' Pat could sense Bill Pigram was looking at her with interest.

Shirley shrugged. 'Women's lib does nothing for me. I can see living with a chap until you can afford a proper wedding and get a place and all but not never getting married.'

'And Sharon felt . . . feels the same?'

'Oh yes, though I tell her, how she'll settle down to just one man, I don't know.'

'And you don't think she's gone off with a man now?'

'Like I said, she told me she was just off for a drink with this chap.'

'Which chap?'

'The one she was going with.'

'And you don't know who that was?'

'Like I told you, she never said.'

'But she has gone out before and not come back?'

'Well, not until the next morning. And she did once go to Morecombe with a sales rep for two nights, he said he'd get her into this smashing hotel on his expenses. But she said it wasn't half as nice as this place.' Shirley gave her surroundings a smug look. Pat was interested that during the interview her manner had undergone a change.

In the hall, talking to the police and Mr Tennant, her voice had been quieter, more educated, it had matched her smart appearance, she had the demeanour one would expect to be met with in such a place as the Manor Park Hotel. Talking about her friend, worried about her whereabouts, her speech had slipped into a more colloquial style. Pat could see her as a natural if slightly shyer partner for the uninhibited and sexy Sharon.

'But you don't think that something similar has happened to her this time?'

Shirley's eyes welled, she pulled out a paper handkerchief from her sleeve and wiped them. 'I don't know!' she wailed. 'I'm just so worried. She hadn't anything with her, no nightie or other clothes, I mean. When she didn't come back on Sunday I did wonder what was happening. Monday I was that worried I nearly rang then. But I thought she'd tear my hair out if she learned I'd put the police on to her and she was somewhere with some chap. Yesterday I did ring but just as I got through, Mr Tennant came into the office and I had to put the phone down. I thought it was meant, you know, that she was going to turn up. But she didn't and this morning I just knew I had to tell someone.'

'You didn't speak to Mr or Mrs Tennant?'

'Sharon said she had the week off, you see. It wasn't as though she was missing from her job. Why should they know where she was?'

Why, indeed!

Bill Pigram placed the photograph in front of Shirley again. 'Please look at this once more very carefully. Do you think it is your friend?'

Shirley gave a last scrub to her eyes, put away her handkerchief and picked up the print. 'What's happened to her?' she asked. 'I'm sure it's Sharon but her face looks all funny. Not like her at all.'

'Do Sharon's parents live nearby?'

'No, they're down beyond Minehead. At least, her mum is, her dad's dead.' She looked at the print again. 'This is the picture

77

of a dead person. Sharon can't be dead, she just can't be, it can't be her.' She flung the photograph on to the desk and looked at them defiantly, then the tears started again.

Pat James glanced at the sergeant in a silent enquiry. He nodded.

She moved to crouch beside the upset girl. 'I'm afraid she probably is. But we'd like you to come and take a look at the body, see if it is your friend or not.'

Shock arrested the flow of tears. 'Me, look at a dead body?'

'You see, we don't know who it is. You say the picture might be of your friend, we have to confirm whether it is or not. If you feel you really can't face it, we will get in touch with her mother and ask her to come to the mortuary. But that will take time and the sooner we know who it is, the sooner we can start finding her murderer.'

Shirley turned the matter over in her mind, her fingers shredding the paper handkerchief. 'You mean I could really help?'

Pat nodded, an arm around the girl.

'All right, then, I'll try.'

'Would you like us to ask Mrs Tennant to come along as well?'

Shirley shook her head. 'I'd rather do it on my own. Except, you'll be there too, won't you?'

Pat gave her a squeeze, 'Good girl. Yes, of course, we'll both be there.' She looked across at the sergeant.

He got up. 'It won't be as bad as you might think. She looks just as though she's sleeping, not at all frightening.'

Pat thought of the naked body slashed from nape to crotch and stifled a shudder. She knew that not only had the dead girl's innards been removed but her brain as well. But she also knew that all incisions would have been neatly sewn up, the hair rearranged, the corpse made to look as normal as possible. None of the violations that had been practised upon it would show. Only the traces of asphyxia from the strangling.

Shirley went quietly with them after a brief word of explanation on the telephone with Mrs Tennant.

In the plain little room known as the Chapel of Rest, the body lay on a covered trolley underneath a plain sheet. Shirley stood beside it, her arms tightly folded across her front, a slight perspiration breaking out on her brow despite the chill of the room. Pat stood on the other side of the trolley and took the sheet in her hands. She looked across at Shirley. The girl closed her eyes for a moment, then opened them, took a deep breath and nodded her head.

It was released in a long, slow sigh as she looked on the face presented to her gaze. 'Yes, that's Sharon,' she said. She reached out to touch the face lightly. 'What happened to her? Why does she look like that?'

'I'm afraid she was strangled,' Pat said and lowered the sheet back over the dead girl.

'Strangled!'

'And we'll now have to ask you to come with us to the police station and let us take your statement,' said Bill Pigram from behind her. He opened the door.

Pat James watched him usher the girl through, remembering the feel of his hand under her arm as they had gone through to the office at the Manor Park earlier that day.

Chapter Eleven

After her tour of the Manor Park, Darina drove back thoughtfully to the Hotel Morgan.

The luxury of the hotel had been a revelation. Adam Tennant had shown her beautifully appointed rooms, each decorated differently but in the same exquisite style. Not a note jarred, everywhere were touches that displayed the thought that had gone into meeting every possible need or desire. Delicious toiletries in the bathroom plus disposable razors, a sewing kit and a hairdryer in each dressing table, with a plug sited conveniently near, a couple of the latest novels by the bed, guide books to the district and a selection of games on low tables in the sitting area. Carefully chosen objets d'art, antique furniture and a collection of nineteenth-century water colours and oils all combined to give an impression guests were staying at a private country house.

'It's a fantasy world,' said Adam as he showed her round. 'When people come here they want to get away from their everyday lives, fulfil some sort of dream. Everything must work towards that end.'

A dream world indeed. As she drove away, Darina thought of the investment and commitment needed to create such perfection. Adam had shown her an entire new wing that had recently been built. He'd told her what it cost, had laughed when she'd asked if he'd brought in other investors. Only the bank, he'd said. She thought of the interest payments charged on such a loan. No doubt the Manor Park produced an income sufficient to finance such an outlay. There was no way she and Ulla could match such expenditure. And the Manor Park was but one luxury country hotel, there were several others within the county. Was there room for another? Was this what they had to aim for? If so, how were they going to achieve it?

But already she knew she had to try. She wanted to see her hotel filled with people enjoying themselves like the clients at the Manor Park. There had been a happy buzz in its public rooms, a quiet hum of satisfaction. Adam had exchanged brief words with many of them, he seemed to know everyone. Most, he said, were business people but there had been locals in the dining room enjoying an early festive season lunch, and some Americans had returned from a visit to Bath exclaiming at the antiques they had found.

Only one incident had suggested there could be serpents in paradise. As they ate their lunch, Darina admiring her fillet of venison, the flesh tender and slightly gamey, the velvet smooth meat beautifully pink, resting in a pool of sauce flushed a deep, clear colour with a depth of flavour that spoke of skilfully made stock, with an accompaniment of jelly both tangy and subtly sweet, she became aware that something on the other side of the room was claiming her host's attention.

More than half of the dining room's tables were occupied. The clientele was mixed: businessmen lunching with each other, a couple of pairs of women chatting busily whilst they ate with gusto, several Americans, recognisable by the informality of their clothes, a table of five Japanese. And in a corner were a young man and girl. The wine waiter was retreating from their table clutching a bottle of wine, an expression of near panic on his face.

Adam Tennant motioned him over and asked him what the problem was. Almost in tears, the man explained the couple had ordered one of the most expensive bottles of wine on the hotel's list, and after tasting it had sent it back and ordered another, almost as expensive. The same thing had happened.

'The young man says they're inferior, he was quite rude.'

'And what's your opinion?'

'I haven't tried this one but the Latour seemed perfect to me.' The waiter was asked to leave the bottle he was clutching and bring the other to Adam's table with fresh glasses. Whilst they waited, Darina looked at the couple again. The young man was talking fast and gesturing expansively. His young companion looked enraptured at his performance. Neither looked as though

81

they formed part of the Manor Park's regular clientele.

'Do you know them?' she asked.

Adam Tennant shook his head. 'They've won a competition. We were asked to present a prize of a free lunch for some fashion promotion. I hope the organisers of the competition realise there was an upper limit on the cost of the lunch. It should have been enough for a splendid meal with a generous allowance for wine but hardly such wines as these.'

Darina looked at the labels as the wine waiter reappeared with a second bottle of claret. A 1961 Château Latour and a Château Lynch Bages of the same year. Adam Tennant poured a little of each into two clean glasses. He held up the first and looked at the colour, swirled the deep red liquid around the glass, thrust his nose into the rim and inhaled deeply. Then he took a mouthful, forcing the wine around his taste buds in the noisily sucking way wine experts assess the grape's harvest.

After sampling the first, he drank some water and repeated the performance with the second wine. His concentration was absolute, nothing existed for him but the two clarets. All artifice, all projection of personality, had been forgotten. He was a total professional, lost in his private world of expertise. Finally he said, 'I can find nothing wrong with either.'

He looked across the room and sat in thought for a moment. Then he turned to the wine waiter. 'Take them back to the table and say now that they have had a chance to settle down you believe they will enjoy them.'

Darina watched as the waiter, with every appearance of total confidence, carried out his instructions. The young man watched the Latour being poured into a fresh glass, sniffed it, tasted it – and smiled. The girl dimpled happily and drank deeply from her glass, hardly seeming to notice what was in it. Darina wished she had been allowed a sip of the two great wines. She asked how much they were.

'The Latour is on the list at £600, the Lynch Bages at £450,' Adam said.

Darina gulped. 'Will they have to pay the difference between the limit and their bill?'

Adam Tennant signalled a waiter and asked for the voucher to be brought. He looked at it and smiled. 'It is the organisers who will have to pay. They have forgotten to state the limit.'

Looking at the young man it seemed unlikely he would have the resources to cover the additional amount. No wonder Adam Tennant seemed relieved as he gave the voucher back to the waiter. 'There are always clients who want to show off, to impress their partners. Half the time all they do is alienate them, though I have to say it doesn't seem to have happened with that girl. Almost breaks my heart to see her drink that wine as though it was Babycham. And I don't suppose he knows it from Beaujolais.'

'Do you have many problems with guests?'

'Not many, no. It's the nouveau riche who cause the most. It's strange but so often they feel they have to make their mark by complaining stridently over quite trivial matters. If guests start over tipping, beware, they'll end by giving you trouble. The others you have to watch out for are the con artists.'

'Have you had much trouble?'

'Not often. There was one chap in the early days who convinced me he was creditworthy and drew a considerable sum of cash before I got wary, too late to do me much good. Luggage can sometimes provide a clue; more than one Vuitton case has proved to contain nothing more than newspaper and a brick. We even had one chap book in with a case quite empty except for a trumpet!'

'Did he blow it?'

'Not even that. We never got to the bottom of him. Now, are you sure I cannot tempt you to a pastry?'

Darina shook her head and drank coffee thoughtfully. There were problems in a hotelier's life that had not occurred to her.

The Hotel Morgan presented a sad contrast with the glittering world of the Manor Park. As Darina entered the reception hall, it seemed even darker and drearier after the light and colour of the luxury hotel. She stood in the doorway and looked around her, her gaze finally coming to rest on the wisp of smoke rising from two small logs in the fireplace. Then she went and looked at the lounge and the library. Then the dining room, the one cheerful and stylish note in the whole place. The trouble was, it showed up the rest of the hotel so badly.

Darina went back to the hall. It wasn't so much the gloom,

she decided, as the incongruity of those chairs with their wooden arms and modern backs and the way everything was arranged. And as for the blue and orange curtains, which had even found their way to the long windows either side of the front door, they belonged in a suburban terraced house. Darina could only think the Morgans had bought the material in a job lot; nobody could actually have *chosen* that pattern.

The flimsy reception cubicle offended her as well. It protruded from the panelled corner like a carbuncle that, if not quite monstrous, was certainly hideous. It wasn't even as though there was a receptionist inside waiting to see to her needs.

Darina stopped being thoughtful and went into action. She piled extra logs on to the fire, jabbing at the smouldering wood with the poker until flames flickered into life and licked at the new fuel. Then she went through to the passage leading to the service areas of the hotel. Almost immediately the sound of voices raised in argument reached her.

In the office Ulla was standing in front of the desk holding forth.

'And if you think I'm going to let you drive your stupid horses across my land in that, that *disgusting* game you call a hunt, Major Brownsword, you have another think arriving.'

Ulla's face was flushed, her fair hair awry, like a child's after a steamy bath. She looked like a small angel in its first battle with a devil.

The devil now had his turn. Major Brownsword was a lean, spare man, very tall and slightly stooped, his thinning black hair brushed straight back from a wind-tanned face. 'Your husband agreed to us meeting at the hotel on Boxing Day, as we have done for years. It is quite impossible for you to change your mind now.'

'Impossible! Why is it impossible?'

'Well, of course it is, arrangements have been made, the Hunt informed, everyone knows.'

'Then you can tell them different. I won't have innocent little foxes made a game of on my land.'

'Madam, if you do this, you will regret it to the end of your days.'

Darina came forward. So intent had the protagonists been on each other, neither had noticed her standing in the doorway.

'Is there some disagreement about the hotel?' she asked ingenuously. 'May I introduce myself, Major Brownsword? Darina Lisle, I'm to be Ulla's partner.'

He gaped at her. 'Partner? Ulla, you said nothing to me about a partner?'

Ulla Mason continued to glare at the Major and said nothing.

He flushed slightly, seemed to recollect his manners and took Darina's outstretched hand. 'Perhaps you can talk some sense into her. The Boxing Day meet is one of the Hunt's most important; it's quite impossible to change the location at this late stage.' His eyes were almost black, the whites threaded with red veins; they looked as if a feather's weight more pressure would cause them to pop out of his head. 'I might also point out it has never been bad business for the hotel bar.' He pulled a flat hat out of the pocket of his riding mac. 'Tony confirmed the arrangements before he died and as far as I am concerned we shall be meeting at the Hotel Morgan at ten thirty on Boxing Day. If you're not prepared to honour traditional commitments, I would suggest you sell up and go elsewhere!' He glared at both girls, jammed his cap on his head and left the office. The odour of brimstone singed the air.

'Whew!' said Darina, collapsing into a chair. 'What was *that* all about?'

Ulla went and sat behind the desk, her breath coming quickly. 'That, that *monster* wants to chase foxes all over my land. I tell him, yust you try.' Darina found Ulla's inability to pronounce the 'j' sound and the collapse of her usually good grasp of the English language when she got excited quite enchanting.

'Do I understand they met here last year?'

'Tony said it was good for business and, anyway, he didn't mind, he quite liked the hunting.' Ulla's voice was despairing.

'But, Ulla, you can't cancel their arrangements at this stage. Organising a hunt is quite a complicated business, I believe,' she added a little doubtfully, her actual knowledge of hunting being limited to a few occasions following the hounds with friends.

'But I had forgotten all about it. There have been so many things since Tony died. Then, this morning, I suddenly remember. I cannot bear that they do this so I ring Major Brownsword and tell him, no.'

'Which brought him straight round here?'

85

'Oh, he was so angry!' There was a tiny gleam of amusement in Ulla's eyes.

'Is he Olivia's father?'

'Yes. Alex says he has handed his brains on to his daughter, that the both of them together couldn't find Cleopatra's needle in a haystack.'

'I can believe that. But, Ulla, don't you think you should reconsider, for this year anyway? Tell the Major that it is the last time, that they must find another location for next year.'

'You really think so?'

'Think how many local people will be upset if you throw the whole thing into confusion now! Just at a time when the hotel needs all the good will it can get. And all the business there is going.'

Ulla looked at her pensively. Finally she gave Darina a tiny smile. 'All right, I send him a letter, put it in writing. Now, let's forget the Major. How was Adam and what did you think of the Manor Park?'

Darina gave a vivid account of her lunch and tour.

'It's the most beautiful hotel. Did Tony really think he could turn Hotel Morgan into something similar?'

'Yes,' said Ulla proudly. 'This hotel was going to be yust as beautiful and well run.'

'It would take a great deal of money,' said Darina doubtfully, 'and would it be profitable in the long run? I was very struck with what Adam said about location.'

'Tony said it could be done.' There was complete conviction in Ulla's voice. 'He said there was a considerable amount of local commercial business in this area, it's growing all the time, and it has many tourist attractions.'

'Hmm.' Darina sat and thought. Then, 'Have you got a local paper?'

'I think it's in the lounge.'

They went through and found it on a table crammed with local information, much of it looking as though it had been there since the time of the Morgans. Darina carefully scanned the classified advertisement section.

'What are you looking for?' asked Ulla.

But Darina merely tore out a page and said, 'Look, I want to go home and pack up some things so I can move into that room in the stable block. I'll be back in time to provide dinner. And I'll be out tomorrow morning.'

'What about your chef? Isn't she coming down?'

'Could Alex meet her at the station tomorrow morning, the Paddington connection? Get her to prepare lunch for George Prendergast and us with whatever she can find. Good test for her. I'll be back by one and we can discuss the situation together in the afternoon. OK?'

'OK,' said a slightly bemused Ulla.

There was one incident Darina had omitted from the description of her visit to the Manor Park. She had made no mention of running into William and his female assistant. As she drove swiftly and competently towards her mother's house, Darina forced herself to re-live the moment she had seen the sergeant place his hand under the arm of the small policewoman and carefully shepherd her through the archway at the rear of the Manor Park's reception hall. She recalled the neat little figure, back held straight, head poised,the hair glossy as a chestnut.

She had seen that guiding hand and felt a deep stab of jealousy, keen and sharp as the edge of a newly-ground butcher's knife. It had shaken her. Shaken her so badly it had taken the effort of concentrating on Adam's amusing and fascinating account of how he turned a near derelict country seat into a luxury hotel for her to recover her composure.

Darina had not known she could suffer jealousy. Or that it could stir her in quite that way. It was not a pleasant revelation.

Chapter Twelve

It was ten days before Christmas and frost lay heavily on the ground. No doubt the world would have looked a winter wonderland, if it had been light enough for Alex to see the landscape. At six a.m. it was too dark to be aware of anything but the frost-limned grass at the edge of the iron-hard path as he made his way from the stable block to the main house of the hotel and to the boiler room.

Here he riddled out the previous night's clinker, fed the ancient boiler with its preferred nuggets of fuel and fired it, waiting to see the ,temperamental apparatus well on its way to heating the bedrooms and bathwater for the three guests they had staying in the hotel. As he waited, Alex leaned against the dusty windowsill and pulled out a battered paperback of Colin Thubron's classic account of his travels through China.

After a little while a particularly loud gurgle of heating water chuckling through the pipes brought him back to his surroundings. He fed the boiler with more nuts, adjusted the dampers and left for the kitchen. Here he put on the kettle and unlocked the fridges. With their present staff level, it hardly seemed worth the precaution but his father had installed the locks and it seemed the least his wayward son could do now was to follow the routine that had been set.

Alex laid a couple of trays for early morning tea and thought about his father. Would he and the old man ever have seen eye to eye? He remembered endless battles about 'proper jobs', 'getting down to life', 'taking a responsible attitude', 'not wasting your education and abilities'. Maybe they would have come to an understanding when Alex had managed to establish himself in his chosen career. If Tony had lived, if Alex had indeed managed to achieve what he wanted.

The kettle boiled. He took the two trays upstairs. He woke first the couple in the Abbot's Room (all the rooms were named rather than numbered, a fact he found twee but which, according to Ulla, his father had insisted gave the hotel more cachet).

Alex placed the tray on the bedside table and drew back the curtains. The whitened world was filtering into view through the lightening gloom and the delicate, icy tracery of leafless trees held exquisite beauty.

A groan from the bed signified its occupants had registered the day's start. They'd turned up yesterday evening, asking if there was a bed available. Had even had dinner. Alex reckoned it had been a spur of the moment decision by a man who should have been on his way home to wife and family but had found a more exciting companion for his bed. The man and the woman could be companions in work, there had been an easy familiarity in the way they'd chatted during dinner. But the way the bedroom was strewn with hastily discarded clothes told another part of the story.

Alex wished them good morning and left. The noise of the gradually heating radiators would prevent them returning to sleep though the temperature was still sufficiently cold to keep them in bed for some little time, even if desire did not. He went along to Camelot, containing another casual arrival. The hotel had hardly any advance bookings until the special Christmas break. Here there was a 'Do Not Disturb' notice hanging on the door. And from the way the occupant had been knocking back the double whiskies the previous evening, Alex was not surprised. The one thing he could say for hotel life was that you kept on meeting interesting people. Usually he was able to enjoy listening to details of lives very different from his own, but there had been little he could get out of this monosyllabic drinker. He placed the tray on the floor by the door and went back downstairs.

Now there were the fires to lay. He fetched the metal bucket and set to work clearing up ash, removing part of the debris and sweeping up the rest into a good pile to provide a base for the paper, kindling and small logs he built into a new fire. Then he swept each hearth and lit the fire laid in the reception hall. Once again he waited to make sure it was well alight, carefully placing two large logs either side of the healthily crackling flames. He rubbed his hands in front of them, relishing the warmth. Ulla had been shocked at the way Darina Lisle had insisted the fires be kept blazing.

'We can't afford it,' she complained when Darina threw on two more logs on her way through the hall during one of the infrequent periods of time she had spent at the hotel over the last few days.

'We can't afford not to keep it looking cheerful and warm,' she had retorted. 'Don't you see what a difference it makes?'

It had puzzled Alex slightly that his Scandinavian stepmother was so mean with the fuel. He expected her to complain about the cold, insist on keeping fires and boiler going full tilt. But she was paranoid about money, seeing the reduction of any expense as a way of keeping the place going.

Alex left the fire burning merrily, went to the back door, shrugged on an old anorak and started to chop logs to fill up the huge baskets Darina had installed beside each of the fires.

As he brought down the axe in swift, economical blows, Alex's mind returned once again to the problem of getting Ulla to sell up the hotel. It was going to be even more difficult now that she appeared to have found a partner. And a partner who showed every appearance of knowing exactly what she wanted and how to get it. Darina might not have been around much the last week but things had happened.

The new chef was a businesslike girl who had taken one look round the kitchen, glanced at the dining room, assessed the quality of the raw materials produced for her attention and announced, 'I can make something of this, if you'll let me.' Darina and she had gone into a huddle, then there had been a rapid consultation with Ulla. Alex reckoned she hadn't so much been asked if she agreed as given an ultimatum. Whatever, she had not given even a slight demur at the suggested fee for a month's trial, which was generous but not excessive, the arrangement being that if Sally Griffiths stayed after that, her salary would include special bonuses to reflect the increased business of the restaurant side of the hotel. Alex was not one who set great store by food, his idea of the perfect meal being an eight-ounce New York hamburger made with rump steak and served with a fresh salad, but he could appreciate the standard of the food that was now being produced.

He wheeled the barrow along the flagstoned passageway, then set it down outside the door to the hall and started ferrying loads of logs into the various baskets. Glancing across the hall, he had to admit that the removal of the little reception cubicle was a great improvement. Without it, the hall had improved its proportions, even regained a certain dignity.

Ulla had been against the innovation. 'But how can we deal with the guests?'

'Why do you need it to deal with guests?' Darina had countered. 'Put a bell on that nice round table and a little notice saying "Please Ring". The keys can stay in the doors until a room is taken. We can install a box for them to be dropped in when guests go out if they want to lock their rooms and have a board in your office to hang them on. They won't take a moment to fetch.'

So Ulla had given in. Indeed, she seemed shell shocked in the face of Darina's energy and determination. Alex didn't know what the new partner was up to, spending so much time away from the hotel but he was certain they would see the results before too long.

Pity that she had appeared on the scene. Without the infusion of spirit and possible cash that Darina had brought, Alex reckoned he could have got Ulla to weaken and place the hotel on the market before the New Year arrived. All right, so the market wasn't brilliant and when the bank was paid off there was unlikely to be a fortune left but his half should still be more than sufficient for his purposes.

He filled the last of the baskets, eased out his aching shoulders and wondered briefly if his purposes could equally well be served by a hotel that was making money. After all, he stood to receive half the profits. Then he reminded himself that profits were unlikely to appear for some little time yet. If the hotel stopped losing money it would be a minor miracle. No, it had to be a sale.

Pity about Darina. In more than one way. If it hadn't been for her involvement with the hotel, he might have tried his luck there. Blondes were very much a weakness of his and that hair was unusual, so long, creamy and silky. He imagined the feel of it running through his fingers. Even her size was attractive, curves were always a turn-on. And she had those in abundance with something more, an elegant ranginess that carried off her height with style. But quite apart from the hotel side of things, there was something in the directness of those grey eyes, her no-nonsense approach that warned Alex off. Not a lady for dalliance. No, Darina was the sort of girl who required a certain commitment and commitment was not a commodity he was willing to indulge in. Sometimes he wondered if he was capable of such a thing. Perhaps it was his background.

He remembered the revulsion with which he had heard the news of his father's marriage to Ulla, not a year since he had been widowed. Could one forget love so quickly? Alex remembered the warmth of his father's previous marriage, the aura of love and understanding that had warmed their home. All forgotten so easily? And for what? A Scandinavian with a good body and a sexual aura so strong it could bring moose from deep forests. And would Ulla now forget his father just as easily? Already he sensed a restlessness in her. He'd noticed the looks Adam Tennant gave her when he popped in, as he tended to do more and more often these day, 'For a quick drink,' he always said. But the drink had never been quick and now seemed to be getting slower and slower.

Alex thought of the way Adam would chat to Ulla, make her laugh, bring her eyes alight. The way her body relaxed as they spoke together. Well, if what she wanted was an affair with a married man, she could get on with it. It only proved what a poor choice his father had made. If only she would sell Tennant the wretched hotel at the same time.

Perhaps he should get closer to Darina, find out exactly how determined she was to invest in Hotel Morgan. It could possibly be a new toy that she would discard as easily as she seemed to have picked it up. Or there might be some way of deflecting her interest.

Alex picked up the handles of the empty wheelbarrow and sighed. If only his friend Andrew Stephens would come through with the goods, none of this might be necessary. But the chances of that happening were too remote even to contemplate.

He returned the wheelbarrow to the yard and went back inside, removing his anorak. It was time to make out the bills for the overnight stayers. Not for the first time Alex decided that his father's fatal heart attack had been brought about by overwork. It was no more than eight o'clock and already he was tired. He still had to help Ulla serve the breakfast, carry down bags, sort out the bar in case anyone came in for a drink before lunch, deal with telephone calls, help Ulla with the correspondence (her written English was very suspect), polish glasses and help prepare the dining room (they did seem to be getting in the Christmas lunch parties, was word of the new chef getting round or was everywhere else booked out?), then man the bar and clear it up, all the while checking the fires, answering the telephone and dealing with queries if Ulla was involved elsewhere with her equally arduous routine of ordering supplies, supervising the cleaning of the rooms and the general running of the hotel. In the afternoon he might just be able to snatch an hour or two off before dealing with incoming guests and their baggage and repeating the whole bar and dining room exercise for the evening.

Every other evening he had to stay up until the last guest had gone to bed. Thank heavens they tended to move up early; perhaps it had something to do with the fact that Ulla insisted the boiler was turned off at ten o'clock.

It was a punishing schedule that could only be lightened by more staff, which required more guests, which could only, he imagined, be wooed by further investment, for which Darina seemed the sole source.

He pushed open the door to the kitchen and found her preparing to cook breakfast.

'Morning,' she said, arranging strips of bacon over neatly halved and cored kidneys on a grill pan. 'What a beautiful day it's going to be.'

'I'm glad you think so.' Alex headed for the kettle and started to make a pot of coffee. 'I wouldn't get too enthusiastic about breakfast. I can't see our third guest making it down for some time and I don't suppose he'll want anything to eat when he does.'

'But I expect you'd like some?'

Alex's eyes lit up. Usually he made do with toast and coffee on the run. 'Are you taking over breakfast duty?'

'I told Ulla I would share it with her. Now that we've got

Sally looking after lunch and dinner, I thought it only fair.' She starting frying bread and by the time Alex had set two tables, just in case Camelot made it down, a plate loaded with a full English breakfast awaited him.

He ate swiftly, then pushed the plate away with a grunt of satisfaction, looking up to see Darina watching him with amusement.

'Best meal of the day and it's a long time since I had such a good one,' he said.

'Good, I think you're going to need it.'

There was a purpose in her voice that alerted him. 'What surprise are you going to spring on us today?'

She laughed. 'Wait and see! But I want you to help me clear some furniture out of the way after breakfast.'

The moment the business couple had left, Alex found himself carrying away the chairs from the hall, the lounge and the library. He and Darina put them up in the large attic that ran the length of the front of the hotel.

'What's going in their place?' he asked as they lugged up the last couple, stacking them as neatly as possible in a dusty corner.

'Ah,' she said mysteriously, 'you'll see.' She looked round the large space, inadequately lit by a single naked bulb. 'What's in those boxes? Your father and Ulla's things?'

He looked at the collection of tea chests gathered together in another part of the attic. 'No, I think they're an inheritance from the hotel. I remember coming up here with my father when he first bought it and he said that they really should go.'

They went over and investigated. Clouds of dust had settled on layers of newspaper covering the tops of the open chests. Underneath were folds of heavy material. Darina lifted out a pile of ancient velvet and shook it open. It was a huge curtain, the dark brown streaked with age. She laid it carefully over the pile of chairs then started pulling more material out of the chests. Alex stood and watched her growing more and more excited at her discoveries.

'These must be the old curtains, before that ghastly orange and blue stuff was put up. The material is practically falling apart but they're still usable. Help me carry them down.'

94

Alex found himself with his arms full of material, the rising dust making him sneeze. 'Now, look,' he started, 'hadn't you better discuss this with Ulla?'

'She's out this morning, getting a whole load of things for Christmas. Let's get them to the first floor landing then I can sort out which belong downstairs.'

The pile on the landing grew. Alex thought it was beginning to look like a particularly seedy jumble sale.

Then, on his way down with yet another load, he saw through the big landing window a huge furniture van come up the drive. Darina saw it too and dashed down the stairs past him. He dumped his armful of curtains and followed her.

He arrived outside in time to see two burly men unlatching the rear doors of the van. They let down the tailgate, then disappeared inside to re-emerge each carrying a wooden armchair heavily carved in the Jacobean style. 'Where do you want them, miss?'

'In here,' Darina led the way into the entrance hall.

As the chairs were gently lowered on to the flagstones, the girl who did the bedrooms appeared.

'Miss Lisle, I don't know what to do. Camelot is still in his room and I can't get in.'

Darina looked towards Alex. 'Is he booked in for tonight as well?'

'No, he definitely said just the one night.'

Darina looked at her watch. 'Eleven thirty. He's supposed to vacate by noon.' She stood looking indecisive.

'He was drinking heavily last night.' Alex was aware of a distinct feeling of unease.

'You've got your pass key?' Darina asked the girl. 'Right then, let's see if we can ginger him up. Will you come, too?' she asked Alex, 'We might need a man.'

The little group went upstairs, passing the collapsed piles of curtains. The sad heaps of worn material lying like remnants from Miss Haversham's home spoke of neglect. The scent of dust hung heavily on the air. It smelt of forgotten years, of disillusion, dry decay, disintegrated days.

Alex realised he had been left behind, that Darina was already knocking at the door of Camelot. As he came up, she was

95

unlocking the door with the pass key, then she led the way into the darkened room followed by the housemaid and Alex.

She switched on the light and they could all see the body lying across the bed, still dressed in his untidy suit, his tie loosened, the shirt collar crumpled. His mouth was open and heavy, short breaths emerged at irregular intervals. Beside the bed was an empty bottle of whisky and an empty glass. The room was pungent with the smell of alcohol.

'He seems to have spilt as much as he has drunk,' said Darina, gently shaking the sleeping man.

Alex drew the curtains, letting in the brilliant sunshine that was rapidly melting the frost wherever it touched. 'I doubt you'll wake him like that,' he said. 'Leave him to me, I've dealt with this sort of thing before. And,' he added, 'I see sofas are now following the chairs into the hall. Hadn't you better see what's happening?'

'Oh, God,' said Darina. 'I'd quite forgotten about them.'

Chapter Thirteen

Max Saunders drove down the A303 to Somerset glorying in the bright sunshine. His immaculate car was going well, the traffic was untroublesome and he was travelling towards the Hotel Morgan. He broke into the first bars of 'God Rest You Merry Gentlemen', couldn't remember how it continued and took up 'The First Noel' instead. The speedometer crept past the ninety m.p.h. mark. In front of him he noticed the blue light of a police car embedded in the middle of a regulation speed covey of cars. He lightened the pressure of his foot on the accelerator of the Volvo and drifted into a position at the rear of the group. There was no way he was going to be caught for speeding, not at the start of his Christmas holiday. He thought of how surprised Ulla and Alex would be to see him and gave an extra flourish to the last series of Noels.

Then he drove in silence for a little as he wondered how they were going to take his news. Ulla would be all right, she would applaud his decision, but he was not at all certain about Alex. For a moment he regretted not having followed through his impulse to come down the other day. He could have told them everything and had it all behind him by now. Have had extra time at the hotel. Then he thrust the thought away from him. Regrets were of no use now. As it was, he had been able to take care of bits of business in London and now he hoped everything was organised for a carefree stay.

He didn't bother to stop for lunch but a hold-up just before the Mere bypass delayed him an hour and it was after three o'clock when he finally arrived outside what he fondly thought of as the Hotel Morgue.

He had followed another car up the drive. As he parked beside it and got out, he realised the other driver was Ulla. She collected various parcels from the boot of her car, straightened up, saw him and dropped them.

'Max, darling, how wonderful!'

He caught her in a bear hug and buried his face in the fair hair, inhaling the sweet scent he always associated with her, a mixture of Calèche, clean hair and something like hay. Why this should be when she never went near hayfields he didn't know but it was so. He felt the fragile bones, the heart beating inside her rib cage like a bird with a broken leg he had once held in his hands whilst his father tied on a splint; he had never felt anything so soft as the down on that bird's breast. Then Ulla struggled free, laughing, 'Oh, Max, it's good to see you. But why so early? We weren't expecting you until Christmas Eve. Come in, it's too cold to stand out here.'

He helped her gather up the things she'd dropped and followed her into the hotel.

As they entered the reception hall he heard Ulla gasp. She stood, staring, her breath coming quickly. 'What the *hell* has happened? Darina, Darina, Darina,' she called, each repetition of the name a little more frantic than the last.

Max looked around him to see what had caused the excitement. The only thing he noticed was that the seedy, run-down, depressingly suburban air the hall had always seemed to wear had vanished. Now it was dignified, elegant in a way that would have been sombre without the warmth of the blazing log fire and the sparkling lights that scintillated and shimmered from the crystal chandelier now hanging from the ceiling.

'I say,' he said. 'What a transformation!'

'Transformation! It's something out of a nightmare. I didn't agree to this; what must it have cost!'

'Very little, I promise you.'

Max saw an amazingly tall girl with a wealth of fair hair clipped back either side of her head who had appeared from the back of the hall; she was grinning with delight.

'What do you think?'

Ulla put down her parcels on the highly polished round table set to one side of the entrance.

'I don't understand. Where did you get all this furniture?' Her glance encompassed twin velvet sofas set either side of the fire,

98

their high backs lashed together with the equally high arms by a swag of two-toned silk rope, matching chairs and a pair of ornately carved wooden armchairs with thick velvet seats and back. 'And that chandelier?'

They all looked up at the coruscating crystal prisms, rainbows of colour edging the cut glass, rays of light dancing out to play hide and seek on the panelled walls and plaster ceiling of the hall as the draught from the front door moved the glass drops.

Darina went and shut the door. 'The local auctioneers put me on to a hotel that's just closed. We've hired most of their armchairs and sofas for the next three months whilst they sort themselves out, with an option to buy if we want after that. It's costing peanuts. All I've bought is the chandelier, which was an absolute bargain. I got it at the reserve price, nobody else was bidding. Come and see what's happened in the lounge and library.'

Max followed the tall girl and Ulla across the hall. He could tell from Ulla's rigidly upright back that she was deeply upset.

'Wherever did you find those curtains?' was Ulla's first comment as they looked round the lounge, where boarding house gloom had been replaced by the same sombre richness as the hall. Velvet armchairs and small sofas, invitingly cushioned, were companionably grouped around the large room, their muted browns and purples offset by old gold velvet curtains topped by deeply fringed pelmets.

'They're the original ones, we found them in the attic. The ones in the library are amazing.'

Darina led the way into the other room.

Max liked the curtains draping the big bay window, their faded parchment silk-sheened, the drapes generous, held back with silk cords that ended in slightly tattered tassels.

'That material is rotting,' said Ulla. 'Tony and I had them out when we first arrived. I thought he had thrown them away.'

'Handled carefully they will last a little longer,' said Darina. 'Arranged as they are, you can't see the tears, can you? Don't they look magnificent?'

Max looked round the rest of the room. The uncomfortable chairs he remembered had disappeared. In their place were groups of dark leather armchairs. The TV was still in the corner but the room now had the air of a gentleman's club. On the walls, as in the lounge, were large oil paintings of anonymous nineteenth-century gentry.

'It's all dreadful, absolutely awful!' Ulla collapsed into one of the chairs and put up a hand to cover her eyes.

The tall girl perched on the arm of another; she looked upset. 'I thought you'd be pleased. Isn't it something to have got rid of those blue and orange curtains?'

'At least they were bright and clean. All this,' Ulla waved a despairing hand around her, 'it's ghastly, looks like something out of Dracula.'

'I think it's got style,' said Max, thinking it reminded him of his grandparents' house. For a brief moment a door in his memory opened and he heard again the stern warnings about Life and Duty and Gratitude that alternated with days spent learning to shoot and ride and other country pursuits with his monosyllabic grandfather.

Ulla shuddered. 'Tony said we would do nothing until we could do it right. Do it as we did the dining room and kitchen. That's style. All this is dreadful.'

'Look,' Darina leaned forward and spoke gently. 'I understand this is not what you want. The dining room is beautiful, I do appreciate that, but that's part of the trouble.'

'Trouble?' Ulla dropped her hand from her eyes.

'Yes, it shows up the rest of the hotel so badly. Those terrible chairs, they weren't even comfortable. And those curtains, they may have been bright but they were all wrong for this place. So maybe it does look like something out of a gothic novel but you're right,' she looked at Max, 'it does now have style. Eccentric, maybe, but is that a bad thing? At least it makes us different.'

She turned back to Ulla. 'People want something of an experience when they stay at a hotel. Establishments like the Manor Park offer superb luxury, designer comfort, they cosset all the senses, your eye feeds on the same refinement of taste as your palate is offered. We can't afford that sort of décor, glazed chintz, toning swags, dragged paintwork, not yet. So we must offer a different sort of experience.'

'It's certainly different,' said Max admiringly. He liked the effect, it made the old building come alive, gave it character.

100

'Well, stepmother, dear, what do you think?'

Max turned towards the door. 'Alex!' he exclaimed joyfully.

His reception was a curt 'What the hell are you doing down here this early?'

'Alex, don't be like that, it's wonderful to have him here.' Ulla reached out and caught Max's hand, drawing him down on to the chair-arm beside her.

He grasped her hand in both of his, giving it gentle caresses.

Alex continued to look at him enquiringly.

Max felt a moment of unease. 'Oh, I managed to get a few days off, thought I'd surprise you. Well, I think it all looks magnificent. Never thought the old place could look so, so . . . ' he hunted for the right word and came up with: 'elegant.'

'What do you think, Alex?' asked Ulla.

'I think "Hotel Morgue" just about sums it up.'

'So you don't like it either?'

'For once, Ulla, I'm in agreement with you.'

Max caught the tall girl giving Alex a sharp look but she didn't say anything.

'I don't think it's your style at all.'

Now it was Ulla giving Alex the sharp look. 'You devil, Alex, you just want me to go off my head, give it all up. You don't care at all, you don't care about anything, anything except yourself.'

Alex leant against the door frame and folded his arms. 'Not true,' he said softly, looking at her, 'but you are right about my wanting you to give up this hotel. It really isn't your style. Just be thankful you weren't here this morning when we had to deal with the drunkest sod it's been my bad luck to come across.'

'Drunk? What happened?'

Max regained his grasp of Ulla's hand and stroked it soothingly.

'Nothing,' said Alex. 'Just one of those little problems that arises with hotels. Mr Jones decided to drown his sorrows and overdid it. He's all right now, gone on his way, but it'll be a few days before you can let the room again.'

'Hardly likely to need it before Christmas anyway,' said Darina. She looked at Max. 'I don't think we've met.' She held out her hand and came towards him. 'I'm Darina Lisle, I may be going into partnership with Ulla. No need to introduce yourself, you must be Alex's brother.'

Max felt inordinately pleased. 'Are we that alike?'

'Same fair hair, same blue eyes, the resemblance is extraordinary, isn't it, Ulla?'

Ulla looked from one young man to the other. 'I suppose it is.'

Alex laughed. 'Ulla's amazed because we're so different in character. She's never thought of us as brothers, isn't that right, stepmother, dear?'

Max watched a slight flush suffuse Ulla's face. He suddenly felt very protective towards her. A memory of her taking him shopping for his first pair of jeans returned to him. What patience she had had, trailing round shop after shop while he searched for a copy of the pair he had seen Alex wear. 'Any chance of a cup of coffee and a sandwich in this super-luxury hotel with tremendous style? I haven't had anything to eat since breakfast and I'm starving.'

'You poor boy,' Ulla rose. 'You've come all the way down from London and I haven't even given you a proper welcome. Come along, there's bound to be something nice left over from lunch, at least the new chef is a success.'

Max happily followed her out of the room. 'I've got such lots to tell you, I've made some really important decisions about my life.'

Chapter Fourteen

That evening Darina found herself with both Alex and Max in one of the local pubs. It was Ulla's turn to be on duty, a task which was not going to prove particularly onerous since the only business the Hotel Morgan had that night was two tables for dinner. Even so, it was an improvement on the previous week. Rarely had there been more than four customers for the evening meal, in addition, of course, to George Prendergast, Ulla and Alex. Lunch business might have picked up, nothing else had. The situation worried her.

Now that Sally Griffiths was settling down so nicely and Darina had temporarily solved the dire decorative state of the hotel, to her satisfaction if not to Ulla's, it was time to turn her attention to the problem of building up the restaurant's business. Her attempt to discuss the issue with Ulla had revealed the Scandinavian's complete lack of any ideas.

'Tony knew all about that side, he had all the marketing ideas. I'm sure we will gradually get more people in. If only that newspaper man hadn't come in when the food was so awful! Adam Tennant said he would be sure to attract lots of business.'

'Was it he who suggested you ask him round?'

'He gave me his name and telephone number.'

'We shall have to ask him back, offer him a free meal for two.'

Ulla had agreed and they'd sent off the letter but Darina did not have any great hopes of it stimulating much new business. More action was needed.

After supper on the day of what she looked on as the hotel's transformation, she found Alex in the office. She wasted no time coming to the point. 'I want to talk to you about improving the restaurant business.'

He looked up from the letter he was studying, the blue eyes suddenly ablaze, his face alight in a way she hadn't seen before. She wondered what the letter contained to cause such a transformation.

'I can't think it will do you any good. You know as far as I am concerned this enterprise is a dead duck but why don't we go out for a drink? And let's ask Max as well.'

He bounded up from the desk, folding the letter he'd been reading and tucking it into his inside jacket pocket, and went through to the hall, where Max and Ulla were having coffee in front of the fire.

Max hesitated in accepting the invitation. He looked at Ulla. 'I thought I'd keep you company this evening.'

She smiled at him. 'Don't be silly, go with Alex and Darina. I have the accounts to work on; we will have time later for a chat.'

Alex drove them to a pub a little way towards Bristol. It was pleasant, with comfortable chairs, an open fire and a happy clientele. The tables were all occupied but they found a couple of spare bar stools and Darina and Max sat down while Alex ordered.

The barman was a cheerful fellow. 'Nice to see you again, stranger; where've you been?'

'Dealing with a new broom.' Alex gave a sidelong grin at Darina and handed her a glass of white wine.

The barman carefully drew a pint of draught lager. 'Gather Ken didn't work out then.'

Alex said nothing, merely handed Max the beer, but Darina's attention had been caught.

'You mean Ken Farthing, the chef?'

'Ho, that's what he's calling himself now, is it?'

'What do you call him?'

'Cook is what he's known as when he works here.'

'You mean you've employed him?' Darina looked round the pub, glancing at the large slate with that night's dishes handwritten on it, good staple choices that were even now being consumed at many of the tables.

'Works here regularly "between engagements" as you might say.' The barman handed Alex his pint of bitter and rang up the drinks.

'Thanks, Dave and have one yourself,' said Alex, handing over a five pound note.

'Thanks, mate, a half of Shires'll hit the spot.' Dave pulled himself a glass of bitter.

'What do you mean, "between engagements"?' asked Darina.

The chap looked around, saw the barmaid was dealing with the other customers and leant his arms on the counter, settling down for a bit of a chat.

'Ken's got the idea he's a bit flash with the kitchen stove, thinks he's competition for Keith Floyd. On the straight and simple stuff, the sort of thing we serve here, he's good, no doubt about it. Never have no complaints. But that's not enough for him. He has to be "creative". Never seems to realise he's hopeless at it. What happens is he hears of a place that wants some arty-farty chef, begging your pardon, Alex, but that's what you was in the market for, no denying it. So off he goes, cooks them his presentation dish that he learnt some place or other, convinces them he's the answer to the maiden's prayers and settles in. Well, it depends on how long it is before he's given his head but as soon as that happens, the game's up, they realise he can't cook that sort of grub to save his soul and he's back here asking if I've a job!'

'And have you?'

'Sometimes I have, sometimes I haven't. He was here the other day and I'd nothing to offer.'

'So where's he gone?'

Dave took a long drag of his beer. 'Said he was off to London, could be something there. God knows, there're enough restaurants and pubs, but I shouldn't be surprised to see him turn up here again before too long.'

'And you'd employ him if you did have a vacancy?'

'Like a shot. Like I said, at this sort of grub he's good, no fooling. And he works! Gets through more work than one and half other cooks. It's his strength. Mind you, you've got to keep him off the booze. Did you have any trouble with him in that direction, Alex?'

Alex broke off his conversation with Max. 'What? Drink and Ken? No, no trouble at all.'

'Don't suppose he was there long enough. Usually starts off all right.'

105

'What happens then?' asked Darina.

'Gets bored, or frustrated, see. Starts slowly then suddenly it's the hard stuff, keeps it in an old wine bottle by the stove, takes a swig when he thinks no one's looking, then another, then another. Before you know it, he's raging drunk and picking a fight with whoever's at hand. Silly sod!'

Darina remembered the size of the incompetent chef. 'I wouldn't care to be the one he picks the fight with, particularly with kitchen knives around.'

'I'll say this for him, he usually relies on his hands, though there was once an incident with a meat cleaver.' Dave gazed reminiscently across the pub.

'What happened?' asked Darina after a moment.

'The serving counter's got a bloody big dent in it, that's what happened. Luckily I managed to get out of the way!'

'And you are still willing to employ him?'

'Like I said, he's a bloody good worker. I reckon it's up to me to keep him off the booze.'

Customers waiting to be served claimed Dave's attention and he moved to the other end of the bar.

'Did you know any of that about Ken Farthing?' Darina asked Alex.

'Not a thing. I've been in here quite often, Dave's a good sort and it's a good pub, but I've never been behind the scenes. Must have eaten Ken's steak and kidney pie, I suppose, from time to time.'

'And if that's the sort of food he's been serving George Prendergast, no wonder he was happy with it.'

Max was looking bewildered. Alex started to fill him in on the saga of Ken Farthing and Darina looked around the pub, admiring its atmosphere of cheerful bonhomie. Then watched in astonishment as William and his new female assistant came into the pub.

She hadn't seen the detective since her visit to the Manor Park. He'd rung her the following evening, given her some of the details of the murder investigation they were conducting, asked her in a fairly perfunctory way how she was getting on with Ulla and the Hotel Morgan, then said he couldn't talk longer as he was still working but would be in touch again when he had a moment.

Darina had put down the telephone with a spurt of emotion she didn't care to analyse.

There had been two more hurried calls, then nothing for several days. Now here he was walking into The Fox and Goose with Constable Pat James. On or off duty?

The pair walked up to the bar.

'Dave Cummings, landlord?' asked William.

The man behind the bar nodded.

William showed him his identification.

'Nothing to do with the licence, I hope?'

'No, just conducting some routine enquiries. Do you recognise this girl?' William turned to Pat James, who produced a snapshot from her handbag and the sergeant handed it across to the landlord.

Dave studied it for several minutes, then he shook his head. 'Couldn't really say. She might have been in here, then again, she might not. We get a lot of casual trade, mostly from Bristol and Bath, the food's good and we're not expensive. Girls looking like her come in every week.'

'So you couldn't say if she was in here Saturday ten days ago?'

'Saturday ten days ago? Have a heart, sergeant, half Somerset gets in here on a Saturday night.'

William sighed and crossed off a name from a list in his notebook. Then he looked up and saw Darina.

There was no hesitation in the way he came across.

'Am I following you or are you following me? But what a sight for overworked eyes you are. I've been missing you. This wretched case means I have no time to call my own. Alex, good to see you.'

Darina eyed him. He seemed as open and warm as ever. She glanced over at his female companion, who appeared deeply interested in the menu board. William followed her glance.

'Pat,' he called, 'come and meet Darina Lisle.'

The two girls shook hands, Pat giving Darina a small smile.

Darina introduced Alex and Max, watching with interest the total lack of impact their quite considerable charms appeared to have on the constable.

Max said, 'Police, how interesting! What are you investigating?'

'Murder,' said William. He held out the snapshot. 'This girl

107

was strangled ten days ago just a few miles from here. We're trying to find out if she was seen in any of the local pubs that Saturday night and with whom.'

'Can I offer you a drink?' asked Alex as he took the photo.

'Kind of you but we're on duty.'

Darina looked over Alex's shoulder at the snapshot. A laughing face with a mass of fair hair looked back at her. Nothing very special about it, but there was a vitality in the eyes that was appealing. Strangled, William had said; Darina gave an inward shudder, then noticed a curious rigidity in Alex as he also looked at the photo. She glanced at him – just as he grimaced and shook his head.

'Did you say she's dead?' he asked, his voice shocked.

'Found in a ditch the Monday I lunched at your place. She was the reason I had to dash away and leave you to drive Darina home.'

'Pretty girl,' Alex said steadily and handed the photo back to Pat James.

'Recognise her?' asked William.

'No, no, can't say I do. Though it's a fairly ordinary face; I doubt it would have registered if I had met her.'

'Her legs might.'

'Legs?'

'She had very long, very shapely legs.'

'Ah, I'm a breast man myself.'

'Alex!' protested Max.

He leaned across and ruffled the younger man's hair. 'Poor form, eh? You're quite right. I apologise, William. I'm sorry the young woman came to such a bad end but I can't help your investigation.'

'Didn't really think you could. How about your brother?' He showed the snapshot to Max, who gave it a cursory glance and shook his head.

'Max isn't often down here, it's not likely he'd know her,' Alex said.

William sighed. 'Come on, constable, it's on to the next one on our list.'

He might have called her constable but once again the way he guided her across the room gave Darina a jealous jolt. She chided herself for being a dog in the manger. It did no good.

'Nice figure, hardly shown off to best advantage in that loose coat, face a bit pale but lovely shape, could be quite a looker if she did something to herself. What did you think, Max?'

'If you mean that policewoman, I hardly noticed her. Bit nondescript if you want my opinion.'

'You're slipping, brother dear, not nearly as perceptive as usual.'

'You're the Romeo, *brother*, not me. You're the one who has to degrade every female he sees.'

'Now that's hardly fair. What do you say, Darina? Have I tried even a morsel of degradation on you?'

The blond hair flopped over the broad forehead above the cynical eyes. He leant against the bar with every appearance of relaxation but a muscle twitched just below his left eye.

Opposite him, perched on a bar stool, Max was almost his mirror image. Same floppy blond hair, same regular features, same strong bones, eyes the same pale blue under colourless lashes but the blue lacked the ice in those of the older man. There was something else lacking, too, a cutting edge of intelligence and worldliness. Or was it just that Max was so much younger?

And hot headed. 'Alex, you're never serious! You never take anything seriously. Why can't you treat girls with some respect?'

'Respect? Is it respect they want? Well, well, well. Remind me to try that line one of these days, my young expert on female psychology.'

Max flushed. 'I know I'm not experienced like you, Alex, but I think I know more about some things.'

'You do, eh?' said very softly. 'And what sort of things would they be?'

'Well, Ulla for one.'

'And what is it about Ulla you understand so well?'

Max sucked in his underlip and hesitated, then plunged in. 'She doesn't deserve the way you treat her.'

'And how do I treat her?'

'Like, like she's something the cat dragged in.'

'Ah, is that how I treat her?'

Darina slipped down from her bar stool and murmured a word about finding the ladies.

Once there, she lingered as long as she could, then emerged to find Alex standing alone at the bar. 'Where's Max?' she asked as she rejoined him.

'Gone back to the hotel in a huff. Said he'd walk or hitch-hike. I'd dared to suggest his beloved Ulla was something less than a complete saint and he couldn't stand to breathe the same air a moment longer.' He finished his drink with a rapid swallow, banged the glass on the counter and shouted, 'Dave, how about some service down this end of the bar? Make it a double whisky and another white wine, or would you, too, prefer something stronger, Darina?'

Darina said she would prefer to stick to the wine. 'And it's my round this time,' she insisted.

'The joys of women's lib,' Alex murmured, downing half his whisky in one go. 'Now, what was it you were so anxious to pick my brains about?'

Darina put the change in her purse and picked up her glass. 'First, tell me why you and Max have such different attitudes to Ulla? Why you resent her so much and he so obviously adores her?'

The ice-blue eyes stared back at her. 'Any reason why I should go into the family history with you?'

'Only that if I'm to become Ulla's partner, it seems reasonable I should know something of the background.'

'But I'm not interested in you becoming Ulla's partner. I'd rather she sold the hotel.'

'So you can have your share?'

'Bang on, Watson.'

'What do you need the money for that is so important?'

'Now that really is none of your business. I might just as well ask what it is about that insignificant little policewoman that has you so up-tight.'

'What do you mean?'

'Don't you know how prim your mouth became as William introduced her? The way you became the glacial goddess? Good God, girl, you have nothing to fear from her, not unless you turn off the warmth with which you are so liberally endowed.'

Darina refused to be diverted. 'I still want to know about Max.'

'God defend me from woman's curiosity. All right, so far as

110

Max is concerned, Ulla is the only real mother he's ever known.'

Darina frowned. 'I don't understand. Why do you resent Ulla taking Trudy's place so much and Max doesn't?'

'Great heavens, girl, you have got it all mixed up. First off, Ulla isn't Max's stepmother.'

'But . . . ' Darina thought rapidly, 'you mean you and he have different *fathers*?'

'Well done.'

'No need to be sarky, it was a natural error!'

'Was it?'

'He seemed so at home.' Darina adjusted some more of her ideas and said, 'You mean Trudy wasn't your mother either?'

'Whatever gave you the idea she was?'

Darina began to think her deductive powers had completely deserted her. 'It was just that you were so resentful of Ulla, I thought she must have supplanted your mother.'

Alex sighed patiently. 'To all intents and purposes, from the age of about three Trudy was my mother. I suppose I felt about her much as Max feels about Ulla. We were,' he hesitated, 'we were a very happy family.'

'I gather she died,' Darina said after a moment.

'Cancer,' said Alex shortly. 'It wasn't very pretty. I thought Dad was as cut up about it as I was. I couldn't believe it when he announced he was getting married again, less than a year after Trudy'd died. To a girl almost half his age.'

'It's supposed to be a tribute to a happy marriage when a widower gets married again quickly.'

'Is it?' he said bitterly. 'I think she trapped him, seduced him.'

'Surely you don't believe that!'

'Haven't you seen the way she looks at men?'

Darina thought instead of Ulla's description of her marriage. 'Wasn't your father happy?'

Alex looked moodily at his drink, 'I wasn't at home much, after university I spent most of the time abroad. Dad and I didn't see eye to eye about a number of things.'

'Then how can you judge? What about when you were home?'

'Who knows what goes on in a marriage; just because they seemed happy enough . . . '

'Then what grounds do you have for supposing it wasn't?'

111

Alex said nothing but kicked at the foot of the bar, looking all at once very like Max.

'What about your actual mother,' asked Darina. 'Is she still alive and how was it that Max spent so much time with your father and Ulla?'

'God, you're inquisitive!'

'Well, you have to admit it's an interesting situation. Not many men would welcome their ex-wife's child by another man!'

'No? Well, Dad took pity on him after I explained what a raw deal he'd been landed with, no mother and an army father who was hardly ever there. I once went up to see him at his grandparents' home. Now there was something out of a gothic novel. Enormous place, both the old folk pure Victoriana, so strict you wouldn't believe, never allowed Max to mix with other youngsters, said they'd lead him into bad habits.'

'How did you persuade them to let him visit you?'

Alex grinned at her, 'My famous charm. Had them eating out of my hand. When I want, I know exactly how to handle people.'

Darina thought what a pity it was he didn't exercise his talent a little more often.

'Now that's enough about our family history. Have another drink.'

Darina asked for a mineral water.

'Sensible girl. You can drive us home, I think I'm going to get drunk. Do you mind?'

Darina looked at him, eyes bright, febrile, fingers beating an insistent pattern on the bar. 'No.'

'Does that refer to your driving or my getting drunk?'

'Either. Personally I don't think drinking solves anything but if it helps you live with whatever devil is bugging you at the moment, who am I to preach?'

'Nasty one,' said Alex appreciatively. 'No wonder I don't want to tangle with you.'

'You don't?'

He flashed her a swift smile, full of unreliable charm. 'Max was quite right, I am something of a devil for the girls. I can't refuse a pretty face.'

'Except for mine – and Ulla's?'

'Except for yours and Ulla's,' he agreed. Then he gave a brief exclamation. 'You're right about drinking, I forgot to tell you, I've got to go to London tomorrow, you'll have to cover with the bar, or get Max to do it.' The air of suppressed excitement he had had earlier that day was back. 'Now, was it really the family history you wanted to discuss tonight?'

Darina consigned marketing strategy to a future occasion. 'Why do you think Ulla is so determined to hang on to the hotel?' she asked instead. 'I agree with you that she doesn't know much about how to run one. If she's had a good offer, why continue the struggle?'

'To spite me.'

'You really believe that?'

Alex looked into the bottom of his empty glass then put it down on the counter with a sigh. 'No, you're right, I don't. I don't know what the answer is, I wish I did. She won't discuss it with me, for which I suppose I can hardly blame her. It's not as though I've been sympathetic to her problems. Have you asked her yourself?'

'She says she wants to carry on your father's work but she also says if she sells up she won't have enough to live on.'

'Ah,' Alex was back at his most cynical, 'there we have it. In the hotel she can live in fine style; without it she'd be condemned to slum it.'

'Hotel Morgan fine style?' Darina thought of the bare little apartment Ulla inhabited in the stable block.

'Look at the space, think of the dining room! And it's living more or less free, even if there isn't much money coming in. Where else could she play hostess with as much aplomb – and Ulla does enjoy playing hostess, you haven't seen that side of her yet.'

'She did say she was looking forward to the Christmas Holiday.'

'God, Christmas!'

'You aren't looking forward to it?' It was a statement rather than a question but Alex treated it as such.

'A whole load of strangers to be kept happy, food and drink coming out of all orifices, the boiler to be kept going overtime, Max in some kind of scrape, oh, it's going to be a bundle of laughs.'

113

'Max in a scrape?'

'I keep wondering why he turned up today. He can't just have been given ten days off. He's articled to a firm of accountants and the end of the year is their busiest time; there's even been some doubt as to whether he'd get enough time off to make it worth coming down at all. He's either walked out or been fired. And didn't you hear him say to Ulla he'd made some big decision about his life?' Alex rubbed at his eyes. 'It'll be time at some stage for big brother to bring him down to earth, sometimes he hasn't got the sense he was born with and there's no one else now to remind him what life's really about. I don't relish the prospect, he's got a hell of a temper, but it'll have to be done.'

'Do as I say, not as I do,' murmured Darina, following him out of the pub and accepting the keys of the station wagon that looked as though a tramp had camped in it for a week.

Chapter Fifteen

They picked up Max trudging wearily down the A37 towards the hotel, sticking out a thumb at the sound of each car coming up behind him without bothering to turn round. He didn't say a word as Darina drew up and Alex opened the rear door, just flung himself on to the back seat; then grunted sharply.

'Honestly, Alex,' he complained, drawing out an empty beer can from the depths of the upholstery behind him. 'Don't you ever clean this thing? What would Tony have said?'

'Dad knew it was on its last legs, he was supposed to get a new one next year. It was Ulla who got to change hers this summer.' Bitterness laced his voice like anchovies in pizza.

'I'll clean it out tomorrow.' It was an unspoken apology.

'Thanks, kid. Can I take yours to the station or will you drive me?'

'Station? Where are you going? I thought we could have a talk.'

'Don't sound so dismayed, I'm only going to London for the day. Business. We'll have a chat, I promise you.'

Later, looking back over the whole story, Darina wondered that she hadn't seen the clues that were offered to her the following day. They had all been there, everything she needed to make sense of both what had happened and the tragedy that was about to happen. If she had realised, would it have made any difference? What an impossible question. Precognition is rarely granted. No, at the time the day had unfolded in what seemed a jumble of disconnected events. Unsettling some of them, not to mention unpleasant, but hardly sinister.

Alex had come down to breakfast in a suit. 'I wouldn't have believed you owned one,' Darina teased him, placing a plate loaded with grilled kidneys, bacon and tomato in front of him.

'It was his father's,' said Ulla sharply, searching for the new luncheon menu.

'You need three of those platefuls to fill it out,' commented Max, sitting down to his own breakfast.

It was true the dark suit had been made for a larger man than the lean Alex. And it was doubtful if its tailor had intended it to be worn over a polo neck sweater and a fisherman's knit.

'You look like sartorial kedgeree,' added Max.

'Sartorial kedgeree? That's good, I like it.'

'There are a few special supplies we need if you have time,' Darina produced a list from her pocket. 'I've given details of where you should be able to get the items.'

Alex glanced at it. 'You can't be serious. I shan't have time to dash around doing your errands and what's couverture anyway?'

'Tempered chocolate, and we really do need some.'

Alex shoved the list into his wallet. 'I don't promise anything. Come on, Max, we're going to miss that train.'

His brother picked up the hold-all Alex had dropped by the table. 'Heavens, this is weighty! What on earth have you got in it?'

The hold-all was snatched from him and Alex headed for the door. Max shrugged his shoulders and followed.

'What he wants to do in London, I can't imagine,' said Ulla crossly as they left. 'Leaving us in the lumber is what it is.'

'When did he last have a day off?'

Ulla ignored the question and waved the menu she had found. 'Darina, is this a good idea? No à la carte and so little choice?'

Darina bent over to look at it, though she knew it by heart. 'Ah, but look at what is being offered: home-made soup or warm mussel salad, roast beef or breast of turkey, with a vegetarian alternative of stuffed ravioli, with treacle tart, mince pies or our own special ice cream for pudding. All right, the mussel salad can be classed as a bit iffy for this area but we have to do something to show we are operating in the Nineties and the rest is sure-fire stuff. What's the matter; regretting you said you'd leave all the decisions on food to Sally and me?'

Darina doubted if Ulla appreciated how skilfully the menu

had been put together to sound traditional yet deliver unexpected touches that she and the new chef believed would bring the most discerning of clients back whilst not alienating the more conservative diners. Like little tarts with puréed leek that would accompany all the main courses, mustard hollandaise to go with the beef, home-made fresh mincemeat in the mince pies and Crème Anglaise to accompany the treacle tart. Darina was confident Sally would soon get them a reputation for gutsy food that was unpretentious but of first-class quality. The Hotel Morgan was to be known as somewhere that offered enjoyable food of impeccable standard – and for a good price.

'I don't believe what we're charging,' said Ulla. 'Are we going to make any money at all?'

'Sally's worked hard on the costings, we will make a reasonable margin. I'm going to circulate copies to all the local offices, we've still got time to improve business before Christmas.'

'More expense!'

Darina looked at Ulla. 'Sit down,' she suggested, drawing out a chair. She poured her a cup of coffee. 'Tell me what's bugging you. You know we've got to increase the restaurant business if we're to improve the hotel bookings. Heads on beds is what we need and food is the way to get them.'

'I yust feel I'm losing control,' Ulla blinked her eyes rapidly. 'I dash here and there getting things you've suggested, come back to find the hotel completely transformed, looking like something Dracula might have been comfortable with; it isn't what I expected!'

'Ulla, I'm sorry.' Darina sat down opposite her. 'I've been so excited, finding Sally, getting the food organised and the furniture and everything, I hadn't realised you weren't happy.' It flashed upon her that she had been totally insensitive to Ulla's feelings and needs. 'When the auctioneer introduced me to that hotel and I saw the furniture, all I could think of was how perfect it would look here. I wanted to surprise you with its effect but now I realise I should have consulted you before rushing ahead. Do you really hate the way it all looks?'

Ulla thought carefully before speaking then said, 'No, it's yust not what Tony and I would have done. I suppose I have to get used to realising it is all different now.' They were sitting in the small staff room off the kitchen and Ulla looked round it like a puppy trying to decide if this was home.

'Would you like to call our arrangement off?' Even as she made the offer, Darina realised how involved she had become with what even she now affectionately thought of as the Hotel Morgue. Unpromising as it had seemed at first, she knew now it could be made into somewhere people would want to stay. She believed that the restaurant could make money and, after that, the hotel side.

She silently cursed her stupidity in barging ahead as though it was hers, for not making sure Ulla felt happy with the changes. Whose hotel was it, after all?

The other girl sat without speaking for several minutes. The longer the silence lasted, the more sure Darina was Ulla would say it would be best if they split up. At last the Scandinavian said, 'No, I don't want you to leave. You are like Tony, you know where you are going and I need that. I don't have your ideas, your energy. It's just,' it was a measure of the care with which she was speaking that for once Ulla managed the 'j' sound perfectly, 'I'm beginning to think perhaps I should sell after all.'

It was the last thing Darina had expected to hear. 'What's made you change your mind?'

A small sigh escaped Ulla; soft as a baby's breath, it carried the failure of someone unable to meet the challenges of a big, wicked world. 'It's such a battle and Alex is pressuring me so much, wouldn't it be the easiest thing? Maybe I could return to being a florist, start another shop.'

Darina sat and thought. No doubt to sell would be best for Ulla. But could she top Adam Tennant's offer and would her house provide enough initial finance? And was she prepared to take on such a large project on her own?

'Let's get Christmas over with before you make any decisions,' she said finally.

Ulla smiled wanly. 'OK,' she said. 'A small delay can't matter that much.'

'And I promise to talk everything over with you, make sure you really want to do what I suggest. And you must tell me your ideas and what you think.'

'It's a bargain.' Ulla gave her first real smile of the day.

'Did you have a good time with Alex and Max last night?'

'It was a nice pub,' said Darina evasively. 'But Alex is worried about his brother. Has Max told you what he is up to?'

'Oh dear, I hoped we could get Christmas over with before that came up. I don't know what he's going to say. Max has left his job.'

So, big brother was right. 'Why?'

'He says accounting is so boring.'

'What does he want to do instead?'

'Join the army, like his father, the General.'

A general, no doubt that explained the neat conservatism of Max's clothes, the cords and cavalry twill trousers, tweed jackets and check shirts and the jeans that were so immaculate, so unlike Alex's well-worn working uniform. Did it also have something to do with his nice manners, so different from those of his half-brother? 'Will Alex approve?'

'He didn't like Max's father.'

'Does that mean he doesn't like the army either?'

'He was such a strange man,' said Ulla inconsequentially. 'Terribly strict with Max. Do you know, he wouldn't let him drink before he was eighteen? Of course, he did with us, Tony believed in letting people find out for themselves how to cope with things like alcohol. Max got drunk a couple of times but he soon settled down. Tony really understood people.' Her voice wavered and Darina took a closer look at her. Tiny shadows bruised the fine skin under eyes that were sheened with unshed tears. Ulla reacted to the scrutiny by fluffing out her hair and turning her face away from the searching gaze.

'Why don't you have a night off?' suggested Darina. 'You haven't been out since I started here.'

'Where would I go?' The query was both plaintive and sulky.

'Why not take Max out?'

'Max? What fun is it to go out with a boy? He's very sweet and I love him but, oh, Darina, what I would give for an evening with an attractive man. To dress up, make myself beautiful and have him look at me as though I was the most desirable woman in the world. Tony was such a *man*, he knew how to treat a woman. The nights are so empty, now, so empty and so *long*. Do you know, before Tony died, men were so attentive to me. Major

119

Brownsword, Olivia's father, he was always round here and so were others. The moment Tony died, when I really needed them, they disappeared. It's only Adam who comes round now. Why? Have I suddenly become ugly?'

'Men often feel safe flirting with a happily married woman. If you had given them any real encouragement, I suspect they would have disappeared sooner.'

'So, you think I am still a little beautiful?'

Darina smiled. 'I think you are very beautiful, just a little tired and depressed after all you have been through. You need a break.'

'I think you are right. But dinner with Max is not an answer.'

Perhaps Alex had been more perceptive about his stepmother than Darina had given him credit for.

Ulla pushed away her empty cup and rose. 'This is no good. Let's go round the hotel and I'll tell you how I'm going to do the Christmas decorations.' She drew Darina's arm through her own, giving the hand a quick squeeze. 'It's good to have a friend to talk with. I enjoy having you here. Without you I think I would hit the sponge.'

Did she mean hit the bottle or chuck in the sponge?

Later Darina went over to the stable block to fetch some notes she had made after their return the previous night. In the yard Max was giving Alex's car the clean-out of its life. As Darina passed, he chucked old beer cans into a plastic bag. 'Some job you've got there,' she called to him on her way over.

The notes were quickly found, then Darina went to close her window; the weather was getting colder and colder. The window was stiff and as she gave it a tug, her line of vision caught Max standing strangely immobile.

He was looking at something in his hands, Darina couldn't see what but had the impression of something soft. On the ground were piles of items removed from the car: map books, torches, tins of boiled sweets. Whatever it was Max had in his hands apparently did not belong with these motoring necessities. He thrust it into a pocket of his jeans, leaving a flash of white hanging out, and then dived back into the car to continue his rubbish hunt.

120

Darina shut the window, then stood listening to the noises coming through from George Prendergast's room next door, gradually registering their significance. She could not have said how long they had been going on but it was impossible now to ignore them. The gasps and groans were unmistakable and must come from more than two people. Could he be having an orgy next door? Darina felt her flesh crawl.

The Hotel Morgan's permanent resident had irritated her increasingly over the last few days. There was an oiliness about him, an ingratiating quality that removed any possible pleasure from the complimentary remarks he had showered on her over the changes she had made in the hotel. He would place his small hand, white and smooth as a courtesan's, on her arm, look at her with spaniel eyes, the putty-coloured skin of his fleshy face unhealthily shining, as though the short walk from wherever he had appeared had been too much for his aging lungs, and talk with breathy confidence. Darina would remove herself from his company as quickly and unobtrusively as possible, disliking herself for her antipathy, aware that it was becoming a problem.

Now she opened her door, to find Dawn, the housemaid who did the stable rooms, about to knock on the civil servant's door.

'Am I hearing what I think I'm hearing?' asked Darina.

The girl turned, unconcerned. 'That's only G.P.'s video, dirty old man.' She knocked loudly on the door. 'Twenty minutes, Mr Prendergast.' The girl went past Darina's room and opened Alex's door. 'I always give him a warning, lets him get himself together while I do these two rooms.'

'You mean he's watching a blue movie?'

'I expect it's the only excitement he gets,' the girl said tolerantly.

Darina followed her into Alex's room. 'Does this happen every morning?'

'Oh, no. But it's been getting more often lately.'

'Doesn't he know you do the rooms at this time?'

'Gives him an extra thrill, I reckon, to know I'm out there, listening to what's going on, filthy sod.' The girl seemed unmoved by any aspect of the sordid episode, getting on with her job of making the bed, then moving on to clean the small shower room.

Darina stood watching her, her mind grappling with the facts, automatically taking in the room's sparse furnishings: the type-writer on the table under the window, a pile of notebooks to one side; the bookshelf crammed with battered volumes by Paul Theroux, Patrick Leigh Fermor, Eric Newby and Jonathan Raban, together with books on America, on China, on Russia. No wonder Alex had such a far away look in his eyes so much of the time.

The housemaid emerged from the shower with her pail of equipment.

'Dawn, does Mr Prendergast ever, well, try anything?'

'Touch me up, you mean? He tried it one time but I told him I'd get my brother to sort him out. Bob is bi-i-ig.' She drew out the word in a way that left no doubt about the size of her brother.

'But he continues to play his video so you can hear it?'

'I can cope with that. It's pathetic really, isn't it?'

'Has he tried anything with any of the other girls?'

'Angela went out to dinner with him once.' Angela was the little waitress with the quiff of yellow hair that had served Darina on her first visit to the hotel with William. 'She warned me not to accept if he asked. So I didn't.'

'Have you mentioned any of this to Mrs Mason?'

'Didn't think it would do much good. If Mr Mason had still been alive, I would've. He could sort G.P. out.' She hesitated for a moment. 'Can't say I wouldn't prefer it if I didn't have to go through the whole silly business.'

'Don't worry,' Darina said grimly. 'I'll see to it you don't have to put up with it a day longer. Come straight back to the main building after you've done my room. Leave Mr Prendergast's.'

She went back across the yard to find Ulla. Max was now busy washing down Alex's car, his face concentrated and thoughtful, the warm water steaming in the cold air, suds sliding down the doors and dripping off to lie on the yard like melting snow. The flash of white still peeked from his pocket and Darina could see now it was nylon, with lace attached.

Ulla was with Olivia Brownsword. The girl had not been much in evidence over the last week. Alex had taken her out one evening, returning to the hotel around one thirty in the morning, just as Darina was clearing up after a couple of businessmen who had sat late beside the hall fire, swapping stories. Alex had helped with the last of the glasses, then turned scratchy when she'd asked him how his evening had gone, muttering something about possessive women.

'Where is he?' Olivia was demanding now as Darina came into the hall. 'He said he would call me and he hasn't.' She was wearing a sheepskin coat, more practical in style than her usual outfits, with a silk scarf tied over her hair. Her leather boots needed cleaning.

'I am not Alex's keeper,' snapped Ulla.

'You're trying to keep him away from me, that's what it is!'

'Nonsense! I will tell him you called when he gets back. Now, would you please go, we have a lot of work to do this morning.' Ulla deliberately turned her back and walked through to the dining room.

Olivia was left looking for something to vent her frustration on and found Darina. 'Are you after him, too?' Her voice was sulky and dispirited, rather than spiteful. 'Just remember I have prior claim and you can tell him that.'

'I have no interest in Alex Mason,' Darina said, watching the girl thrust her hands deep into her coat pockets. 'But I don't think he's the sort of man who would admit any woman could have a claim on him.' Olivia was stupid but Darina couldn't help feeling a little sorry for her; Alex was treating her very badly. Was he the first man she had met who didn't come running whenever she lifted her finger? Darina hesitated to put the matter more crudely even to herself.

Olivia turned away with an angry exclamation. 'Just tell him to ring me, tell him I've got to speak to him.' Her feet tripped over the rug that covered the flagstones in front of the big entrance door, she stumbled, recovered herself, yanked at the door handle then turned to deliver a parting shot. 'If he's not careful, he'll have father sorting him out and you can tell him I said so!' She wrenched open the door and left.

Darina sighed and went to find Angela, then asked for the story of her date with George Prendergast.

'It was silly of me,' said the little waitress frankly, 'but he offered to take me to the Manor Park.' She sounded like a window shopper offered her pick of Harrod's. 'And he was really quite nice while we were eating, even flirted with our waitress, not that I could blame him, she was really pretty, much prettier than me,' Angela sighed. 'It wasn't until afterwards that he got fresh. He stopped at this layby on the way home. I wouldn't have minded the odd kiss and cuddle, well, you don't expect to get an expensive meal without paying something for it, do you?' So much for the emancipation of women! 'But I wasn't going to take the things he was trying to get me to do. And I told him so, straight out.' Her spiky hair quivered with indignation. 'And then I think the worst of it was he burst into tears! Said he was sorry, didn't know what had come over him and he knew I'd never forgive him. He made me promise I'd never tell anyone what happened. Then he drove me home.'

'And you didn't tell anyone, just went on serving him lunch?' It was incredible a modern girl could accept such treatment.

Unexpectedly Angela giggled. 'He avoided my eye and never said a word for weeks and weeks. I just pretended nothing had happened. Well, it hadn't, not really. But when I knew Dawn did his room, I warned her. He seems such a gentleman, see, until you know.'

'Yes,' said Darina.

Ulla was checking the table settings in the dining room. 'Alex has no heart,' she said, jerking a frayed napkin off a table and replacing it with one from the dresser. 'That Olivia is all twisted up.'

Darina turned to the matter of George Prendergast. After a short discussion a course of action was agreed on and Darina set off once again for the stable block to deal with the matter, fanning indignation to block out reluctance, knowing Ulla was not up to dealing with the situation. She was not sure she was.

Halfway across the yard, now clear of Alex's car, she met the civil servant coming towards her, his face puffed with petulant annoyance.

'Miss Lisle, my room hasn't been done this morning, it's too bad.'

'No, Mr Prendergast, and until you can refrain from insulting our staff, it won't be.'

Shock stopped him speaking, then understanding dawned, a light beading of sweat broke out on his forehead, his eyes shifted uneasily under her accusing gaze.

'I am not sure I understand you, Miss Lisle,' he said thickly, the tip of his tongue sliding over his upper lip.

Darina looked away, wondering how she could ever have thought his rubbery face pleasant looking. 'I think you do, Mr Prendergast. Mrs Mason and I have discussed the matter and we are agreed that any further trouble will mean you have to leave without notice.' She had pressed for his instant dismissal but Ulla had insisted his weekly payments were too valuable. The unwanted pensioner was now providing indispensable income.

'I must ask that in future you arrange to be out of your room before it is time for Dawn to clean it,' Darina continued and brought herself to look at him again.

His gaze was fixed on some point behind her. Something seemed to have caught his attention, deflecting it from what she was saying. His discomfiture had increased. The sweat was now bedewing his upper lip, the coarse pores of his face oozed grease. If a fly landed there, it would surely slide down and fall off his chin.

George Prendergast's mouth opened, then closed, then opened again. Finally he gave a high squeak like a mouse that had been goosed, tore his gaze away from whatever had fixed it, gave a quick glance at Darina that refused to connect with hers and lifted a shoulder in a gesture of futility. 'I can assure you the case is nothing like you think,' he started, then seemed to decide there was little point in protesting and set off back to the stable block, his short legs moving stiffly.

What a relief, thought Darina. It hadn't been as bad as she had expected. Turning back to the hotel she, too, had her attention caught. She started to laugh then stopped herself. Dangling obscenely down from one of the large, flip-topped rubbish bins standing outside the kitchen was a pair of lace-trimmed panties.

She went across and tucked in the flimsy item. That must be what Max had found in the back of Alex's car. For a moment she wondered whether to rescue and return the pants to Olivia, then thought better of the impulse. Who knew if they were in fact hers? How ironic they should have been hanging there for that dirty old man to look at. Did he think she had planted them?

Then she thought of his room next to hers, the thin wall between them. She told herself it was nothing to worry about, that George Prendergast had been put in his place, and went back into the hotel.

In the bar with Ulla was Adam Tennant. He sat lazily on the corner banquette, his arm stretched out along its back, his other hand holding a beer glass. He was laughing. Ulla was flushed, her eyes shining. Adam saw Darina and stood. 'Ah, the Valkyrie. Will you join us for a drink?'

Darina poured herself a glass of white wine.

'Like the changes,' said the Manor Park's proprietor with a touch of condescension. 'Quite a gothic charm.'

'Are you staying for lunch? We have a new chef.'

Adam Tennant placed his empty beer mug on the little table in front of him; his eyes avoided hers. 'You have?'

'Oh, that Ken Farthing, he was dreadful! You can have no idea what he did to the food!' Ulla launched into an excited recital of Ken's disastrous menu. Soon she had Adam laughing at her confrontation with the chef.

'Do you know where he has gone?' he asked carelessly as she finished her account.

Ulla shook her head. 'If I never see him again, it will be too soon. But do stay to lunch, Adam, you will like Sally's food, I promise you.'

He gave her a regretful smile. 'Would that I could, my dear. I am in fact on my way to Taunton and I'm late already. I'll come another time.' He rose and Ulla accompanied him to the hall, flirting delightfully.

Darina cleared away the glasses and got the bar ready, then allowed Max, smart in a dark jacket, to act as barman while she took the luncheon orders. They had six casuals in plus four who had booked. Business was definitely looking up.

After lunch she went into Yeovil to organise the mailing of the menu to local businesses and stock up on supplies for Christmas. It seemed to be rushing upon them with horrifying speed. Then it was back to the hotel in time to help Ulla welcome the three sets of guests who had booked in for that night and get the arrangements for dinner under way. The Christmas tree had been delivered that afternoon and now stood in the corner beside the front door. Dense, tall and dark green, undecorated it seemed alien, an intruder from some Scandinavian forest, its

126

fresh, resinous scent pervading the large, high-ceilinged hall.

Ulla stood beside it, breathing rapturously. 'How wonderful! Max, tomorrow you and I will decorate it.' She linked her hand with his and leant her head against his upper arm.

He smiled down at her. 'It will be our first Christmas together.'

Her eyes closed briefly. 'My first Christmas without Tony.' She straightened up, dropped his hand, spoke briskly. 'Wait till you see what I have planned for the decorations. But now we must get organised for this evening. Darina, you hold the fort here while I get changed, then it'll be your turn. We must put our best feet in front. Adam may call in on his way back from Taunton.'

But he didn't. By the end of a busy evening, Ulla had lost her brief sparkle. She asked Darina to check the money and went off to bed.

As she locked up the cash in the safe and entered the credit card vouchers, Darina realised she had not seen Alex return from London. Max had been around the whole evening, he hadn't had a call to collect his half-brother from the station. But as Darina went across to the stable block, she saw Alex's light was on. He must have managed to find a taxi at the station and gone straight to his room. Had he wanted to avoid questions about his business in London?

Chapter Sixteen

It was December 20th and at the Manor Park Hotel Detective Constable James was waiting with William Pigram to talk to Mr and Mrs Tennant. They had now talked to every member of the hotel's staff except the owners. They had been given a small bedroom to work in, on the strict understanding it was to be vacated before Christmas, when every room was needed for the holiday party that would fill the hotel.

Despite the nature of their task, Pat was enjoying herself. She had become used to the luxury of the hotel and now looked forward to arriving there each day, to working in the charming bedroom with its sitting area and en suite bathroom. She felt the boundaries of her experience were expanding. The ambiance of the hotel no longer frightened her, it made her feel sophisticated. She could understand the lure of working long hours for low wages in such surroundings, was fascinated by the relationships they discovered flourishing amongst the staff. As affairs past and present, both hetero- and homosexual, were slowly uncovered, sometimes unknowingly revealed by protagonists, other times deliberately betrayed by discarded or frustrated lovers, she began to wonder how any of the staff had time to do their jobs, so involved did they seem with leaping in and out of bed.

And she was enjoying working with Sergeant William Pigram. The inspector and others might call him, Bill, but she had quickly discovered he preferred to be known by his full name. She took pleasure in using it; she would not have admitted even to herself that she felt it placed her on terms of equality with the tall, blonde girl who was such an obviously close friend of the sergeant's. But she did congratulate herself on how well their partnership was working out.

'Isn't it strange,' she said as they spent the time waiting for Rosemary Tennant reviewing printouts of their reports. 'We have all these details of the staff affairs and the only member it's been suggested Sharon Fry could have been involved with is that chef who worked here when she first arrived. And Shirley said they only went out together because they came from the same village, had a "history". Has he been found yet?'

William looked up from the report he was studying. 'No, he's worked elsewhere in the area but it seems he's now in London. There's an Action out to trace him but I don't think it's much of a lead, the affair seems to have been over for several months. The other suggestion that's come up is much more interesting. But what is so frustrating is not finding anyone who saw Sharon the night she was killed.'

That morning the inspector was holding a television photo call with a woman police officer more or less the same size as the murdered girl, dressed in the clothes Sharon had been wearing when she was killed. She would be filmed hitching a lift and getting into and out of a car. Then the inspector would make a plea for anyone who thought they might have seen Sharon on the night of her death to get in touch with the police.

A pub-to-pub enquiry was also being conducted throughout the area. And each lunchtime William and Pat themselves visited those in the vicinity, grabbing a quick sandwich at the same time. Police expenses did not run to eating at the Manor Park; the inspector was going to query the account for tea and coffee as it was, it seemed to mount alarmingly. How could it cost so much to provide such simple drinks? Though Pat had to admit they tasted better than any she had drunk before. She wondered if she could find out what brands they used. If William Pigram ever visited her flat she would like to be able to serve him something that tasted as it should. She could not see him relishing her usual powdered instant or the breakfast tea bags she used.

The bedroom door opened and Rosemary Tennant entered.

'I believe you want to talk to me?' she said and sat herself down.

Pat James studied her unobtrusively as she waited for her interview to begin, aware that the headache that had hovered around her temples on waking that morning was now settling into an iron band which was gradually tightening itself around her head. She found it difficult to realise that this small, nondescript woman could be married to the charismatic Adam Tennant. She looked more like a housekeeper. A navy suit, too bright to be chic, did little to camouflage middle-aged spread. The short brown hair was dull and in need of a good cut. Sallow skin was emphasised rather than disguised by make-up and the hazel eyes were tired.

The sergeant had stood up as she came into the room (his manners were always perfect, Pat told herself approvingly, as she did each time she noticed an unexpected courtesy), now he settled himself again behind the writing table he was using as a desk.

'We would like to know everything you can tell us about Sharon Fry,' he began.

Rosemary Tennant pursed her thin mouth, given false fullness by her lipstick. 'Could you tell me what sort of thing you want to know?' she asked warily.

'I understand she has been a waitress here for some six months. Were you satisfied with her work?'

The plump shoulders gave a little shrug. 'No worse than some of the others. It's difficult to get properly trained girls in this area.'

'I understand she'd just started a week's holiday when she met her death. When was that arranged?'

Rosemary Tennant's eyes flickered for a moment. 'I'm not sure I remember. Some of the staff ask for time off to visit families before Christmas, we need everyone on duty over that period.'

'So there was nothing unusual in Sharon asking for a week's holiday?'

'Nothing at all.'

'And she would have approached you for the time off? You rather than your husband?'

'That is the usual procedure, I am the one who supervises the staff.'

There was a pause. Pat looked at the shorthand in her notebook and waited for the sergeant to start another line of questioning. She could tell anything useful was going to have to be prised out of Mrs Tennant like crab meat out of its shell.

William leaned back in his chair as though the serious part

130

of the questioning had finished. 'I must congratulate you and Mr Tennant on a very beautiful hotel which seems most efficiently run.'

Rosemary Tennant inclined her head slightly. 'Thank you.'

'When did your husband acquire the place?' enquired William idly.

'We bought it fifteen years ago.'

'You bought it together?'

Pat watched the woman's chin rise at the note of mild surprise in the sergeant's voice.

'We are joint partners.'

'You obviously know a great deal about the business.'

'I have worked in hotels all my life, that is where I met my husband.'

'How long have you been married?'

There was nothing but casual friendliness in the question but the woman shifted uneasily in her chair. 'Nearly twenty years. Does this have anything to do with Sharon's murder?'

'Just background,' said William easily. 'It seems to have been a most productive partnership. You have obviously made a very valuable contribution, we have been impressed with how happy the staff seem to be here.' The woman began to relax again. 'You don't have children?' Pat already knew the answer to that one.

'No.' Pat waited for her to protest again at the line of questioning but Mrs Tennant said nothing else. Nor did the sergeant. The silence stretched out until Rosemary Tennant said carefully, 'My husband felt hotels were not a suitable place to bring up children.'

'And you agreed?'

She looked at the detective steadily. 'I enjoyed the way we were able to work together.'

'Did you know Sharon Fry was pregnant?'

There was a sharp intake of breath. 'The little slut!'

'So you didn't know?'

'No.' Again a pause, then, 'There were a couple of mornings recently when . . . well, she claimed to have hang-overs. I warned her to watch her behaviour.'

'She was a girl for hang-overs?'

'For more than that!' The words slipped out, then the thin

mouth was firmly closed as though other words she might regret later would escape unless carefully watched.

'You mean . . . ?' prompted the sergeant.

Rosemary Tennant looked down at the hands lying in her lap. She fiddled with a diamond ring she wore beside her wedding band, then made a decision. 'I'm afraid even in a hotel like this there are men who will take advantage of an opportunity if it is offered.'

'You mean Sharon Fry was willing to serve more than food?'

Mrs Tennant said nothing more.

'And you frown on that sort of activity?'

'Sergeant, we are more than a respectable hotel, we are above reproach!'

'Yet she still worked here?'

'I had no proof. It couldn't have occurred often. But there were certain men who developed a passing phase of lunching here alone. Then there were times when Sharon made sure she waited on a particular customer. I . . . ' she hesitated then said, 'I mentioned it to my husband.'

'And he did what?'

'Said he would make sure she behaved.'

'And did he?'

The shoulders shrugged.

'Would Sharon Fry have received money from these men?' Pat asked, leaning slightly forward.

Rosemary Tennant turned towards her; she had obviously forgotten there was someone else in the room. 'Been paid as a whore, you mean? She was an ambitious girl, always talking of the smart house she would live in one day, the way she would travel round the world. She liked money.'

'But you had no proof?'

She dropped her head, lids masking the tired eyes that had briefly been lit by some excitement. 'If I had she would not still have been working here. As it was, I told her that if I ever found she had made overtures to, or accepted them from, any of our guests, she would leave without a reference. Until then, well, staff are hard to find.'

'What about the other members of your staff, was she particularly friendly with any of the men?'

Rosemary Tennant's lip curled. 'Her taste ran to men with money.'

'So as far as you were aware, she was not involved with anyone at the hotel?'

Was there a fraction of a pause before she said no? Pat could not be sure, her headache was gaining momentum and she was finding it difficult to concentrate. She made notes automatically whilst William went back over the same ground they had already covered without eliciting any further information. Mrs Tennant had no idea what plans Sharon Fry might have had for her week's holiday, she certainly would not know of any pub the girl patronised or of any boyfriend she had or who could possibly have been the father of the unborn child. 'And I'd be very surprised if she knew,' she added sharply.

'Sorry we have kept you so long, Mrs Tennant,' said the sergeant finally. 'We shall need to examine your restaurant records, check who ate here over the last six months.'

Rosemary Tennant started to protest, then thought better of it. 'Of course, sergeant,' she said.

'Would your husband be free now?' asked William courteously.

Rosemary Tennant rose, smoothing down the skirt that had rucked itself into creases around her hips. Her face was drained and exhausted. 'He has an appointment for lunch.'

'Afterwards, then?'

'He's very busy,' her tone was both harassed and protective.

'We have been trying to see him now for several days.' There was an edge of steel to the sergeant's voice, a reminder that police investigations had official status.

'I'll tell him.'

'Shall we say two thirty this afternoon?'

'I'll tell him,' she repeated and left the room.

Pat closed her notebook and went into the bathroom to take a couple of aspirin, hoping she wasn't coming down with one of the winter bugs that were going around – this was an important stage of their investigations.

She drank some water, renewed her lipstick, then followed William out to his old Bentley parked in the forecourt of the hotel. After a moment spent checking the map, the sergeant started the car and drove to the next pub on their list.

133

'What was your impression of Mrs Tennant,' he asked steering the big car easily through the narrow lanes.

'She really disliked Sharon Fry. I would have said her days at the Manor Park were numbered even if she hadn't died.'

'We've got quite a picture of her now, haven't we? An attractive girl, out for a good time but only with a certain type of man, one with money, status. A girl who worked somewhere they were readily available. And one who was pregnant.'

'But Shirley said she thought she had a couple of regular boyfriends. Could they have been hotel guests?'

William steered the car without answering for a few minutes, then said slowly, 'I think it's unlikely. You heard what Mrs Tennant said, if she'd formed a liaison with a regular guest, she'd have been fired. And I doubt if she'd been able to keep an affair with someone staying in the hotel secret, not in such a hotbed of gossip. But locals in for lunch or dinner would be another matter. We'll get all the names put on the computer and do a little research into them.'

'You didn't tackle Mrs Tennant on that other rumour.'

'That Sharon was having an affair with her husband? No,' agreed William. 'I thought we would go back to her on that after we have had our chat with him.'

'I was surprised he didn't object to giving a sample for the DNA tests.'

'Not much he could do without it looking as if he knew he could be the father of the unborn child. Better to give in gracefully and hope for the best, if indeed he realised exactly what the tests could prove. The results are going to be interesting.'

'We get them after Christmas, you said?'

'I hope immediately after.'

'What a difference DNA tests have made to our job. We can prove exactly who the father is and who had intercourse with her just before she died.'

'We still need the right samples for matching. If it wasn't someone at the hotel, we may be in for a long search. Ah, here we are.'

It was a small pub, quite a few miles from the hotel and tucked away in a little village. Grey stone and withered creeper on the outside, cosy seating and a blazing fire inside. Only a couple of other drinkers and a landlord who was happy to take their order for sandwiches and a glass of beer and to study the snapshot. He didn't need more than a quick glance.

'Oh, yes, know her all right. In here quite often.'

Pat James felt a frisson of excitement lift the hair on the back of her neck. At last!

'On her own?' she asked, leaning forward.

'Not that one. Pretty thing, great legs, always wears very short skirts. Has a smashing laugh. Why d'you want her?'

'She was strangled just over two weeks ago.'

The landlord appeared genuinely shocked. 'Not that case I read about in the local paper? Didn't they publish a snapshot of her this week? Not very good, it never occurred to me it was her. Found in a ditch, wasn't she? Shame, pretty girl like her come to an end like that.'

'Was she always with the same man?'

'I think so.'

'Can you give us a description?' asked Pat, taking out her notebook.

'Well, now you're asking. Didn't pay much attention to him, she was the looker. Well-dressed sort of bloke, I remember.'

'Age?'

'More or less mine, I'd have said, despite his white hair.'

The landlord looked to be in his mid-forties and once again Pat felt the hairs on the back of her neck rise.

'Can you tell us anything else about him?'

He gave the matter some thought. 'I'd have said he was something of a sugar daddy. Different class from her. Not particularly tall but with a presence, you know? Thinks himself someone. Likes the good life, I'd have said. Always drank malt whisky. She liked Babycham,' he smiled reminiscently. 'He tried to get her on to scotch, said she would never get anywhere unless she learned to ask for a proper drink but she said what she liked was Babycham.'

'Were they in here Saturday evening just over two weeks ago?'

'Saturday? Let me think.'

Back at the Manor Park by two thirty, William Pigram and Pat James found that Adam Tennant was still tied up with his luncheon appointment.

135

'We'll wait,' said William, his tone grimmer than usual.

Pat tried to forget her rapidly deteriorating physical state, took another couple of asprin and helped to tidy up the bedroom, enjoying restoring it to its previous immaculate state.

At ten to three the bedside telephone went. One of the receptionists announced that Mr Tennant awaited the police in his office.

'So that's the way he wants to play it.' William ran a hand over his unruly hair. 'Let's go along and let him think he's calling the shots.'

Pat followed him along the deeply carpeted corridor, down the mahogany balustraded staircase and into Adam Tennant's small but impeccable office. He was standing by his desk studying a wine list as they entered.

'Sorry to keep you waiting around.' He flung the large folder down on his desk and came forward. 'Most important meeting with the chairman of our hotel consortium, planning future marketing strategy. We have to go international, link up with hotels in Europe and the Far East as well as the States. But you don't want to hear about that. Sit down and tell me how I can help in this dreadful tragedy.'

He'd changed his tune from the other day, thought Pat as he drew out a chair for her. She sat beside William in front of the desk. Having seen her settled, Adam Tennant sat himself in a large leather chair behind his highly polished desk.

His manner was suave, his white hair sleeked back, his tailoring smooth, but a more than slight uneveness in his breathing was betrayed by the gold chain flashing across his waistcoat. His right eye twitched and his fingers drummed a rhythmless pattern on the wood as he sat back with an enquiring smile, awaiting their questions.

William Pigram placed a sheet of notes in front of him, deliberately arranging the paper with care.

'Mr Tennant, we have spoken to all your staff and to your wife. After our talk this afternoon I do not anticipate we shall need again the room you have so kindly placed at our disposal.'

Adam Tennant gave a graceful, acknowledging dip of his head.

'As I said,' William continued, 'our last formality is this talk with yourself.'

136

'Anything I can do to help. I am exceedingly regretful it has taken so long to find time to place myself at your disposal.'

'Good of you to make yourself available now, sir,' William's tone was dismissive. 'To bring you up to date with our investigation . . . oh, by the way, I should I suppose give you the official stuff about you not being bound to tell us anything but that if you do your words will be noted and may be used in evidence at a later date. Well, as I was saying, no one at the hotel claims to have seen Sharon after six o'clock on the Saturday evening, when her friend, the receptionist Shirley, says she left to go on a date with a boyfriend. She assumes the boyfriend picked Sharon up since she had no car herself.'

'No idea who the boyfriend was?' The question was negligently put.

'Shirley does not know. To be honest, we have heard many times that Sharon, who was obviously extremely attractive,' Pat liked the way William made a small point of that fact, it suggested no man could be blamed for finding her so, 'knew a great many men but there have not been many names to follow up. Either they were one night stands, as you might say, or she was unusually discreet.'

Was that a flash of relief that passed over Adam Tennant's face? If so it was premature.

'Until lunchtime today we had no leads on who she could have met the evening she was killed.'

'Until lunchtime, you say?' Adam Tennant repeated the phrase without inflection.

'We have been checking pubs in the vicinity of the hotel. And today we went to,' William looked at his notes then gave the name of the pub and its village. 'There the landlord not only recognised a snapshot of Sharon, he was able to describe her escort and give us an account of their last visit to his pub on the evening of her death.'

'He described the man with Sharon?'

'Yes, Mr Tennant.' William held the hotel proprietor's gaze with his own.

There was a moment's silence. Adam Tennant picked up a paper knife and toyed with it. 'Do you have a name for this man?'

'The description fits yourself, sir.' The courtesy bounced off the bland façade of the man sitting opposite them but the knife was suddenly held quite still.

'I find that incredible.'

'We can, of course, call an identity parade.'

The paper knife was carefully laid back on the desk and Adam Tennant looked at the police sergeant with a rueful, man to man smile. 'Might as well come clean, then, eh?'

'It would save us a great deal of time, sir.'

'The truth of the matter,' a phrase that in Pat James's experience usually presaged a lie of greater or lesser degree, 'Sharon was giving me some advice on a Christmas present for my wife. It seemed safest to discuss the subject outside the hotel and that pub was convenient. That's all there was to it.' His gaze was open and frank.

'You had more than one discussion?'

'I believe we did.'

'And the last time was the Saturday evening of her death?'

'If the landlord swears that was when he saw us last, it must have been.'

'And how long did you discuss the problem of your wife's Christmas present, sir?'

'Oh, can't have been long, say three quarters of an hour, no more. She was certainly very alive when we parted.'

'And where would that have been, sir?' William made some notes.

'Where?'

'Yes, did you take her home? I assume you originally picked her up in the village?'

'That's right.' Adam Tennant checked himself for a moment, then continued smoothly, 'I left her in the pub. She said she didn't need a lift home. I assumed she was going to meet a boyfriend.' He made a little gesture with his hand, as much as to say, you see how impossible it is there should be anything between us.

'So,' William finished his notes and looked up, his voice friendly and matter-of-fact. 'On the evening in question, you picked up Miss Fry in the village at, what would it have been, around six fifteen? Right, around six fifteen, drove to The Feathers and discussed your wife's Christmas present for about three quarters of an hour over a drink. You then left about half past seven, without Miss Fry, who was waiting for someone else to join her. Would that be the full story, sir?'

'To the last comma, sergeant.'

'This would have been the third or fourth time you and Miss Fry had discussions on this topic at The Feathers?'

'I don't think it could have been as often as that. Say two or maybe three times. No more.'

'And what did you choose in the end?'

'I beg your pardon?'

'What did Miss Fry advise you to buy your wife; it seems to have taken a great deal of discussion?'

'Ah, of course, I see what you mean, sergeant. Miss Fry suggested I buy Rosemary a Janet Reger nightgown and negligee set.'

'A Janet Reger nightgown and negligee set, I see, sir. And have you done so?'

'In fact, I have, sergeant. It's here, hiding in the desk.'

Adam Tennant bent down, opened the bottom drawer and, with the air of a triumphant conjurer, took out a slim, glossy box. He placed it on the desk, took off the lid and drew out a shimmery slither of pale ecru satin trimmed with a rose made from the same material. William gently took it from him.

'Very nice, sir. What do you think of that, constable?' He tossed over the light as a leaf garment to Pat. 'You're about the same height as Mrs Tennant, hold it up against yourself, let's get an idea of the effect.'

Pat stood up and held the narrow straps of the insubstantial nightgown on her shoulders. The lovely material flowed down her slight body, ending in a neat concertina of folds on the floor.

'Ah, you need a taller model, I'm afraid, but it looks a good fit – for the constable.' Pat could feel herself blushing. 'And a negligee as well?' He picked up the second garment from the box and let the soft material fall from his fingers. Pat had a sudden vision of herself dressed, or rather undressed, in both nightgown and robe in the bedroom upstairs, the silk caressing her skin, her body bathed and perfumed, waiting, waiting for, what? She blamed her abstraction on the fever that was clearly infecting her mind as well as her body and brought herself back to the job on hand. William was searching the folds of tissue paper.

'I'm afraid that's all, sergeant. There weren't matching slippers.' Adam Tennant's voice was cool and ironical.

'I wasn't looking for slippers, sir, it was the bill.'

'The bill?'

'If we could find the bill,' William was apologetic, 'it could give a little more credence to your story, you see.'

'You have the proof in your hands, what more do you want?'

'Well, now, you've told us a story and you've shown us a lovely and undoubtedly extremely expensive set of lingerie. It would help you if you could prove it had been purchased after your last talk with Miss Fry. But if you bought it before she died, then we'd have to ask you again why you took her for a drink that evening.'

Adam Tennant looked uneasy.

'Don't worry about looking for the bill, though,' said William cheerfully, as though saving him the trouble of searching his drawers and filing cabinet, neither of which actions Adam Tennant showed the slightest sign of indulging in. 'I can see from the box where you bought it. I'm sure they will have a record of the sale of such an exclusive present. We'll ask them to check. Constable, make a note of the details.'

Adam Tennant closed his eyes. Then he opened them and tried to recapture his frank and open gaze.

'Well, now, sergeant, when I come to think about it, I actually bought the set before that last meeting. I wanted to show Sharon, Miss Fry, what I had chosen.'

'So she could approve your choice?'

'Quite.'

'And did she have any comments?'

'She thought it most appropriate.'

'Even though it is several sizes too small and too long for your wife?'

Adam Tennant said nothing.

William flung down his pencil. 'Let's stop playing games, shall we? We both know that the last thing you and Sharon Fry discussed in The Feathers was your wife's Christmas present. It is much more likely that that lingerie set was bought for Miss Fry herself.'

140

Adam Tennant started blustering.

William raised a hand. 'Please, listen to me. You can cooperate here in this office or we can take you down to the station and interrogate you there. Either way we shall get a statement. Do I make myself clear?'

Pat James waited for the hotel proprietor to insist on his solicitor being present. Surely he must realise what a dangerous situation he was in?

Adam Tennant pinched the bridge of his nose between the finger and thumb of his right hand. When he looked at the sergeant again, he seemed to have shrunk. 'I understand.' He leaned back in the chair and looked up at the ceiling, closing his eyes and taking a deep breath.

'As you have guessed, Sharon Fry and I had a brief affair. It was nothing serious but she was a captivating little bitch. Legs that went on for ever and a mischievous glint in her eyes that could undo any man. She was willing enough, God knows. I'd meet her somewhere inconspicuous in my car and we'd go off to a quiet spot. And I have to say we both enjoyed ourselves. But she'd want a drink as well and a bit of a chat. She was an ambitious girl' (exactly the phrase his wife had used), 'thought she was a cut above being a waitress. That last time, we had a bit of an argument. She had the idea I'd promised her a job as a receptionist after her first six months, which were just up. I had to tell her it was no deal. Would have given our guests quite the wrong impression. She didn't take it very well. She said a drink was as much as I would get that night, she knew where she could find herself a much better evening and I'd better go. Her exact words, in fact, were to piss off.'

Pat's pencil paused as the flow of words ceased. She looked at the hotel proprietor. He had his hands clasped in front of him on the blotting paper pad and was staring at his thumbs. What fools men were. What was it about a moment or two of excitement in the back of a parked car, so uncomfortable after the luxury of a place like this? For all his apparent sophistication, this was a man with the instincts of an alley cat.

Adam Tennant raised his head and looked straight at William. 'Believe me, it was a serious jolt when you showed me that damned photograph the other day and said she'd been strangled. I couldn't

141

help feeling in some way responsible. If only I hadn't left her in that pub.'

'What do you think happened?' William's voice was level and emotionless.

'God knows. I don't know if she was serious about meeting some other chap, she couldn't have had anything lined up. Normally I would drop her off a little way from her place on my way back to the hotel. She might have intended to pick someone up. She was like that. Or she could have tried to hitch-hike back. Either way she could have got involved with some pervert, some psychopath.'

'But you claim to have left her around seven thirty in the pub?'

'The landlord should be able to confirm that if he really does remember me so well.'

William turned to Pat. 'Constable, read us the landlord's statement.'

Pat produced the relevant document. 'They were here about three quarters of an hour,' she began reading in a level voice. 'Certainly no more than an hour. It was all smiles when they arrived but later I noticed they were in the middle of a right old barney. First she was pleading and he was angry, then she got angry as well. I couldn't hear what it was all about but I remember him hissing at her, "there's no way I can believe *that*". A short while later I saw him walk out and leave her. She ran after him, I heard a screech of tyres and then she came back into the pub.

'She sat down again and lit a cigarette. I was about to offer her a drink on the house when she asked if there was a phone. I told her there was one in the corridor next to the ladies. After a few minutes she returned and I gave her a Babycham on the house. I could see she was upset but she said not to worry, she'd got it all arranged. She took the drink over to the windowseat. Then the pub got busy. Next time I look, she's gone. Reckon she saw her friend arrive and went out to meet him.'

'Now, Mr Tennant,' said William, 'let's go back to your account of that evening. You said you had a row, which the landlord confirms. You say it was because Miss Fry wanted a job in reception. I suggest it was because Sharon Fry told you she was pregnant and claimed you were the father.'

Again Adam Tennant pinched the bridge of his nose. He looked very tired now. 'There was no way that girl could know who got her pregnant. I wasn't her only boyfriend, she never pretended I was. But I sure as hell wasn't going to accept responsibility for her carelessness. She'd told me she was on the pill. But I always wore protection. These days it's playing Russian roulette not to. Especially with a tart like Sharon. I asked her once if she wasn't afraid, she only laughed and said Aids was a gay disease and she didn't go with gays. She had no idea of the dangers she ran, she was a child. In many ways, that was part of her attraction.' He sat and mused on it for a moment.

'If you always wore protection, how could she claim you were the father?'

'There was once it broke. Inferior product, I nearly wrote to the manufacturers. Anything could have happened.'

'Sharon Fry seemed to think it had.'

'She was merely using it as an excuse, a pretext.'

'What did she want you to do?'

'Only divorce Rosemary and marry her!'

'And I take it you didn't want to leave your wife?'

'Want to? Sergeant, I can't!'

'Can't?'

'We are partners in this hotel. I would have to buy her out and I can't afford to. I'm over-extended with the bank and these wretched interest rates mean our cash flow is damnably tight.'

Did he realise what a damaging admission that was? He appeared punch drunk, beyond assessing the implications of what he said. He might be a good hotelier but he showed very little sense of self-preservation. No wonder he had been reluctant to meet them.

Too late, he appeared to sense danger. 'Besides,' he added hastily, 'I don't want a divorce. Rosemary and I are extremely happy. Just because I have a little fling every now and then doesn't mean I don't love my wife.'

'And what are you giving her for Christmas?' asked William courteously.

'I have to admit I haven't chosen anything yet. I shall be in London on Monday and will find something nice then.'

William stood up and Pat followed suit. At the door, the

143

sergeant turned. 'One other thing,' he said as if an afterthought had struck him. 'Did you have intercourse with Miss Fry during your last date?'

If the question had been intended to catch Adam Tennant off balance, it failed. 'No,' he said steadily. 'We went straight to the pub and the rest you know.' He hesitated, then said with every appearance of complete frankness, 'I will say that if I had had my way, we would have postponed the drink until later but Sharon was insistent on us talking first.'

The sergeant returned the gaze for a moment, then came back to the chair he had vacated a moment before and said, 'Well, sir, all we have to do now is prepare your statement and get you to sign it.'

As they went through the formalities, Pat was aware that through the insistent throbbing of her head there was a deep sense of disappointment. During the questioning, she had become convinced they had reached the end of the investigation, that Adam Tennant had strangled Sharon. The girl had threatened his comfortable life, his marriage and, it appeared, his business. Yet he claimed the child could not be his and that he had not had intercourse with her on the fatal night. Two statements of fact that could easily be confirmed or denied by the results of the DNA tests. Could he be bluffing? But what about the landlord's evidence? Who could Sharon have phoned after Adam Tennant left her at the pub? And how were they going to find out who it was?

It seemed as soon as one question was answered, the answer turned into another query. It was frustrating. The haze in Pat's head grew into an all-enveloping fog. Vaguely she became aware that William Pigram was asking if she felt all right.

Chapter Seventeen

By Saturday, December 22nd, the Hotel Morgan arrangements for Christmas were nearly complete. Darina and Ulla were exhausted and Alex and Max scrapping with each other but the decorations were in place, the staff enrolled, the supplies commandeered and every detail of the Christmas break organised down to the last petit four to be served. Their group of guests were to be pampered and entertained as no group had been before.

'I just hope my mother will behave herself,' commented Darina gloomily as the four of them sat in the office after an early supper, gathering strength before the bustle of the evening got under way. There were several tables booked for dinner that night.

Max looked up. 'Is she likely to disgrace you?' he asked eagerly. 'Dance on the table or do a striptease?'

'She will either be the life and soul of the party or go into a monumental sulk and bitch to anyone whose ear she can bend.'

'I am sure she will not sulk, not when we have arranged such a wonderful time.'

'Stepmother has spoken, you have nothing to worry about.' Alex was slumped beside the fire, a picture of weary depression.

'Do buck yourself along, Alex. Ever since your visit to London you've been impossible. Either up in the sky or under the earth, we can hardly speak a word without having our heads snapped off, even Max. For goodness' sake, tell us what happened there.'

The long figure raised his head and looked at Ulla. 'All right, I might as well tell you. I saw some publishers. They've given me a contract for a book on my American trip.'

The only reaction was complete bewilderment from each of his audience. Ulla said, 'A book?'

'It's a discovery of modern middle America. Travelling around

Colorado, Arizona, Utah, I met characters who could have stepped straight out of an old-fashioned Western but used the most modern technology to run their lives. Then there were people who've never been outside some hick town in the middle west, who only know the rest of the world through television.' He had risen and stood in front of the fire, his face alive with excitement, pushing back the blond hair that flopped over his forehead. The cynicism had fallen away, he seemed years younger, almost of an age with Max.

'Until you drive through, you can have no idea of the isolation of those western states, their space. How arid the land is, how extraordinary the rock formations, there's just the rocks, cactus and dirt. You see the name of a place on a map, the focal point of an area over two hundred miles square. It looks as though it's some sort of town, civilisation. When you get there, it's a trading post, just a garage with a shop selling the basic necessities. Nothing more. Imagine living there. A city like New York or Chicago is as exotic to those people as Hong Kong or Delhi is to us. Life is lived on its most basic level; drama, literature, any culture whatsoever, has no relevance. The local radio station offers what they need, a diet of pop music, country and western, local news and advertising. Television offers escapism. You know those Western films, where life is reduced to simple issues, where the shoot-out is between the good guy and the bad guy and it's the good guy who walks away? That's life as it is understood there. To those people Ronald Reagan wasn't an aberration, a monumental joke played on the American people by a god who thought that as they'd set up celluloid figures as idols they could have one for their President; he was a hero, ridden out of the folk art they understood, who reduced political conundrums to simple issues. I tell you, life there is simple! Despite all their modern technology, education, communications and freedom, it bears comparison with that of the most primitive inhabitant of the inmost regions of Khazakstan.'

Alex stopped talking and gave a short, embarrassed laugh. 'Well, I took notes everywhere and photographs. When I got back, I knocked it into some sort of shape, typed it out and sent it to an old university chum who's become a literary agent. I had a letter from him the other day telling me he had someone interested in it and could I come up and have a talk with them. That's what I was doing in London.'

'And you never said a word.' Ulla was reproachful.

'God, Alex, how fantastic. I always knew you would do something great!' Max grinned at his half-brother. 'When's it coming out?'

'Not for ages yet, they want quite a bit more work done on it. But I've got a contract and an advance.'

'You'll be rich!'

The light faded out of Alex's face and he threw himself back into his chair, hunching his shoulders dispiritedly. 'That's the rub. I only got a few hundreds. I had no idea publishers could offer so little. There'll be a bit more when I produce an acceptable manuscript and they'll double it when it's published, but that's not for at least a year.' He bit at a hangnail and looked at them in turn.

'At least it's a start,' said Darina. 'And you will be published; I think that's marvellous!'

'But I've got to find the money for my next trip. I want to see what's happening in China and the same publishers could be interested in a book afterwards but they won't give me an advance, they want to see how the first book does. I've been studying Chinese and I know I could produce something really worthwhile but how do I finance it? I used up all the money I had going round America.'

'So that's why you want me to sell the hotel,' said Ulla slowly.

He rose and placed his hands on the desk in front of her, leant his weight on them and looked deep into her eyes, the ice blue of his now burning, searing. 'Don't you see? If I had my share, I could finance myself until I get established as a writer. I know I can do it but I'm not going to start making real money from books for years. And in order to write them I've got to travel.'

Ulla closed her eyes briefly, as if to block out the intensity of his gaze.

'It's not as though your heart is really in hotels,' Alex went on. 'Look how exhausted you are now. Think how it's going to be over the next year, trying to make something of this place, even with Darina to help.'

Ulla glanced over towards the tall girl, then back at the man standing in front of her. She sighed deeply. 'All right, Alex, I'll think about it, I really will.'

'You will?' He gave a whoop of delight, went round the desk, lifted Ulla out of her chair, swung her round, kissed her soundly, then slowly put her down, his arms continuing to clasp her slim figure.

Nobody spoke, electricity flared in the small room. Then Angela, the little waitress, stuck her head round the door. 'We've got customers for the bar, the Johnson party has arrived and someone's asking for Mrs Mason and Miss Lisle.'

Alex released Ulla. 'Come on, Max, you can be barman while I act as Maitre d'.' The two young men swept out of the office, laughing and giving each other friendly punches on the upper arm.

'So you are still thinking of selling?' said Darina slowly.

Like a sleepwalker opening her eyes after several thousand years, Ulla tried to focus her gaze. 'Oh, I don't know. I'm yust so tired and Alex was so, so upsetting. Maybe I won't after all. Come, let us see who is here.'

She went out to the hall and Darina followed slowly.

Standing by the Christmas tree, now hung with silver icicles and golden balls, was William.

Ulla greeted him with real warmth. Darina could not feel so uninhibited.

Running beneath all her hectic activity over the last week or so had been the nagging sense that something valuable was slipping away from her. Several times she had rung William, only to reach his answering machine. She had refused to leave a message on the impersonal tape. She had refused to ring him at the station, terrified he might feel she was trying to involve herself in the investigation. Intellectually she knew he was totally involved in that investigation. She had read the accounts the local paper had printed, seen requests for information on the murdered girl. She knew how detailed were the enquiries that were being conducted, how pressured his time must be. It did not help.

Strangely, it did not help either that she was enjoying throwing herself into the transformation of Hotel Morgan. That she recognised she had found what could be her life's ambition, and knew she was not prepared to abandon it for marriage. She and William

148

were on steel plates spinning in different planes. The nearer their lives were to meshing, the more disastrous would be the result. The two brief glimpses she had had of him since that lunch when he had introduced her to the hotel had made her feel their week together in the Lake District belonged to a time that had no relevance to her present life.

'Hello, William,' she said. 'Are you here officially?' She knew it must be so, otherwise why ask for both of them? She looked around, bracing herself for the sight of the little policewoman who seemed permanently attached to him these days. But she wasn't there.

He smiled at her. Why didn't he kiss her? 'Is there somewhere we could have a few words?' he asked Ulla.

So it was official business.

They went to the office and he explained the police were trying to trace the whereabouts of a chef, Ken Farthing, who he believed had worked briefly at the Hotel Morgan. Did they know where he was now.

Darina and Ulla looked at each other. 'Is he a suspect?' Darina asked.

'No, not yet. But he and Sharon Fry appear to have been very friendly at one time and we want to speak to him. We traced him to a London restaurant but he was fired from there and seems to have disappeared again.'

'He left here that day you came to lunch,' said Ulla.

William made a note. 'And you haven't seen him since?'

Ulla shook her head.

'If he left here that Monday, he must have been working for you on the Saturday?'

Ulla nodded.

'Was he here all that evening?'

She pulled out a record book, flicked over some pages. 'We had two tables in that night, both booked for seven thirty. He probably left about nine thirty, ten o'clock, maybe earlier. All the desserts would have been prepared beforehand, the waitress would make the coffee.'

'Is the same waitress on tonight?'

Darina went and fetched Angela.

Yes, she remembered the evening. Chef had been excited

149

because it was the last dinner before his new menus, they didn't open on Sunday evenings. He'd invited her for a drink after she'd finished but she wanted to get home and put her feet up. He must have left the hotel shortly after nine thirty. She'd gone at ten fifteen, leaving Mrs Mason to look after the final drink orders, it'd been young Mr Mason's evening off.

'You were friendly with Ken Farthing?' William asked her.

Angela grinned at him. Police questioning did not seem to worry her. 'We had the odd drink together, I wouldn't have called him a friend exactly.'

'Would you say he had many friends?'

She shook her head. 'Bit of a loner, I'd say. He never talked about girls. He was hardly a dream boat with that face but, then, there's no accounting for tastes and some go for the rough type, don't they? He was always talking about what was going to happen when he made his name.' She gave a laugh of kindly contempt. 'He was going to have his own TV programme, write books, go everywhere. I knew he wouldn't last.'

'You didn't think he was a good chef?'

'Cooked a lovely steak! If I was offered my least meal on earth, I'd have one of Ken's steaks, straight up. But as for the rest,' she looked at Ulla Mason. 'If you'd asked me, I could have told you he'd be no good. Well, they'd turned him off from the Manor Park, hadn't they?'

'They had?' asked Ulla faintly.

'Didn't last there more than a couple of weeks. He didn't tell no one, reckoned it didn't sound good, but I knew 'cos he told me one night when he'd had a jar or two.' She was enjoying holding court.

'Did he tell you where he was going when he left here?'

'No. Just left.'

'Where was he staying?'

'At the pub down the road. Had a room there.'

'Your staff don't live in?' William asked Ulla.

'Not normally. He didn't ask for accommodation and I prefer not to offer it. Of course, we have our present chef living in the stable block, Darina also.'

'Does Ken Farthing have a car?'

'He had this motorbike,' said Angela. 'Thinks ever such a

150

lot of it. Gave me a ride one night, went really fast. But I didn't like the helmet you have to wear, did awful things to my hair.' She gave a quick gesture of reassurance to her yellow quiff.

William made another note.

'Is there anything else, because I should be getting back to my tables?'

He looked up and gave her his best smile, the one Darina felt welcomed you into his thoughts, said you had a special place there. Was it something he handed round without selection, to anyone?

'There's nothing for the moment. I may come back and ask you something else later, if I may?' The saucy smile she gave told him he was welcome any time.

What was he going to do now? There couldn't be much more he needed at the Hotel Morgan. If he just said he must be going and goodnight, Darina didn't know what she was going to do. She felt like a teenager, fathoms deep in her first love, unsure of herself, of the object of her affections, of the orbiting power of the earth. Ulla's plaint of the long and empty quality of her nights came back.

This was ridiculous! She was a grown girl in charge of her life and in a relationship with an intelligent, rational man. 'Can we offer you a drink?' she heard herself say. 'Or have you time to stop for dinner?'

He looked at her. 'I wish I could!'

She felt absurdly comforted by the warmth of his voice.

'But I still have another call to make tonight.' He hesitated then asked, 'You wouldn't like to come too, would you? We've found a pub Sharon Fry visited on her last evening. I have to go and see if there's anyone there tonight who remembers her meeting someone that other Saturday. It's not likely to be much fun for you but it would give us a little time together and I know how interested you are in murder investigations.' He gave her a teasing smile.

Darina felt he had opened a door in his life to her. She glanced at Ulla.

'It's your evening off,' said the Scandinavian. 'And it's time you had a bit of fun.' She looked wistfully at the tall, attractive detective.

151

Darina fetched her coat and climbed into the ancient Bentley, relishing the smell of real leather, supple with age. William switched on the engine, then turned it off again.

'I can't wait any longer,' he said and drew her to him.

'I didn't know one could get addicted to caviar,' she murmured a moment later.

'The appetite grows on what it feeds, isn't that what the poet says?'

'In that case, perhaps it would be best to starve.' She drew away, flushed and shot with unsatisfied desire.

He stroked back a long lock of cream-coloured hair, joining it with its fellows lying loose over her shoulders, his breath coming quickly. 'When I was on the beat I sometimes had to shine my torch in parked cars, move on couples who'd stopped to sample caviar and other godlike comestibles. I always felt a heel.'

'Why did you have to move them on?'

'Offence against public decency – or possible offence. And that's why I'm starting this car.'

After a moment Darina asked him where his assistant was.

'Gone down with some sort of bug. Hope it won't last too long, she's damned good.'

Darina said she had no doubt the constable would be back quite soon. Then, slightly hesitantly, she asked him about the progress of the case. By the time they reached The Feathers, she'd heard about Adam Tennant's account of their last date and the landlord's evidence.

'So you think her murderer arrived after Adam left her there?'

William locked the car and started for the pub. 'It must be a strong possibility.'

'He's a strange man, Adam Tennant,' said Darina as she followed him. 'There's a sense of danger about him, you feel he enjoys taking risks, challenging people. And from what you've said, it sounds as though he had a pretty strong motive for getting rid of Sharon. I don't suppose his wife would be at all generous over the hotel if she found out about his affair, especially if he'd made her pregnant.' Darina thought of the tired woman she'd met at the hotel, of the effort she must have put into building up the business over the years, losing her looks and charm in the process. No children of her own. She thought of the hotel, of Adam's pride in it, his commitment. How difficult would it be for him to raise enough capital to buy out his wife? How much trouble could Sharon Fry have caused?

The pub was doing good business. A wide cross section of customers appeared to be enjoying themselves. Darina asked for a glass of wine and refused the offer of something to eat. 'But you go ahead,' she added, noting the way the detective's eyes lingered on plate of steak and kidney pie.

He ordered for himself, had a word with the landlord and handed Darina her glass of wine. 'There are a number of locals here who could have been in that Saturday night. Now, if we go and sit over there, we can fall into conversation with that little lot.'

Darina sat down and watched him go into action. There was no concealment of his status as a policeman but his friendliness and informality disarmed his potential witnesses and created an atmosphere of interest and helpfulness. They had all heard of the murder and the possibility of being connected with its investigation brought a frisson of excitement.

It took an hour before William found someone who'd seen Sharon leaving the pub.

'Must have been just before eight. I left home at seven thirty. Ma was late with the tea; usually I'm here by then. I noticed her because she had this short skirt and lots of fair hair. Real looker.'

'Did you see her meet anyone?'

Darina watched the young man's pleasant face assume an expression of great concentration. 'I think she got into a car.'

'Are you sure?'

'Don't know as I can be certain. I think she gave a little wave as she came out. Yes, that's it,' he became excited as memory gradually came back to him. 'That's what happened. She gave a little wave and shouted "Yoo hoo", then ran across the road to a car.'

'What sort of car?'

The youth shook his head regretfully. 'It was that dark out there, I couldn't have recognised my own tractor. It wasn't right in front of the pub, see. It was over the other side of the road.' He thought some more. William gestured towards his nearly empty beer mug and the young man accepted the offer of a refill.

As the detective brought back the fresh pint he looked up and said, 'I *think* it might have been a station wagon. But I couldn't be sure, mind.'

'And you didn't hear her call a name?'

'Nah, nothing like that.'

And that was it. There was nothing else useful William could discover from either the young man or anyone else in the pub that night.

Back in the car William said, 'Tired, or would you like another drink?'

'What other piece of investigation do you want to follow through?'

It was too dark to see his face but she knew he was smiling. 'You know me too well. I just thought it might be interesting to call in at the Manor Park and let Adam Tennant know that his story of how he left Sharon at The Feathers waiting for someone else has been confirmed. Reassure him, you know?'

'Why do I have the feeling you are not at all concerned about reassuring him? That your motive is rather more devious? Have you got some hunch about him?'

'The police don't follow hunches, that's for amateur detectives.' There was a smile in his voice. 'We rely on careful investigation, the checking out of facts. What about it, are you on?'

It was not a question that needed asking. As William started the car, Darina thought about Sharon Fry being picked up at The Feathers, met by a car which may or may not have been a station wagon, then taken – where? 'Do we pass that layby?' she asked.

William did not have to ask which she meant. 'No, we come out further up the road. I've been thinking about that, too. I reckon whoever she met took her for a drive of some sort. Either to another pub – we're still checking all those in the vicinity – or to somewhere to make love.'

Darina glanced around the interior of the Bentley. She thought about stopping for a chat, finding herself involved in a quarrel and then being strangled. What could Sharon have said or threatened that drove her companion to murder? Or had he lost control some other way.

'Do you know if she had made love before she died?'

There was a moment's pause, then William said, 'We believe she had had intercourse.' There was police restraint in the bald statement.

'And Adam Tennant denied he had?'

William nodded.

'And you think it's quite possible that one moment she's trying to persuade him he's the father of her child and he ought to marry her and the next she's making mad passionate love to someone else? Ensuring he can be given the same story, perhaps? I'm not surprised she came to a sticky end.'

They drew up outside the luxury hotel. William turned off the engine and sat looking at the big windows spilling light on to the forecourt.

'How much do you think all this means to Adam Tennant?' he asked Darina.

'Would he murder to keep it, you mean?' Darina sighed. 'It's a funny business running a hotel. I suppose if you built up a company making ball bearings or importing handbags, you would have a certain emotional attachment to it, but I can't think it would give you anything like the same thrill as a hotel. Particularly this kind of hotel that demands a strong commitment from the hotelier; you invest your personality as much as your money. Offering hospitality is quite special. In a way it's offering yourself. It calls for so much expenditure of time and energy, capacity for taking pains, for thinking of guests' needs, endless patience with staff to get that extra effort from them that makes the difference between the acceptable and the first rate. Customers are not always appreciative but when they are, it's wonderful. The joy of creating a place like this, seeing it every day, seeing people enjoying themselves as a result of your efforts must give a tremendous buzz.

'I would think,' Darina ended slowly, 'that Adam Tennant would be prepared to go to considerable lengths to retain this place.'

William looked at his companion thoughtfully. Then he got out and opened Darina's door for her.

The Manor Park was ready for Christmas. In the hall was a great, golden tinsel tree trimmed with chic green tartan bows. Wreaths of green adorned each door and a sunburst of Christmas cards had been arranged on one of the walls. Sounds of discreet merriment came from the bar.

Adam Tennant was sitting at a table in the far corner, talking to a man with a growth behind one ear. He looked faintly familiar to Darina. William sat her down at a table not too far away and ordered two glasses of white wine.

It didn't take long for the hotel proprietor to notice them and come across.

'Darina, my dear, how pleasant to see you. And the sergeant too – is this a professional call?'

'Not really,' said William smoothly. 'But you might be interested to know we have been able to confirm that Sharon Fry was picked up from The Feathers after you left her there.'

Adam Tennant glanced around but such was the placement of the tables it was unlikely anyone else could have heard the quietly uttered words.

'Confirmation is always reassuring but I was totally confident of nothing less. Your drinks, of course, are on the house.'

'Very generous of you, sir, but our visit is my treat.'

He gave the detective a sharp look, then turned to Darina. 'I hope the Hotel Morgan is flourishing? Give the beautiful Ulla my regards.' Without waiting for a response, he went back to his guest. More drinks arrived at the corner table. Adam brought out a cigar, his gestures grew expansive. Whether the news William had given him had been reassuring or whether he had already been feeling relaxed was difficult to say, but he certainly seemed to enjoy his conversation. There was no sign of Mrs Tennant.

'That was quite a speech of yours before we came in,' William said slowly. 'Do I gather you have committed yourself to the Hotel Morgan?'

'I think I may have,' said Darina carefully.

'Hmmm,' William sampled his wine. 'I did myself a considerable disservice when I took you there.'

'If it hadn't been the Hotel Morgan it might have been some-where much further away.'

'So you are determined to pursue your hotel ambitions?'

'I have to, at least for the moment. It has nothing to do with how I feel about you.' And soon there might not be a

Hotel Morgan for her to invest in but it would only complicate matters to mention the possibility.

William said nothing.

The evening lay in ashes around them. There was nothing else to do but drink up and leave. The barman refused payment but William dropped a five pound note on the table. Adam Tennant's eyes narrowed as he noticed the gesture.

About ten minutes down the A37, William said, 'That's the layby.' But he didn't stop the car and there was little Darina could see as they sped by.

Nothing more was said on the drive then, as William drew up outside the Hotel Morgan, he asked, 'Have you a table free for lunch on Christmas Day?'

'I don't think so, we've had bookings coming in all week. Word really does seem to be spreading about our food. You aren't serious, are you?'

'Quite serious. With this case I'm lucky to get Christmas Day off. There certainly won't be time to drive home to the parents and I thought you might be able to supply me with a slice of turkey.'

Darina's spirits rose. 'That's wonderful. I shan't have time to sit with you but I'll put you at my mother's table. She'll be thrilled!'

Chapter Eighteen

The Christmas Party at Hotel Morgan started well. Guests began arriving in the mid-afternoon of Christmas Eve. They were shown to their rooms exclaiming on the way over the Christmas tree and the enormous arrangements of greenery so skilfully contrived by Ulla.

In the rooms were small Christmas presents for each guest, with a bowl of fruit and an arrangement of dried flowers mixed with tiny glass balls in glowing colours. There was also a bottle of the local mineral water and a miniature sherry.

When the guests came down to the lounge, they found an old-fashioned English tea. 'Let's go for traditional English food,' Darina had said to Sally Griffiths during their initial discussions.

'Reinterpreted in the modern style?'

'It should look stylish and sit more lightly on the digestion but not too many nods to fashion. Let's have proper steak and kidney pudding, well-cooked duck with fruit sauces, rack of lamb, sirloin on the bone, beef Wellington, salmon with cucumber sauce.'

'Treacle tart, Sussex Pond Pudding, proper English trifle,' Sally started to become enthusiastic. 'Syllabubs. We'll have to offer some lighter dishes as well but it could be great.' And the food had proved instantly popular. The Christmas Eve tea had been another of Darina's ideas.

'If it goes well, we could think of introducing it as a regular weekend event,' she said. So now a table had been laid with a snowy cloth and bore dainty sandwiches, scones, strawberry jam and clotted cream, and a variety of cakes. China or Indian tea was offered to guests as they arrived and gradually the room filled with people.

Here, too, there were large arrangements of greenery set off

158

with silk flowers (a worthwhile investment, Ulla had declared). And Darina had asked Ulla to look out for antique cushion covers on her buying expeditions. The results of her searches were now scattered amongst the sombre velvet sofas and chairs, the faded colours of old tapestry, silk and damask lightening the atmosphere and giving the room an air of eccentric splendour.

The guests were turning out to be a mixed bunch. Mainly middle aged, they sat in tight little groups, casting suspicious glances at each newcomer as they were shepherded in by Darina or Ulla.

It was the Hon. Ann Lisle who got the party going. 'How delightful,' Darina's mother said as she entered with her companion, General Sir Gerald Stocks. 'We are all going to have such fun. Do let me introduce myself,' and she proceeded to progress round the room, chatting to each party, performing the role of hostess. By the time she had finished, everyone not only knew who both she and Gerry Stocks were, they had been introduced to each other and fraternisation had begun.

Darina sighed with thankfulness, took on board the lesson and returned to the hall where a woman in her fifties was warming her hands at the blazing fire. She was attractively plump and dressed expensively with silvery fair hair swept back in a sophisticated chignon. 'Thank heavens for a proper fire; it's so cold I wouldn't be surprised if it snows.'

'Too cold for snow,' said a bulky man examining the Christmas tree. He bore all the marks of a successful businessman, his coat looked cashmere, his gloves pigskin. His hair was trimmed at just the right length, his skin was smooth and tanned. Darina gave a glance out of the hall window as she went towards them. Sure enough, sitting on the drive was a Rolls Royce with this year's registration.

'Happy Christmas,' she said, her mind swiftly running through the list of guests yet to arrive, mentally assessing handwriting, names and addresses. She could not think of any that matched the style of this couple. She wondered what had brought them to the Hotel Morgan.

Then the door at the rear of the hall opened and in came Alex with a tray of ice for the bar. He kicked the door shut behind him, caught sight of the woman and said, 'My God, Vivian!'

159

'Darling, come and kiss me.'

Darina watched Alex hesitate, look at his tray, then place it on a table, come over and plant a cool kiss on the soft cheek offered for his salutation.

'You look very well, my darling,' the woman said, stepping back a pace to study him properly.

Alex held out his hand to her companion. 'How do you do, sir, good to see you again.'

'Alex, how are you doing?' the man shook hands with him, his greeting courteous rather than warm.

'We were in the area and thought what a good idea to come and see how you were,' said the woman, sitting down on one of the sofas by the fire.

'I'm fine.' Alex remained standing by the sofa.

'You might act as though you were pleased.' The woman patted the cushion beside her. 'Come and sit down and tell me all about yourself.'

'Now, now, Viv, we've taken the boy by surprise, he's probably in the middle of a thousand and one things.'

'Can I get you some tea?' offered Darina, wondering if, in fact, this was a good move. Alex did not seem at all anxious to detain the couple. But they had come to a hotel, after all.

'That would be lovely,' said the woman. 'Surely you can spare us a few minutes, Alex? We so seldom see you.'

He glanced at the tray with the ice bucket and sighed. 'Let me introduce Darina Lisle, she wants to go into partnership with Ulla. Darina, Vivian and Arthur Fairchild.'

Darina smiled at them. 'I'll order the tea,' she said, then went and added some more logs to the fire.

Alex sighed. 'You really mustn't stay long.'

'Nothing like being made welcome.' The woman gave a pretty little pout.

'It's not that,' said Alex, sitting on the sofa beside her. 'It's just . . . just that Max is here.'

'Max?' exclaimed the woman; there was a peculiar note in her voice, something between delight and consternation.

'Didn't you know he'd be here for Christmas?'

'I didn't think.'

160

'You never have, have you?' commented Alex sourly. 'Where else does he have to go now his father's dead?'

'Is he here at the moment?' The woman looked round the hall with a mixture of anticipation and apprehension.

'He's gone to collect some cream, we had a late panic over supplies. He won't be long.'

Darina picked up the tray with the ice bucket and took it to the bar, then went to the kitchen. She arranged with Angela for tea to be brought to the little party in the hall, then arrived back there in time to greet the next arrivals, a party of two middle-aged couples with a pair of older women. She took them upstairs. They were booked into three of the smaller, more modern doubles on the second floor. There was an immediate protest from one of the older women over the stairs. 'Barry,' she said, 'I thought you promised me a lift. I must have a lift.'

Darina apologised. 'Mr Johnson asked for our most modern accommodation,' she said.

'Can you put my mother and Mrs Franks in a room on the first floor?' asked Mr Johnson, a jolly looking fellow. He patted his mother's hand. 'There, there, precious, we'll get things properly arranged, don't you worry.' The middle-aged woman Darina had marked as his wife sighed deeply and exchanged a glance with her friend.

Darina thought quickly. The only unclaimed room on the first floor had been booked by a Mr and Mrs Taylor, whose reservation form had asked for a large room. Both the deposit and the balance of the cost of the Christmas holiday, due in advance, had been paid in cash via registered envelopes. The correspondence had been nicely typed but the paper had been very ordinary, the modest sounding address not printed but typed on the top right corner. It added up to unpretentious guests. Perhaps they could safely be switched to the room intended for the senior Misses Johnson and Franks.

She took the older ladies downstairs and installed them in the commodious room at the top of the stairs. 'It's next to the lift,' she pointed out. 'You should be very comfortable here.'

Mrs Johnson inspected the bathroom, emerging with pursed lips. 'Jerry built,' she announced. 'Does that extraordinary noise go on all night?' she pointed to the gurgling radiators. 'I shall never be able to get a wink of sleep.'

Darina said the heating was turned off in the late evening.

'And I suppose that means we freeze in the night. I told Barry it was no good staying at anything less than the best. But he was all for the "old-fashioned Christmas" bit. I tried to tell him old-fashioned meant out of date. However, Joyce will no doubt have to do without her jacuzzi and sauna.' The satisfaction in her voice was unmistakable.

'If he'd only left matters to my John, we'd have been somewhere top class,' offered Mrs Franks.

'Your John would have booked us into some third-rate seaside monstrosity,' retorted Mrs Johnson. 'Remember what happened when we went to Torquay and those computer keys would never open our room? Three times they changed them. And the towels in the health spa were disgraceful and the food dreadful.'

'I'll get your cases sent up,' said Darina, escaping to the hall.

'I'm sorry to interrupt, Alex,' she said, seeing the tea party still comfortably installed in front of the fire, 'but we need cases taken upstairs for the Johnson and Franks party. And I've had to switch Mrs Johnson and Mrs Franks senior to the Monks Room, one of them can't manage stairs.'

Alex rose without hesitation. 'Sorry, to cut your visit short, Vivian, but I'm on duty.'

'I quite understand, darling. There'll be plenty of time to chat later.'

Alex stood stock still. The woman laughed up at him. 'You didn't think we'd just dropped in at this extraordinary hour on the off chance of seeing you, did you?'

Her companion stood up. 'We're the Taylors,' he announced to Darina.

She didn't understand. 'I thought you were called Fairchild?'

Vivian laughed. 'We wanted it to be a surprise. If we'd booked under Fairchild, Alex would have known. So we called ourselves Taylor. Arthur got his secretary to do the booking from her address and we sent cash so you wouldn't see the name on the cheque.'

Alex was looking at her with horror. 'You mean you're staying all over Christmas?'

'Of course, you silly boy, isn't it wonderful?'

'Oh, my God,' said Darina. 'I've just put Mrs Johnson and Mrs Franks in your room!'

It was at that moment that Max walked into the hall. Vivian saw him first. 'Max!' she said and held out a hand.

He looked across and went paper white. Arthur and Alex stood quite still. Mrs Fairchild took a step forward.

'Darling?' her voice was pleading.

He appeared frozen, staring at the space she occupied as though unable to register her presence, then turned without a word and went through the door at the back of the hall.

Vivian Fairchild's hand dropped, her husband moved towards her. She motioned him away. 'Don't, don't,' she said and sat on the sofa, shading her eyes with one hand. He sat beside her, taking her other hand in his.

'I did warn you,' said Alex.

Darina felt it time to take a hand in whatever drama was being played out in front of her.

'I don't understand what is going on but can I show you to your room?' she asked.

Mr and Mrs Fairchild aka Taylor meekly followed her upstairs. They took the lift to the first floor then the stairs. Darina showed them into the room. 'I'm sorry I didn't know who you were when you first arrived. I know you asked for a large room but Mrs Johnson can't manage the stairs and it seemed the only possibility was to switch her room with yours.'

'It's charming,' said Vivian Fairchild automatically without looking around her.

'Modern plumbing,' said her husband, emerging from an inspection of the bathroom.

Darina hesitated then said, 'I'm sorry but I would like to know exactly what is going on. What is the relationship between you, Alex and Max?'

Beautiful blue eyes set wide apart under a broad brow blinked. 'You mean you don't know? Oh, what must you have been thinking! I'm their mother.'

'She's a dreadful woman,' said Ulla in the lull before dinner as she and Darina checked the dining room. 'She ran off with

163

some poet when Alex was only two. I don't think he's ever really forgiven her.'

'Arthur Fairchild doesn't look like a poet.'

'She's been through several since his time.'

'Where along the line did Max arrive?' asked Darina, adjusting the placing of a napkin on one of the tables. She stood back and admired the scene; each of the round tables bore an arrangement of holly leaves and glowing red baubles and in the big bay window was a massed arrangement of poinsettias.

'I think she married his father after the poet ditched her.'

'How long did that last?'

'I am not sure, I don't think Max was very old.'

'He went quite white when he saw her.'

'He never mentions his mother. His father was very bitter too.'

'Did you know him?'

'I met him once or twice. Very upright, military and very strict with Max. They were devoted to each other, though. Max was desolated when the general died last spring. It's most awkward her coming here. Heaven only knows what will happen. There, I think we're ready.'

The Johnson/Franks party came into the dining room halfway through the service. Barry Johnson had asked for two tables, one for four and the other for two. He led his party into the dining room with his mother clinging to his arm.

'Now, precious,' he said as they approached the tables Darina indicated were theirs, 'we thought you and Doris would like to sit together.'

Mrs Johnson senior looked at the table for two and then at Darina. 'I shall sit at Barry's table,' she announced. 'My son asked me to spend Christmas with him.' She waited, a small, mutinous woman dressed in iron grey with a musquash wrap.

Mrs Johnson junior sighed deeply, then in a nasal whine said, 'Barry, you know what we agreed, the mothers should sit together and we four should sit together.'

Her husband lost a little of his jollity. 'Mother, precious, are you sure you and Doris wouldn't like to sit together? You'll have much more fun, think how you can tear the rest of us to pieces!'

'Barry, if you don't want me, all you have to do is say. I

164

thought when you asked me to join you and Joyce for Christmas you wanted my company.'

'Precious, of course we do.'

By now most of the dining room was more or less openly awaiting the outcome of the little scene.

'Really, Muriel, you never have known how to behave,' was Mrs Franks senior's contribution. She ostentatiously sat down at the table for two and picked up the menu, virtuous in her compliance with the arrangements.

'Just because you and John never have got on, there's no need to try and spoil Barry's and my relationship. We have always been very close.' Muriel Johnson laid her hand on her son's arm.

He capitulated and turned to Darina 'Sorry about this. Could we turn it into a table for six?' he asked.

'No trouble, sir. Would you like to return to the hall for a moment or two whilst we rearrange things?'

Five minutes later a larger top and cloth had been supplied to the table planned for four, it had been re-laid and the smaller table whisked away. The Johnson/Franks party was settled with only the minimum of flurry about the adjusted seating arrangements.

The carol singers appeared towards the end of the meal, standing at the end of the restaurant and singing a selection of well-known carols, unaccompanied. Then they were served mulled wine and mince pies round the Christmas tree and ended off with some lesser known carols, the guests standing and sitting around them, drinking coffee. Finally the singers pulled on coats and hats and left.

Ulla announced that midnight service started at eleven thirty in the church just down the road and torches would be supplied to all to the light the way. 'Do drive if you would like, but it's not far and you may enjoy the walk.'

But when the first of the guests ready for the service pulled open the heavy front door, in drifted flakes of snow.

'Oh, look,' said Vivian Fairchild, 'a white Christmas!'

Chapter Nineteen

The snow did not last the night. By the time Darina walked across to the hotel from the stable block on Christmas morning, a thaw had set in and the ground was slush. At least, she thought, the bitter cold had given way to warmer weather. Perhaps they would manage to keep everyone happy with the central heating, after all; there had been several comments the previous night on chilly bedrooms.

Her hopes were dashed by Alex. 'The boiler's bust,' he said the moment she entered the main building.

Darina stared at him. 'Tell me this is a joke,' she pleaded.

'No joke. I've been trying to get it to go for the past thirty minutes.'

'Is there an emergency service?'

'Heaven only knows.'

'Well, go to the office and look for one. No, you get the open fires going and I'll look for one.'

A desperate search through the Yellow Pages yielded several companies offering a twenty-four hour service. Heartened, Darina dialled numbers, to find that even so early in the morning no one could promise a call before the end of the day at the earliest. 'It's the change in the weather,' explained one of the companies. 'Because of Christmas we're short staffed anyway and last night pipes started bursting and radiators leaking all over the county.' Darina's pleas that their case was far more serious than a leaking radiator failed to elicit more than a statement that they would see what they could do but couldn't promise anything. By the time she rang the fifth company she was offering any fee they liked to name and a tired voice promised to send their man around when he got back from his current call, but not to expect him for several hours.

She put back the telephone, fighting rising panic. They had a hotel full of guests, all of whom would soon wake to Christmas morning with cold bedrooms and no hot water.

She went in search of Alex, finding him in the library, where he had just applied a match to his pile of paper, kindling and logs. 'Are the fireplaces in the first-floor bedrooms functional?'

He thought for a moment. 'Yes, Dad had boards put in the chimneys to stop the draughts but with those out the fires could be lit.'

'Right! Get some kindling and logs up there and we'll go in with morning tea and light them.'

'What about the second floor?'

'Haven't they got electric convection fires?'

'You're right, I'd forgotten about those. Dad thought there could be trouble with the hot water rising that far. And they've all got electric showers that heat the water as it comes out.'

'Thank God,' said Darina. 'Well, we'd better put on pans of hot water for the first-floor rooms. If we can't get the boiler repaired quickly, perhaps the second-floor rooms wouldn't mind if the first-floor guests used their showers. I suppose things could be worse.'

Whilst Ulla began to prepare breakfast and Max laid tables, Alex and Darina started on the job of taking in the morning trays. Happy Christmas sounded pretty hollow in the chill rooms. Darina laid the first of the fires and lit it, watched by the Misses Johnson and Franks, for once struck dumb with incredulity. Before they could regain their voices, she whisked on to the next room.

'That's so lovely,' said the female guest watching her apply the match. 'Reminds me of being ill as a child, a live fire in the bedroom, the flames flickering and casting shadows on the walls.'

'What's wrong with the boiler?' asked her more prosaic husband.

'I don't know,' said Darina honestly. 'I'm afraid it's rather ancient, an absolute monster.'

He swung his pyjama'ed legs out of bed and reached for his dressing gown. 'I'd better come and have a look at it.'

'Chris, you'll catch your death. Come back here this minute.'

'Now, now, Marjorie, I'm only going to have a look.' He

dug his feet into slippers. 'Now, young lady, lead me to your monster.'

Darina took him though the hall into the maze of corridors and back rooms that led to the boiler room.

'Are you an engineer, Mr Chubb?' she asked as he peered at the rusty contraption.

'Got my own central heating company. Years since I've seen one of these in action. You've obviously lost the oxygen supply. Probably rust – have you got a wire brush?'

Darina went to find Alex, thinking the man looked really happy for the first time since he'd arrived.

Breakfast gradually got under way. Two electric fires fought valiantly to provide sufficient heat to make the dining room acceptable but most guests had opted to have theirs in bed.

As Darina was clearing away the last place, a smutty, greasy but triumphant Chris Chubb emerged from the back reaches of the hotel, rubbing his hands with a filthy rag, and announced that the boiler was back in commission.

'You wonderful man,' screeched Ulla. 'I could yust, yust kiss you.'

'Can't say I'd mind if you did,' he grinned.

'You are an absolute genius,' said Darina and looked at the dressing gown now decorated with a fetching pattern of black smudges. 'You'd better let us have that after you're dressed and we'll see what we can do with it. What your wife is going to say I daren't imagine.'

'Don't you worry about that. It was her idea to come here. With both kids spending Christmas with their in-laws she said it was time she had a holiday herself, got away from cooking the turkey. I'd have been quite happy putting my feet up at home without all the trimmings. Though I have to say you seem to be doing us quite nicely; really enjoyed my meal last night. No, what I want to say is, you need to think about replacing that outdated wreck out there. I can't promise how long it'll continue.'

Darina gave him a level look. 'Would you like to come back after Christmas and give us an estimate for a new system?'

'Sure thing. I'll make a date before we leave. You're welcome to get quotes from other companies as well, of course, but I'll tell you this for nothing, no one will offer better value for money.'

The news that both the water and the radiators would soon be hot was greeted with loud relief by the guests.

'Just as well you moved us to the second floor,' commented Vivian Fairchild when she came downstairs, dressed in beautifully draped wool crepe, carrying her toning, soft tweed coat and wreathed in an aura of Patou's Joy. 'I've never been so grateful for a shower before, not to mention an electric heater.' She gave a graphic shudder and went to stand by the hall fire. A few minutes later Arthur Fairchild joined her and they went outside.

'Just remembered who that woman is or, rather, was!'

Darina turned to find General Sir Gerald Stocks by her elbow. 'Who, Gerry?'

'That woman, what does she call herself now, Vivian Fairchild? Soon as I saw her, said to myself, know you! Couldn't give her a name. Then just now it came. Vivian Saunders, or she was when I knew her, married to Richard Saunders, Brigadier he was then.'

'He was Max's father.'

'Max?'

'Alex's half-brother.'

'Good lord, that youngster old Richard's son?'

'Tell me about his mother.'

'Wrong un through and through. Discovered in flagrante with a major.'

'Good heavens.'

'Richard was badly cut up over it. Became something of a recluse after that, not that he was ever the life and soul of the party.' The General stood smoothing his moustache, lost for a moment in memories. 'Caused a bit of a flurry when he married her, we all thought he'd lost his mind. Think he had. Beautiful woman, of course, but with a past even then. Can't think why she married him, would never have made an army wife, too . . . ' the general grappled with the problem of finding a word to describe the woman he remembered as Vivian Saunders. 'Couldn't take the discipline,' he finally said.

'Perhaps she didn't know what it would be like?'

'Could have a point there. Army's bit like marriage, don't know what you've enlisted for until it's too late. Don't know why but ladies always went for Richard, he was lean as a whip and dark, very dark.' The General tended to rotundity and his complexion was ruddily fair. 'Always wanted to mother him, I think. Never looked at any of them until this one came along.'

'Max must take after his mother.'

'Quite, my dear, what we all said at the time.' Darina understood that there had been other comments the General was too much of the gentleman to repeat.

'I believe Max wants to join the army himself,' she said.

'Does he, by God; I must have a word with him. Is he around?'

Max was managing to keep himself well out of the way, safe from any possibility of coming across his mother. Darina explained he was laying the tables for Christmas lunch at the moment and then asked the General if he was enjoying himself.

'Indeed I am! Grand idea of your mother's to come here.' He paused, smoothed his moustache again, then said, 'She's really very excited about this venture of yours y'know?'

'She is?' Darina found it difficult to sound anything but doubtful.

The General ploughed on. 'Finds it difficult to express herself sometimes, y'know? Doesn't like to admit she misses you. Knows you have to lead your own life of course, doesn't want to interfere, that's why this idea works so well. Sees her daughter in action, y'know, is even part of the action, in a way. Great for her.' The General cleared his throat, started to say something else, thought better of it, gave Darina a little salute and marched off to the library, leaving her staring at his departing figure.

If it hadn't been so funny, Darina would have been angry. He had made it sound as though Ann Lisle was really interested in her daughter's activities. And even as if the said daughter was neglecting her! Darina remembered the way her mother had of dismissing her young, excited descriptions of some childish enterprise until she learned to reserve them for her father, who always responded with gratifying interest. After he died friends had not quite taken his place but they had offered interested ears in return for hers on other occasions. Visits home had become duty occasions. Darina liked the General but felt he had a lot to learn about her mother.

More guests came down, some to go out walking, taking advantage of the assembly of variously sized green Wellingtons Ulla and Darina had provided by the front door, others to congregate in the lounge and library. Darina wished the rest would

170

hurry up, the staff doing upstairs were going to be all behind. She thought of the Christmas dinners waiting for them at home and wondered how many rooms she and Ulla would have to do.

In the kitchen all was organised chaos. Sally and her assistant had dissected several turkeys and were preparing to roast the legs and braise the breasts, cutting the cooking time in the red hot professional ovens to some forty minutes and ensuring both were cooked to perfection. All the trimmings were prepared, and a set of Christmas puddings steamed gently away.

'You going to help us dish up?' asked the chef. 'With this lot to serve all at once, we're going to need an extra pair of hands.'

'Darina, have you got the key to the wine cupboard? I need to get the champagne on ice.'

'Darina, the Kendalls have asked four friends to join them for Christmas lunch and swear they told us.'

'Miss Lisle, Paternoster has dropped a bottle of aftershave in their basin and it's cracked right across.'

'Darina, the Smallbones say they're not just vegetarians, they're vegans and stuffed wild mushroom pancakes are quite unacceptable unless made with soya milk.'

By the time William arrived, Darina was feeling as though she'd been through a mincer. But all the problems seemed to have been sorted out, all the rooms cleaned, the temperature in the hotel was again comfortable and Alex was serving champagne cocktails in a pleasurable air of festivity.

It remained through lunch, what was left of the afternoon and into the evening, when, after an elaborate cold table, Darina and Ulla organised a bridge drive in the lounge, a beetle drive in the library and charades in the hall. As one of the guests said, it really was proving an old-fashioned Christmas.

Only a few brave souls could be enticed into the charades. Olivia Brownsword had arrived with a present for Alex, a silk tie she insisted he wore with his official dinner jacket, removing his black bow tie for him with a great flourish. As far as Darina knew, Alex had not been in touch with her recently, nor did he produce a present. Perhaps he had sent one round to Northwood Hall, ancestral home of the Brownswords.

Olivia was flushed and noisy and immediately enthusiastic

about the prospect of charades. One of the more extrovert of the middle-aged couples also agreed to play, William said he was game and so was Max and a couple of elderly maiden ladies who swore they hadn't had so much fun for years. Darina and Ulla were busy helping Angela supply drinks and coffee but on their way through the hall to and from the other rooms they caught glimpses of manic scenes that raised considerable laughter.

The noise gradually enticed guests from the lounge and library. Darina brought through more chairs from the dining room as the audience grew.

She paused to watch for a moment. 'Wish I could act like her,' said Angela as Olivia threw herself into a histrionic scene with Alex. Darina had noticed all that particular team's dramas had involved Olivia draping herself over Alex for one reason or another.

'Come on,' cried Max after shrieks of delight had greeted the successful answer to the charade. 'Our turn again now.' His face was flushed. At last he, too, seemed to have caught the Christmas spirit.

'Isn't it about time we called it a day or, rather, a night?' pleaded William.

'They started the game, we should have one more go ourselves. Remember what we decided?'

William allowed himself to be taken through the door at the back of the hall. Each of the teams had arranged their dramas in the wide corridor behind the hall. And each had dressed up. Gradually rooms had been plundered for costumes. Max and Alex had obviously been across to the stable block and brought back an amazing range of garments, including some from Ulla's wardrobe. Darina half expected to see some of her own clothes appear.

She left the hall audience buzzing with happy chatter and went to check on the lounge, where two tables of card players remained. Mrs Johnson senior was leading out ace after ace saying, 'I think I'll make these whilst I can.'

'You silly old bat,' whined her daughter-in-law partner. 'You're just giving them the hand.'

'Mother,' her son said patiently. 'We're playing no trumps, those aces are good any time.'

'Only if I can play them,' Mrs Johnson picked up her third trick and laid it complacently with the others.

'It's quite hopeless,' the junior Mrs Johnson complained. 'She has no idea at all. I said it would be useless letting her play.' Her underlip thrust out in a pout that threatened to become a permanent feature.

At the other table, Darina's mother laid down her hand and said, 'I think the rest are mine,' only to be immediately challenged by Arthur Fairchild. Having been asked to describe her strategy, Mrs Lisle then looked on flummoxed as it was demonstrated how she could have been defeated in the contract.

'Oh well,' she said with dangerous charm, 'if you are taking it all that seriously, I think it's time we finished. How much do we owe, Gerry?'

It seemed they were badly down. The General gallantly paid up for his partner and himself. 'What's going on in the hall, Darina? Lots of jollity, by the sound of it. Why don't we join them, eh? And could the bar produce a whisky? What about you m'dear? And Vivian, Arthur?'

They were in time for the start of the new charade. By the time Darina brought two whiskies, the dry martini that was her mother's favourite tipple, and a brandy and soda for Vivian Fairchild through to the hall, the audience was convulsed over a scene with Max dressed in one of Ulla's bras stuffed with napkins and a lace negligee, his lower limbs covered with a tablecloth draped sarong style. Paper streamers had been cobbled into a semblance of a wig, he was outrageously made up and posturing in a grotesque parody of sexual allure, draping himself over the sofa that formed part of their stage.

'Evening all,' William entered, a party hat in the shape of a policeman's helmet on his head. 'What's all this here, then?' More shouts of merriment, all were by now well aware of his job. Mrs Lisle had gone round introducing him to everyone after lunch, patently charmed by him.

'Darling, I can't think why you haven't brought this delicious man home before,' she said to Darina when her daughter at last had time to join their table for a glass of wine. 'She's such a difficult girl,' she added to William. 'So secretive, I never know what she's up to or who she's seeing.' She gave her daughter an arch look.

173

Darina bit her lip and Gerry Stocks stepped in smartly. 'Now then, Ann, Darina hasn't had too much time for keeping you up to date.'

'Darina never has had time for keeping me in touch with her activities,' said her mother tartly. 'I did think now she had given up her catering I'd see something of her but spending time with an aged mother is obviously not an attractive occupation.'

'With two such charming men, I'm surprised you've even noticed I wasn't with you!'

'Now then,' murmured the General.

'If you're not careful, William will think you're too sharp to be comfortable company,' Ann Lisle turned to the silent man. 'Don't you stand any of her nonsense!'

'Your daughter and I understand each other very well,' he said quietly and took Darina's hand. 'That was a delicious meal. All the traditional ingredients and some unusual touches. I loved the citrus jellies at the end. What was the sauce?'

'A lime sabayon. We thought its sharpness would be just right after the richness of the Christmas pudding.' Darina allowed the warmth of his hand and the look in his eyes to comfort her and fingered one of the gold and pearl earrings he had presented her with on his arrival.

The stage policeman, she noticed now, was using the silver fountain pen she had given him to take notes on the back of a cracker motto. He wound up his badinage by arresting the sexy wench for importuning and they moved on to the last scene. This seemed to consist of all the players pretending to be dogs, going round on all fours shouting 'Pow Wow, Pow Wow.'

'No idea what it is, far too clever for me,' announced Gerry Stocks as the players scrambled to their feet for their final bows.

Helpful comments were bandied about: 'They said it was a building . . . What sort of a building? . . . Two words, three syllables . . . Buckingham Palace?' The last suggestion came from Vivian Fairchild and was immediately shouted down as too many syllables.

'I think it's Manor Park,' shouted Ulla suddenly.

'Right!' said Max excitedly.

There was a moment's puzzled silence.

'What's Manor Park?' asked someone.

Ulla explained.

'I got the "man" bit; that came when they were pretending to be Jamaicans and slapping each other's hands. But where did the rest come in?' asked someone else.

'Pow wow,' exclaimed another guest, 'instead of bow wow; park instead of bark!'

'But what about the "or"?' demanded Vivian.

Max looked straight at his mother. 'I was a whore,' he said.

Was it only Darina who noticed the painful flush that washed up Vivian Fairchild's throat and face? Who felt the moment when son looked at mother stretch to infinity before Vivian Fairchild looked away? But it could only have been a few seconds before general conversation started and the party broke up into little groups.

Max disappeared and was not seen again that night.

Alex resumed his duties as barman and Darina had a moment to spend with William. 'I think I should be going,' he said. 'I have to be in the office early tomorrow.'

'You're not working on Boxing Day, surely?'

'There's no holiday in a murder investigation. Half of us have had today off and the other half hope for tomorrow. However, if we get a break, it could be we shall all have to work. At least the rest of the station's fairly quiet. Domestic troubles are usually the main problem over the holiday period.'

'Christmas gets to families, doesn't it?'

'Don't let it get to you, it's all going splendidly.'

He started to put on his coat.

Darina placed a hand on his arm. 'You wouldn't like to stay tonight?'

He hesitated.

'I'd love to,' he said finally, 'but I think you should get a proper rest, you're looking very tired.'

Thank you very much, thought Darina, that's all I need. What she said was, 'You will be coming to our dance tomorrow night?'

'I've had an idea,' he said. 'Why don't I bring along Pat James?'

'I thought she was ill.'

'She rang yesterday to say she's much better and will be in tomorrow.'

175

'Why on earth should you want to ask her?' Darina couldn't keep resentment out of her voice.

'I thought Max might like a partner.'

She looked at him suspiciously, 'Max?'

'He's a nice lad, needs a bit of feminine company, don't you think?'

Darina hadn't thought, nor did she want to. She wanted this evening to end. The Christmas holiday she had planned so carefully, worked so hard for, was turning into a nightmare.

'Ask whoever you like,' she said ungraciously. 'Just remember it's black tie.'

He sighed and looked at her for a moment, then planted a swift kiss on her stubbornly shut mouth and left.

Darina closed the door after him, stood quite still for several minutes, then started tidying the hall.

Her mother came up. 'Thank you, darling, for a wonderful day, I've been so proud of you.' She gave her startled daughter a kiss. 'And I liked William very much, I hope you will bring him home sometime. Now, I must go to bed, get some rest so I can enjoy all the fun you've organised for us tomorrow. Come along, Gerry, we'll take the lift, the second flight of stairs is quite enough exercise for me. Next time we come, Darina must give us rooms on the first floor.'

Darina watched them go, a peculiar expression on her face.

Chapter Twenty

The Hunt started arriving for the Boxing Day meet around ten o'clock, the numbers rapidly increasing as the time for them to move off approached. Boxes were parked in the lower drive and on the road leading to the hotel. Horses were led down, blankets whipped off, saddles thrown on, girths adjusted. Anoraks were discarded, hunting jackets carefully buttoned, hard hats strapped into place.

Some members hacked up, horse and rider already immaculately turned out. The large lawn in front of the hotel was gradually covered with mounted riders and foot followers, greeting each other with cheerful shouts and mock groans, tales of over indulgence being swapped with stories of family catastrophes. From the yard behind the hotel came the excited noise of the hounds.

The hotel staff donned Wellingtons and moved amongst the Hunt, offering whisky macs and port. 'This is going to cost a fortune,' complained Ulla.

'Write it off to goodwill,' instructed Darina and brought out another tray of the hot sausage rolls she had baked that morning, the forcemeat mixed with mushrooms, herbs and garlic, the pastry flaky and buttery.

A big woman, shoulders straining at her Barbour jacket, tweed hat pulled down above a handsome face, complimented her. 'Done the Hunt proud, you have.'

'It's nice to have you here, gives our guests a bit of excitement.' Most of them were standing outside the hotel, watching the scene of circling horses, riders busy with final adjustments and encouraging slaps to their mounts, followers chatting happily, as though it was a show staged entirely for their benefit. Some had borrowed hotel Wellingtons; all were grasping drinks.

177

'I don't think we've met,' said the large woman. 'Sarah Brownsword, my husband's the Master.'

Darina looked at her with interest. 'How nice to meet you. I know Olivia, of course.'

'Of course,' said Olivia's mother dryly. She looked across at her daughter, mounted on a large bay with a bony head and powerful shoulders, coat shining, dark mane and tail neatly plaited. Olivia was equally well turned out, her hunting stock secured with a gold pin, hair for once as much under control as her horse's, caught up in a coarse snood under her riding hat. Darina thought a topper would have sat rather well on her.

'She's very attractive.'

Her mother smiled a thin smile. 'Children are a certain sorrow and an uncertain joy.'

Ann Lisle would certainly have agreed with that.

'What's happening with the hotel?' asked Mrs Brownsword. Darina explained her position.

'Ah,' said the Master's wife thoughtfully, 'Ulla Mason. She *is* continuing in business, then?'

'Did you think she mightn't be?'

'Heard a rumour she could be selling up. Something my husband said.' Her gaze went back to where her daughter was now laughing at the Master, his heavy black hunter sidling and snorting beside Olivia's bay. On his other side, mounted on a patient horse offering no trouble to his rider, was the weasel-faced man Darina had seen the day she had lunched at the hotel with William. Olivia seemed to have made some joke because Michael Brownsword roared with laughter, throwing back his head, his adam's apple bobbing above the white stock, his hunting pink jacket rising and falling with his chest. His horse disliked the noise and started moving sideways, pushing Olivia's out of his way. He was brought under control by his rider in a moment.

'Don't your husband and daughter look marvellous!' Darina's mother in a dashing pair of short white rubber boots had picked her way across the churned-up turf and now ignored her daughter in favour of the Master's wife.

Mrs Brownsword greeted her with a cry of glad surprise, the two women exchanged courtesy kisses, then looked again at the hunters. 'Michael's dotty about her, always has been, she gets anything she wants from him.'

'No doubt you apply the right correctives, my dear?'

'What can anyone do these days, Ann? She's got a small income of her own, I've no control over her. I suppose I should be thankful she hasn't enough money to move away from home, not with her tastes, until she finds a rich husband.' Olivia surely couldn't think Alex had money?

'Still no job?' Darina heard her mother ask. She was offering her rolls to some of the hunters but the two voices carried across to her.

'Oh, she does the odd bit of promotion work, I believe she's very good at it, but nothing serious. She's not been too well lately. Been looking very peaky and she turned down quite a good job they offered her just before Christmas.'

'And Michael, how's he? Behaving himself these days?' How well Darina knew the subtle innuendo with which her mother could invest the most casual of remarks.

'Now, now, Ann. You know it never means anything and it's amazing what a salutary lesson availability instils. No trouble now at all. I'm slightly surprised the Hunt's still meeting here though.'

'You mean *she* was the one? No! I had no idea!' Ann Lisle was clearly set for a good gossip but Mrs Brownsword had turned to a nearby couple clad in the ubiquitous green waxed jackets.

'Do let me introduce the Howards, they're being such a help with the Conservatives.'

Darina heard no more.

'Jolly decent sausage rolls. Would it be too greedy to have another?' asked a man leaning on a heavy stick, one foot clad in plaster.

'Help yourself, please, we've plenty more. Are you a victim of the Hunt?'

'Got caught in a gate, twisted the foot right back, stretched the tendons like a piece of elastic.' He flexed the foot experimentally. 'It's nearly better, tried to get the doctor to take the plaster off last week. Wouldn't, said it would only have to go on again at the taxpayer's expense. A hundred pounds, he said. Would only do it if I agreed to go privately for the replacement! Pity, I would

179

like to have been out with them. It's going to be a dirty day but it should be a good hunt. Blow away the Christmas cobwebs.'

He had a hawk nose and witty dark eyes. 'Good meeting place this,' he said, pastry spitting out of his mouth.

'Nice that Ulla changed her mind about you meeting here.'

'Thought we'd be too much for her, did she?'

'Would have been rather awkward for you, I suppose, if she'd said no?'

'Not at all, we'd just have met down the road. Missed all your nice drinks and rolls, of course, but it wouldn't have worried us.'

Darina stared at him. 'It wouldn't?'

'Good God, no.'

So much for goodwill, but in that case what on earth had all that fuss been about?

There was a flurry and the horses started to move off.

'I think I shall retire to your bar and have another of those excellent whisky macs.' The hawk-nosed man started to move across the lawn in a series of agile hops.

One paying customer at least. Darina offered the last of her rolls to a couple stuffing their pockets for later and went inside to find the bar nicely busy, with Ulla doing the honours in great good humour.

Hotel Morgan was offering bar snacks today instead of a proper luncheon menu, with Darina and Ulla interested to see how popular they were with the locals and whether it was worth making bar food a regular feature. The hotel guests had been encouraged to go out by being supplied with a map of the area and a list of possible places and events of interest, plus pubs that were offering food. Sally and her assistant were busy with the buffet for the evening, when the hotel was holding a black tie dinner and disco. The regular guests were to be augmented by a number of non-residents and Darina and Ulla hoped the evening would make a handsome profit.

Darina left the noisy bar and found the Fairchilds in the hall. They asked Darina for their bar account.

'You're not going?'

'We think it's for the best,' said Arthur Fairchild. 'I don't expect a refund, I quite understand how these holidays are budgeted.'

180

'It hasn't worked out,' said his wife, her large eyes, the colour of a madonna's robe, remote and blank.

'We'll have your bill ready in five minutes.' Darina went into the office. Alex was there, entering telephone charges and the previous day's drink accounts on to separate sheets for each guest.

'Mr and Mrs Fairchild are leaving, they want their account,' Darina told him.

He looked up, his eyes, so much colder than his mother's, unsurprised. 'Probably best.'

'That's what your stepfather said.'

'No flies on Arthur, he knows exactly how to manage Vivian, gives her just enough rope.'

'Do you get on well with him?'

'Arthur?' he found the right sheet and started totting up the amounts. Darina glanced at the unused computer sitting in the corner of the office. In the New Year she must get someone round to show how that worked. 'We rub along together.'

'Have you thought of asking him for a loan to finance your Chinese trip?'

Alex gave a short laugh. 'My dear Darina, Arthur's a business-man. To him travel writing is something you do in your spare time. He doesn't interfere in my life as long as I don't expect him to contribute anything towards it. His feelings for Vivian do not extend to her sons. Not that he sees anything of Max.'

Darina perched on the edge of the desk. 'Why does Max hate his mother so? It can't just be because she was unfaithful to his father. After all, the same thing happened with Tony and you seem to manage some sort of relationship with her.'

Alex searched among the chits on the desk to make sure everything had been entered on the Fairchilds' bill.

'I, my dear Darina, did not discover her in bed with another man.'

'That's what happened with Max?'

Alex put down the pen and leaned back in his chair with a slight sigh. 'He and his father went out bird watching, something they often did. They were supposed to be away all day but Richard Saunders sprained his wrist in a fall quite soon after they started. With some difficulty he drove the two of them back and sent Max

181

upstairs to find a crepe bandage in their en suite bathroom. Max never got further than the bedroom where Vivian was entertaining her major.' Alex's eyes were chips from a glacier. 'He was only seven. The worst of it was that he probably didn't understand too much of what it meant, then. But his father and grandmother made quite certain every sordid detail was explained as he grew older. Vivian never stood a chance.' He resumed totalling the bill.

Darina could not think of anything to say.

'That's the lot, quite a tidy little sum.' Alex finished his accounting and handed the bill to her.

She stood with it in her hand. 'Do you think we should offer to offset this against the cost of tonight?'

'Don't be a fool,' Alex was curt. 'Arthur won't expect it. Neither would he thank you. He'd accept, of course, and reckon you'll be out of business in a couple of months. After all, we're not going to let their room for tonight, are we?'

Darina shook her head.

'Tell her I'll be out in a minute to say goodbye.'

Arthur Fairchild paid the bill without hesitation, then took two twenty pound notes out of his pocket book. 'For the staff,' he said.

Darina returned the money. Ulla had explained Tony Mason's policy over gratuities. 'We don't expect or accept tips,' she repeated Ulla's words almost verbatim. 'The staff work for reasonable wages and we prefer that they know exactly what they will receive.'

He gave her a quizzical look. 'It's a policy I approve of. In fact I approve of most of what you are doing here. If I may make a suggestion, contact local businesses in your area and encourage them to book meetings and small conferences with you. Lots of companies need somewhere they can get salesmen together, make a presentation to clients or hold a meeting outside their offices. That library could be made into a very suitable room. Stress your good food and the quiet. And if you could offer fax and word processing facilites, so much the better.'

Darina thanked him and receipted the bill. Alex came through to say goodbye to his mother and she took the cheque to the office.

When she returned to the hall, the Fairchilds had left and Alex was staring reflectively at the leaping flames of the fire. 'What's your theory on heredity?' he asked.

182

'Are children like their parents, you mean?' Darina perched on the arm of one of the carved wooden chairs.

Alex nodded.

'I sincerely hope I'm not like my mother.'

'But she's charming!' he exclaimed, genuinely surprised.

'You don't live with her. In fact I'm supposed to be like my father.' She thought of the fun she used to have with her doctor father in the school holidays, cooking him odd messes for lunch when Mrs Lisle was out, involved in one of her many activities. 'Which parent do you think you resemble?'

Alex sighed, 'There's too much of Vivian in me.'

'Too much of the philanderer?'

'An inability to form serious relationships. Anyone starts being possessive and I run a mile.'

'Is that what makes you want to travel?'

'Partly, I suppose. It's easy not to get involved if you move around. I've been here quite long enough.' He glanced around the panelled hall as though bars might suddenly appear and imprison him.

'Yet the other night you sounded interested in people. How can you not get involved?'

'I like finding out what makes them tick – as long as they don't start making demands on me. I want to be an observer, not a player.'

'Can you really go through life like that? It sounds awfully empty.'

'It's what I want,' Alex asserted.

'Have a drink?' offered Ulla. She stood in the doorway of the bar, her face flushed. She was wearing a pale green dress of some soft material with a V-neck that showed off her breasts like swelling spring buds. There was an abstracted smile on her face and a lilt to her voice that suggested the bar's clientele, getting noisier by the minute, had been generous with their offers of 'one for yourself'.

'Why don't I take over from you?' Alex strode across the hall and entered the bar.

Ulla gave the smallest and most elegant of hiccups. 'Oh dear,' she said. 'I seem to have upset him.' She smiled at Darina, 'Do come and join us, we're having such fun.'

Darina explained she had promised to help Sally in the kitchen.

Chapter Twenty One

The Boxing Night dance was proclaimed a success by the guests. To Darina it was a nightmare.

She had suggested an afternoon rest to Ulla, hoping it would sober her up. The Hotel Morgan's proprietor had appeared later in dazzling form, wearing the wispiest of dresses. A chiffon halter neck, it was almost backless and a minor miracle would be required for the front to remain in place should Ulla undertake any but the most modest of movements. As soon as the dancing started, it was obvious she wouldn't. The life and soul of the party, Ulla asked man after man to stand up with her. All were delighted.

Ann Lisle took great pleasure in pointing out Ulla's disgraceful behaviour to her daughter and asking if she shouldn't do something about it.

At first Darina tried giving Ulla small tasks. When she was waved away with an airy, 'Much better if you do it yourself, you're so much better at everything than silly little me,' for the third time, she realised she was doing more harm than good.

It didn't help that William had arrived with his police assistant dressed in a simple long red dress that suited her perfectly. Hair glossy, eyes bright, she seemed in as good condition as the hunters that morning. Darina had arranged for her to sit next to Max at her own table. William, the Chubbs and another couple made it up to eight.

Max had hardly spoken since his mother's departure. His excitement of the previous night had burned itself out. He'd been fed Alka Seltzer, concern and sympathy by Ulla, given a bracing walk by Alex and treated with matter-of-factness by Darina. None of the therapies had worked; he sat looking as though the evening was some exam for which he had failed to

184

prepare. And if William had asked Pat James as a partner for Max, he seemed to have failed to make that clear to her. She monopolised the sergeant and hardly spoke to the young man on her left.

The table placings had been arranged by Ulla and Darina in the early afternoon. They and Alex each hosted a different table.

With some guile, Darina had asked her mother to host one of the other tables so she was at least spared barbed comments from her. And when she looked across the dining room, Mrs Lisle seemed to be the centre of a riotously happy group, the General a contented spectator as Darina's mother led the conversation.

Various of the hotel guests had made friends and the tables had not been difficult to arrange. The only problem had been where they put George Prendergast. Darina had endured an awkward conversation with him the day after their confrontation in the yard. She had come into the library to find him sitting with some papers. As she came in, he rose. 'Miss Lisle, please, may I say a few words?'

She'd hesitated.

'I know how it must have seemed, my video, but really it was not like that.' A light sweat broke out on his forehead, he drew out a silk handkerchief and mopped at it. 'These things do get blown up out of all proportion, don't they? I'd hate to upset any of the staff.' His spaniel eyes pleaded with her.

'Mr Prendergast, I think it would be best if we forgot the whole distasteful episode.'

He flinched. 'But you do believe me, it wasn't what it seemed?'

'I prefer not to think about it,' Darina said repressively and left the room. Afterwards she'd wondered if there hadn't been some way she could have suggested he saw a psychiatrist. But it was probably years too late for that. They had to accept the man as he was or give him his marching orders.

For Christmas Dawn had received an enormous box of chocolates decorated with a red bow from the civil servant. It seemed to have impressed her. Angela had also been presented with one. Darina could only be grateful he'd had the tact not to offer one to Ulla or herself.

Whilst George Prendergast had chatted civilly to the other

185

guests, he had not managed to be drawn into any of the little circles that formed. Disconsolate, he had gone to his room quite early on Christmas night. Darina did not like to consider what form of amusement he found there but she did wish he had chosen to do the same on Boxing Day night. Instead he had booked for the dinner-dance, paying the required supplement without hesitation. After considerable deliberation she and Ulla placed him between the two maiden ladies.

Now Darina noted him courteously talking first to one, then the other of his dinner partners. That table, too, appeared to be enjoying the evening. She went and checked the buffet for the umpteenth needless time. Sally had prepared a Scandinavian smörgåsbord. Ulla had helped with dishes and advice and Darina had contributed some recipes of her own, garnered some years before from a Swedish friend.

Pickled and marinated herrings were offered in a variety of sauces together with gravad lax and dill sauce. Although the marinated salmon had become almost a restaurant cliché, Ulla said no smörgåsbord would be complete without it. Mild Swedish anchovies had been used in the most irresistible gratin ever, 'Jansson's temptation'. Who, Darina wondered now, had Jansson been and why had he had to be tempted? Ulla had not known. Eel swam submerged in aspic, a huge bowl of Dublin Bay prawns in their shells sat next to a variety of mayonnaises. There were fish balls in a wine sauce, tiny meatballs served hot with a mushroom sauce; a gratin of tongue, mushrooms, onions and red vermouth topped with Parmesan and a hearty dish of lamb and cabbage studded with peppercorns that was a speciality of Ulla's.

There were cold dishes: a spiced ham; loin of pork stuffed with prunes and apples, glossily succulent and topped with slivers of separately cooked crackling as crisp as arctic snow; liver pâté, smooth as foie gras, lay next to smoked goose. And in between all the main dishes were side ones of pickled beetroots, cucumber in lemon, potato salad, marinated mushrooms, glazed new potatoes, tomato salad, green salad. The centrepiece was a huge, untouched ham beautifully decorated. A cheese board, covered with the best of local cheeses: Coleford blue, the Capricorn goat's cheese that resembled a brie, an unpasteurised farmhouse Cheddar, and Hurstone – made on the Somerset/Devon border from Jersey milk to a Scottish Dunlop recipe – all surrounded by hard breads of various kinds, including Sally's special oat cakes. For dessert there were light-as-air mousses; the Danish apple pudding known as 'Peasant Girl in a Veil'; a Swedish almond and chocolate confection in the shape of a giant heart decorated with split almonds; bowls of home-made ice cream resting in ice and a Swedish rice pudding that had buried in it somewhere a sweet almond which was to bring luck to the finder. 'There should be a bitter one in it as well,' explained Ulla during their menu discussions. 'My Swedish mother would never include it because it was supposed to bring bad luck. Now, of course, you can't buy bitter almonds anyway.' Finally there was a mouth-watering selection of gâteaux and Wienerbröd, the pastries known to the rest of the world as Danish.

All were plundered heartily, with Darina encouraging guests to return to the buffet table for second and even third helpings. Then double doors between the dining room and hall were thrown open to reveal a small dance floor placed on the flagstones between tree and fire. A discotheque operated in one corner and strobe lights flashed but the music was a mixture of gentle old-fashioned waltzes and quicksteps intermingled with more modern melodies and rhythms.

There was no reason for Darina to feel jealous at William leading Pat James on to the floor, she had little time to dance with him herself. Could she be getting possessive? She remembered Alex's hatred of those who made demands on him. William, she was sure, was different but she would do herself no good by openly resenting his attentions to the comely WDC. If only Max would buck up his ideas and ask her to dance.

Max sat stubbornly at the table. Through the open doors, dancers circled briefly into view before once again vanishing, to re-emerge at the far side of the dancing area. For a moment Ulla and Alex provided a cameo in the doorway. It was a quieter number and they swayed gently together, not speaking, her fair head laid against his collar bone, his jaw resting on her hair. The questing, icy eyes were almost closed. The couple vanished to be replaced by William and Pat, the policewoman doll-like beside his length.

'Come on, Max,' Darina said decisively. 'It's time we had

a dance.' She gave him no opportunity to refuse. They were of a height and Max, once on his feet, performed a more than competent quickstep. 'I didn't think anyone learned dancing these days,' said Darina, conscious that her all too few ballroom dancing lessons in her last year at school left her at a disadvantage.

'My grandfather insisted. He said all young men should be able to dance, shoot, order a dinner and hail a taxi.'

'Did your father agree?'

'He was abroad most of the time. I spent the summer holidays with him, the shorter ones with my grandparents, until Alex invited me home with him and first Trudy then Ulla took me in. It was great, lots of fun and meeting people and eating out. And it was marvellous getting to know Alex. But I still went and stayed with Grandfather and Grandmother for part of the time, until they died.'

'Where did they live?'

'They had a big house in Derbyshire. It was even gloomier than this place,' he glanced at the panelled hall, 'but they liked it like that.'

'What did you do in the holidays?'

'Learned to fish and shoot. Read a lot, listened to Grandmother telling me about Father as a boy.'

It sounded a lonely life. 'And when you were with your father?'

'A lot of bird watching, it depended where he was. In Germany I'd go walking, in Hong Kong I liked to sail.'

'Did you make friends?'

'Father's friends all had children much older than me so there really weren't many opportunities.'

'But you liked army life enough to want to join yourself?'

He executed a skilful variation in step that Darina just about followed, then said, 'It offers a lot of things that I think would be good for me.'

'Such as?'

'Well, the discipline for one. There's a set routine for nearly everything, you know where you are. I thought accountancy might be something the same but there's not nearly the variety and the work is so boring. In the army you do dozens of different things.'

Was it the same restlessness that was in Alex?

'And what does your brother think about your change of career?'

'Alex? I haven't had time to discuss it with him yet. I keep waiting for the right opportunity but there's been so much to do we haven't had a chance for a good talk. I don't think he's all that pleased, he doesn't think much of service life. But I know it's right for me.'

'Does it matter what he thinks?'

A shadow crossed Max's face. 'It does to me. He's been so good to me. I thought about it an awfully long time, you know. I wanted to make up my mind on my own, I didn't want him to influence me but after I decided I wanted to tell him as soon as possible. I nearly,' he paused briefly as he guided Darina into a neat spin then picked up the thread of their conversation again, 'nearly wrote to him but then thought it would be better to talk to him. And to Ulla.'

'Excuse me,' said William, appearing alongside them with Pat James. 'If you've time to dance with Max, you've time to dance with me. How about making a swap?' In one easy manoeuvre he placed Pat in Max's arms and took Darina in his. 'I was beginning to think you had asked me here under false pretences,' he said. 'Come on now, relax, let that stiffness go, the evening's a success. In fact, from what I've seen, the whole Christmas period has been. Everyone is very happy so start looking happy yourself.'

Darina said nothing. She concentrated on following his steps, as deft as Max's had been, and felt some of her tension begin to drain away. 'Did your grandfather insist on your learning ballroom dancing?' she asked after a few minutes' circling the floor.

'What?'

'Never mind, it doesn't matter. I was just complimenting you on your dancing.'

'I had a girlfriend once who was mad keen. We even entered a competition or two. She soon realised I was a basic handicap and went off with a chap the same size as her. Did I tell you she was five foot two?'

She'd forgotten how comfortable it could be with William. Tales of past girlfriends didn't disturb her. It was the way Pat James leaned towards him to recapture his attention when they

189

went back to the table that reawakened the temporarily lulled devil which inhabited some region of her lower chest.

Max had slumped back in his chair, then noticed Ulla was for once on her own. He was over at her side in a moment, asking her to dance. Left at the table were Darina, William and Pat James.

Darina asked how the day had gone.

'Very successful, actually. We had a real break. Sharon's handbag has turned up.'

'I didn't know it had been missing.'

'We hadn't exactly advertised the fact. It was found in London. Some tramp had it in his set of plastic bags. He was done for a bit of opportunistic thieving Christmas Eve and given a right going over. The bag was empty, of course. It was identified from a couple of those sticky name-and-address labels at the bottom of an outside pocket.'

'Did the murderer take it to London?'

'We can't say,' Pat James brought herself into the conversation. 'Someone on his way up to London could have picked it up from the layby after the murder. It could have dropped out of the car unnoticed and lain on the ground for some time.'

'Where did the tramp pick it up and when?'

'He says he found it in a rubbish heap in Hyde Park, two days before he was picked up,' said William. 'Who knows how long it could have been there? London rang Frome this morning to ask us to let Miss Fry know they had her handbag. Got quite a jolt when they were told she was a murder victim. A CID team have gone straight up to London to question the tramp and bring back the bag.'

'If only her pants would turn up,' said Pat, 'we might really get somewhere.'

'Pants?' queried Darina.

'We haven't given it out generally,' there was a note of warning in William's voice, 'but the body wasn't wearing any panties when it was found.'

Darina knew there was something about that piece of information which meant something to her but the evening had produced so many tensions and pressures, her mind could not concentrate. Nor was she to be given the chance to consider it further.

190

From the dance floor came some kind of commotion. People stopped dancing and stood still. The music continued but above its lively beat came Olivia's voice. 'You're a cruel, cruel man,' she was shouting. 'Well, I don't need you. But someday you'll need me and I won't be there. I won't! I should never have come here, I should have gone to the Manor Park with Daddy and Mummy.' She came walking unsteadily into the dining room, picked up a ruffled wrap that matched her tobacco brown taffeta dress, tossed it round her shoulders with hands that shook, picked up her bag and left.

There was a sniff from Mrs Johnson senior together with a loudly uttered, 'If she was my daughter, she'd have something coming her way, I can tell you!'

Then the dancers resumed their gyrations and Alex came across to Darina's table with a look of exasperation as he settled down at a discarded place.

'Aren't you going to see if she's all right?'

'That's what she wants but she can find her own way home. She's got her car.'

'She seemed very upset.'

'Just needs a lesson or two in handling herself and getting rid of this ridiculous idea she owns me.'

'And no one must have a single claim on you, must they, Alex?' Max was back with Ulla at his side. Her eyes were too bright, the exercise had dislodged the chiffon of her dress and a breast threatened to escape the caressing folds.

'Sit down, stepmother dear, you're falling out of your dress.' Alex reached up a hand and pulled Ulla down beside him, adjusting the material with an amazingly skilful sleight of hand.

'You are a bastard, Alex. That girl wanted to talk to you and you wouldn't let her.' Ulla's tone was not as indignant as her words.

'Dance floor's no place for a serious chat,' he said lazily.

Max sat down in the chair on Ulla's other side. 'I can't imagine what girls see in you, Alex, you treat them like dirt and they come back for more.'

'Learn a lesson, little brother.'

'Well, well, well, police at Hotel Morgan. Finding other suspects, sergeant?'

191

Unnoticed by any of them, Adam Tennant had arrived. Like the other men in the room he, too, was in black tie, a white carnation in his lapel. He was smoking a cigar and Darina could smell whisky on his breath as he sat down beside her. 'Don't mind if I join you, I'm sure. Thought I would come along and see how you were doing. Such a boring lot at my place.' His voice was smooth, his gaze wandered round the room. Beneath the aura of bonhomie, Darina was aware those eyes were taking in everything: the dance floor and disco, the happy relaxation of the guests, the remains of the sumptuous buffet.

Ulla straightened herself in her chair, a mischievous look on her face. 'Sure you didn't come to make me another offer for the hotel, Adam?'

His gaze sharpened. 'My original one is still open.'

She placed both elbows on the table and rested her chin in her hands, leaning forward so the cleft between her breasts was clearly visible, indeed it was amazing that you couldn't see her navel. 'How about improving it, darling Adam?'

His face never moved a muscle but the ash fell from his cigar on to the pink tablecloth. He brushed it away and said casually, 'I could raise it ten per cent.'

Ulla looked at him steadily, a calculating smile on her face. Beside her Darina watched Alex grow tense, his eyelids half closed. He looked down at the cigarette in his fingers then with a sudden motion stubbed it out, pushing and squirming at the butt like a man trying to kill a snake by grinding it into the ground. She knew how he felt, every muscle in her body was tense as she waited for Ulla's answer. This was it. She could sense that, drunk or not, this would be a decision the proprietor of Hotel Morgan would stand by.

Ulla laughed silently and sat back in her chair. She snapped her finger and thumb in the air at Adam Tennant. 'That for your ten per cent.' Another snap. 'That for your offer. I'm not selling. I shall never sell. Darina and I will build this hotel into something. Something you will really envy, Adam Tennant. You will really regret not being able to buy Hotel Morgue.'

Not a flicker of expression crossed his face. 'You're drunk, dear Ulla. I may repeat my offer when you are sober.'

Her face assumed a look of cunning, she leaned forward

and pointed her finger at him, jabbing at the air. 'I believe you have been trying to mine me, blow me up. It was you who sent me Ken Farthing as chef, wasn't it? You knew he was no good, a wet firework, you hoped it would be the last piece of hay for me, didn't you? Instead I found Darina. Repeat your offer as many times as you like, I shan't accept. I'm a hotelier, I enjoy being a hotelier.' She ended on a triumphant note and sat back with an expression of great satisfaction.

Adam Tennant opened his mouth, seemed to think better of whatever he was going to say and closed it again.

Alex's face was bleak. With a jerky movement he pushed the ashtray with its murdered fag end away from him, got to his feet and stood looking down at his stepmother. Ulla twisted round so she could look at him. 'Yes, Alex, you have something to say?' she asked gently.

A spasm crossed his face, he turned on his heel and left the dining room. Ulla rose and took a step away from the table, looked back at those left sitting round it, said, 'Such a silly boy, yust a boy, I will tell him everything will be all right.' She followed him out of the dining room. Neither was seen again that night.

Adam Tennant turned to Darina. 'When Ulla is sober you might tell her I had no hand in her hiring of Ken Farthing. I had no idea he had applied for a job here, I would certainly have warned her against employing him if I had known. To suggest I'd stoop to a trick like that is ridiculous. As you know, I've only offered to buy this place to help her out.'

Darina looked at him. More ash fell from the end of his cigar, he ignored it and held her gaze, his eyes open and frank. Darina decided to leave the question of possible sabotage for another occasion and asked if he would like a drink.

'How kind, a whisky would be welcome,' he said, his voice as steady as that of a captain on the bridge of a small boat in the teeth of a Force Ten gale.

William leant back in his chair. 'And how are things at the Manor Park?' he asked conversationally. 'Have you had a good Christmas with your boring guests?'

Adam unbuttoned his dinner jacket and leant back also, lifting the glass of whisky Darina placed in front of him. 'Amazingly well, thank you. I left a very happy party in full flow.'

'I think we should celebrate the success of your Christmas, Darina. Would you have a bottle of champagne on ice?'

'William, what a lovely idea. Max, you know where it's kept, would you get it for us?'

The silent boy went off, returning shortly with a silver bucket full of ice and the chilled bottle of champagne, a white cloth draped over in regulation style.

William maintained a flow of easy conversation with Adam Tennant. He had been drinking mineral water during the evening but now sipped at a glass of the sparkling wine. 'I can understand the attractions of staying at a place like this or, indeed, your beautiful establishment,' he said to Adam at one point. 'No need to watch your alcohol intake, you merely have to negotiate the stairs at the end of the evening.'

Darina wondered if it was a hint to the hotelier to watch his drinking. Any breathalyser presented to his mouth would turn green long before he actually breathed into it. She could only guess at how much he had drunk before arriving at their hotel. Now he was consuming more whisky and champagne.

'Come on, Pat, we have an early start in the morning, time we left,' the sergeant eventually said.

Darina wondered whether he had tired of the effort of keeping the conversation going or of the evening as a whole. She should try and express gratitude to him but she was too tired. Too emotional. With a certain sense of perverse satisfaction she refused to allow him to pay for the constable's evening, insisting they were both her guests, but accepted payment for the bottle of champagne he'd ordered.

Then she accompanied the couple to the door, wondering if Pat James would have the tact to disappear to the ladies for a moment so they could say goodbye. No chance.

'Goodnight,' the policewoman said at the front door. 'It was such a nice evening, I enjoyed myself ever so much.' Darina decided the look she gave William at that point could only be called arch.

'Very nice to have met you,' she muttered. More than anything she wanted William to say he would send the silly girl home in a taxi and stay the night with her. She closed the door behind them and started clearing discarded glasses from the hall. The last waitress had left, the kitchen was immaculate, the dining room cleared apart from the drinks, the disco ended, the equipment now waiting for collection next day. But still some guests lingered over drinks and it was going to take an effort to get the rooms ready for the morning breakfast routine. Darina looked around and sighed. Ulla and Alex were supposed to be helping, what the hell had happend to them?

The front door was pushed open and William appeared. He took her in his arms. 'Couldn't leave you like that,' he murmured into her hair. 'She really is quite an intelligent girl, very good at her job, but not too bright where lovers saying goodnight are concerned.' Darina forgave Pat James everything, could even feel sorry for her. She led the way through the door at the back of the hall and melted against him.

'Can't you stay?' she said at last.

'I'd give anything to but I promised to take Pat home and we really do have another early start tomorrow.' He gave her a final kiss, promised to ring the following day and left for the second time.

It was with renewed energy that Darina went back to her clearing up. She found Max removing empty glasses from the tables. Adam Tennant was still drinking where she had left him, but had been joined by the weasel-faced man she had seen sitting on his horse beside the Master that morning. He had been in one of the local parties. They broke off their conversation as she cleared the table, apologising to them for the interruption.

'Can I get you gentlemen anything else?' she asked as she picked up the last dirty glass.

Adam Tennant gave her a calculating look. 'Can this hotel produce some black coffee?'

'No problem, sir.'

Two hours later the last of the non-residents, including Adam, had left, the hotel guests were all safely in bed and Darina and Max had restored a certain order to the reception rooms. The boy looked exhausted when they had finished.

'Would you like a nightcap?' Darina asked.

He shook his head.

'I don't know what I would have done without you,' she said. 'You've been marvellous.'

'I enjoy helping, makes me feel part of the team, part of the family.' He gave her a tired smile that had all his mother's charm.

Darina locked the back door after the two of them and they walked across to the stable block. Though the almanac declared the moon was full, it was a dark night, cloudy and stormy. There was something threatening in the way the wind blew through the trees, bending down leafless branches, the evergreens in the shrubbery rustling like papers blown into a corner of a pleasure park after a bank holiday weekend. Not normally a nervous person, Darina was grateful tonight she had company on the little walk over to the stable block. As they skirted the shrubbery, the wind blew the clouds from the face of the moon and for a moment clear light bathed the scene.

Max clutched at her arm and stood still. 'What was that?'

Darina, too, thought she had seen something, a movement in the shrubbery. They peered at the waving bushes. Nothing. Then the moon disappeared again, leaving the night even darker than it had been before.

'Come on,' said Darina. 'It's time we were in bed, we're seeing phantoms.'

Once in her room, she sat and made some notes on an idea that had come to her earlier that day, then undressed and went into the little shower room. The sounds coming through from the next room stopped her in the middle of applying cleansing cream to cotton wool. George Prendergast had one of his blue movies on. For an instant she saw red. Almost she dashed out to bang on his door. Then she looked down at her naked body and smiled ruefully. That really would set him going. She was too tired to do anything about it, she decided. Once she'd shut the shower room door, the sounds wouldn't reach her and, anyway, nothing would keep her awake tonight.

All the same, once she was in bed, sleep didn't come easily. The events of the day replayed themselves in her mind, images coming and going with dizzying speed. Then the replay slowed down and lingered over the way her mother had drawn down her head to plant a warm kiss on her daughter's forehead before she went to bed.

'Thank you, my darling, for another lovely evening. I wish your father could have been here, he'd have enjoyed it all so much.'

Her mother almost never talked of her husband. It was as if she had blanked out her marriage the moment the funeral was over.

'You were so close,' she was saying now, 'sometimes I was even a little jealous. Then I'd hoped I'd be able in some way to take his place. Foolish, I know, we are so different. But now I've seen you in action, I can understand you better. Don't stay up too long, you look very tired. Careers are all very well but I hope you aren't going to let William Pigram slip through your fingers. Men like him are rare and it's not as though you've had men queuing up for the privilege of taking you out.'

Darina had watched her leave the hall, followed by the general, with a mixture of familiar exasperation and a quite new surprise.

In bed she heard again the wistful note in her mother's voice as she talked of her dead husband's relationship with his daughter. Had she really been jealous? Witty, charming, demanding, restless Ann Lisle? Who made both husband and daughter feel hopelessly inadequate?

What of Vivian Fairchild, rejected in some degree by both her sons? Did she feel life had been unfair to her? Or did she inhabit some romantic world where everything would come out all right in the end? What impossible dream had brought her to Hotel Morgue?

The carousel of images stilled and Darina slept.

Chapter Twenty-Two

The daily briefing meeting of the murder enquiry was over. All those involved with the Sharon Fry case had been given new impetus and energy from the appearance of the dead girl's handbag. From threatening to become bogged down through lack of leads into a stultifying routine of dogged enquiries to eliminate unlikely suspects, the case had suddenly come alive once more.

'Bill and Pat, you come with me.' Inspector Grant led the way out of the large briefing room, now rapidly emptying of the many detectives and uniformed officers that had attended the meeting. The two detectives followed him to his small, bare office.

Grant threw a file on his desk and sat in his chair. 'I've got the DNA results through.'

'That's quick work, especially over Christmas!'

'Payment was authorised for an outside lab to work on them.'

'Well?' William pressed.

'Your boy, Adam Tennant, is involved up to his neck.'

An inappropriate figure of speech, thought William. 'He was the father of the child?'

'Right on! *And* he had intercourse with her before she died.'

'Ahhh.'

'You don't seem surprised?' Pat James commented.

'He lied to us about almost everything else, it was more than likely he would lie about that.'

'Then we've got him!' Pat and William both looked triumphant.

'Not quite,' said Grant. 'She had also had intercourse with someone else.'

'Are they sure?'

'Quite sure. There's no doubt.'

'Do we know who?'

198

'No.'

The detectives sat in silence for a moment, considering the implications of the results.

'We can, of course, go back and question Adam Tennant again,' said William. 'We had another interview with his wife after we took his statement. According to Rosemary Tennant, rather to her surprise he returned around eight o'clock. She'd been expecting him to stay out most of the evening, it's a not uncommon practice of his. In their cottage in the grounds they ate a meal sent over from the hotel kitchens and went to bed at around eleven p.m. But they have separate bedrooms and he could have left again without her knowledge. We know that the hotel has considerable bank loans and business has fallen off over the last six months; there have been a number of new hotels opening up in the area. The high interest rates must be hurting more than somewhat and Sharon Fry could have rocked an already leaking boat.' William paused, then added, 'Rosemary Tennant struck me as a woman pushed to her limit. And it seemed that the news of the victim's pregnancy upset her considerably.'

'So you think it's possible he could have left the house later that evening and strangled Sharon Fry then?' Grant's voice was sceptical.

'Shirley, who shared the house with her, says that after her duty that night she went out with friends and didn't get back until about three o'clock in the morning. Sharon could well have returned home earlier that evening and received a visit from her murderer. They could have gone out together or he could have murdered her at the cottage and then removed her body. Unlikely, perhaps, but it has to be a possibility. It could be that that was when Tennant had intercourse with her and he was telling the truth when he said it had not taken place during the earlier meeting. He's a tricky customer.'

William thought of Adam Tennant as he had appeared at their table the previous night, a pedigree Persian cat joining a party of moggies. Something had seethed and fluttered beneath that excellently tailored jacket and cummerbund. He'd been too taut, with a fine-drawn nervousness that had become more apparent as alcohol loosened his control.

Just why had Adam Tennant come down to the Hotel Morgan?

What was his real interest in the place: Ulla Mason or something else? Could he really have sent Ken Farthing there in a ploy to get Ulla to sell? Surely buying the hotel couldn't be a realistic proposition with his stretched financial resources?

There was something about that damned hotel that made William uneasy. And Darina appeared totally wrapped up in it. It was no fun being with her there, her eyes were constantly checking that guests had drinks, that the food didn't need looking after, that . . . well, it could be any of a thousand details. All he knew was that her attention was not his.

She'd looked so elegant last night in a long black dress of some silky jersey, her skin glowing with pearly translucence against its matte sheen, her hair caught up into a confining caul of black silk roses. What was happening to them? Why hadn't he wanted to stay with her on Christmas night? It had been true she'd looked tired but the real reason had been the hotel. It had an unsettling presence. If the Hotel Morgan had been human, he would not care to leave a child in its care. And he did not feel Darina could be his under its roof. It was unlike William to feel so overwhelmed by the atmosphere of a place. He'd seen all Darina had done to give it a certain eccentric style but he still felt chilled. Just why was Tennant so interested in it?

Grant was examining once again Sharon Fry's handbag. He opened it and turned it in his hands as though he had never seen it before. William switched his attention to its consideration. Black, leather and expensive, it hardly matched the clothes the victim had been wearing the night she met her murderer. For one thing, it had handles. He would have expected Sharon to carry the sort of bag that could be slung over her shoulder. Then it had lots of pockets, open ones at either side, zipped ones inside. A regular organiser of a handbag. Sharon would surely have chosen a bag she could chuck her life into in one messy pile. He thought of her room at the cottage she'd shared with Shirley. A jumble of clothes and accessories, the expensive treated as carelessly as the cheap. Sharon might have longed for the good life, she didn't know how to look after it. Pat James had tutted at the way a pair of patent leather shoes had been slung without trees into the back of the wardrobe. She'd taken them out and stroked the scarred skin, mourning its misuse. Almost he'd expected her to try them on.

'Cleaned out, of course,' said Grant. 'Except for those little labels found at the bottom of this pocket.' He stretched the fine leather on one side of the bag. 'Was it the murderer who removed the evidence or a petty thief? And how did it get to London?'

'It's an expensive bag,' said Pat James. 'I would have thought a thief would have tried to sell it, not chuck it in a pile of rubbish.'

Grant suddenly thrust the bag towards her. 'As you say, constable, it's expensive. Get on to the manufacturers and try to trace where it was sold and to whom.'

Pat left the office with the bag in her hand. William was about to return to the matter of Adam Tennant when the telephone rang.

The inspector lifted the receiver, 'Grant! Is there, by God?' The inspector was all attention as he listened. 'Right, we're on our way down.'

He put back the receiver. 'There's a man downstairs says he saw the victim getting into a car that Saturday night!'

James Dent was in his fifties, a cheerful, chunky man. 'It was recorded on the video, the police programme, you know? Yesterday evening we wanted to watch the BBC Christmas Day film. We had all the relations round the previous day. Not but they wouldn't have all liked to see it, but you know how it is?'

'As far as I can judge, these days most families do nothing but watch the box,' growled Grant.

'We're a bit old fashioned then,' James Dent's eyes crinkled with amusement.

William wished he would get on with his story.

'Not that our TV habits have much to do with anything, except I wanted to explain how it was I hadn't seen the appeal before. For people that had seen her, you know?'

'You mean the police reconstruction?'

'Right! I switched on the video and found the kids had changed the tape without my realising it. They'd been messing around replaying something recorded before Christmas. I was about to take it out when I saw this girl in a red striped anorak with long fair hair and long legs. There was only a few minutes before the tape ran out, the kids had either started their recording early or let it run on, that wasn't the programme they were interested in, see?'

'But you thought you recognised the girl?' William prompted.

'There was just something about her. Then I heard them asking for anyone who thought they could have seen her either getting into or out of a car with someone in a pub or walking along a road on that Saturday to come forward, and suddenly it all clicked.'

'Clicked?'

Finally Dent gave them the details. He had been returning from driving his mother home when his headlights had picked up a girl in a red anorak walking beside the road.

'Had to swerve to avoid her. She stuck out a thumb but I don't pick up hitch-hikers. You daren't these days, do you? Reckon anyone who does deserves anything he gets. But there was something about her. She had a really dispirited look to her. And I hadn't left her far behind when I thought I maybe ought to give her a lift. She reminded me a little of my daughter, Kate. Older but with the same long fair hair and long legs. Kate takes after her mother,' he added with a certain pride, glancing down at his own short and sturdy limbs. 'So I stopped and reversed a little way, then thought that was a bit dangerous so I drew into the side and waited, then thought I'd walk back and meet her. It was only a moment or two before I saw her in the headlights of an approaching car. She turned and stuck out a thumb and he stopped just short of her. She ran towards the car a little way, then it seemed as though she changed her mind and started walking again. The driver got out and shouted at her to stop.'

'What did he shout?' asked Grant.

'I've thought about that. I can't be certain, it all happened so quickly, but I think he called her by name, Shirley, it sounded like, and she stopped and faced him.'

'Did she say anything?'

'I think it was, "No, I won't" or it may have been "No, you can't". I thought I ought to call out, tell her not to worry, I was there, but then suddenly she laughed and ran towards the car and got in and so did he. So I went back to my car.'

Grant produced a photograph of Sharon Fry. 'Is that the girl you saw?'

James Dent studied it. 'Reckon so. Certainly looks like her.'

'Can you describe the man?' asked William.

'About six foot tall, young, mid-twenties probably, perhaps less, very fair hair.'

'How did he behave towards the girl?'

'Nothing out of the ordinary.'

'He didn't seem excited or angry?'

'No, if anything he was pleased.'

'Did you see the car?'

'I think it was a Volvo. I couldn't see much, it was dark and the only light was from the headlights but I think I saw that oblique chrome bar they have on the front.'

'Did it pass you on the road?'

'No, once she was in the car, he reversed into a little lane and drove off in the other direction.'

James Dent was not able to give them much further information. He thought the young man had been wearing jeans and an anorak but he couldn't swear. He didn't know what model the car was, had only seen that it was a reasonable size and might have been an estate. Couldn't even swear it was a Volvo. Certainly didn't notice the number. The only thing he was reasonably positive about was the identity of the girl.

They left him closeted with the photo-fit officer.

William went with Grant to the Incident Room, busy with operators entering the reports from the previous days' enquiries on to the mainframe computer, and studied the large scale map of the area hung on one wall.

Grant located the spot where James Dent said he had seen the girl and inserted a coloured marker.

'Just west of Bruton,' said William. 'Some way from the Manor Park. But not a vast distance from The Feathers. And there are some nice quiet lanes off there, ideal for lovers.'

'The layby where Sharon's body was found is on a route from there to the Manor Park.' Grant hummed tunelessly, knocking a pencil against his teeth and studying the map. 'She gets picked up from The Feathers around seven thirty, then is seen several miles away here at ten o'clock. Two and a half hours. Spent doing what?'

'It seems she knew the man who picked her up and that they had had a quarrel of some sort. If they'd been parked up here,' William indicated a small lane on the map, 'and she'd run off, he could have followed and met up with her at the spot James Dent saw them.'

'Shouldn't have taken him that long to catch her up.'

'If she left her pants behind, he may well have had to do a certain amount of adjustment to his dress before he could start the car. And probably have to turn it around, not an easy operation in a narrow lane in the dark.'

'So, she makes it up with him, they drive off again and then he decides to strangle her? To prevent her doing whatever she'd threatened to do before leaving his car? It could be a possibility.'

Grant went over to one of the researchers. 'Run through the descriptions, see if you've got a match for a young man, mid-twenties, six foot tall, blond hair.'

The two detectives gathered round the video display unit and watched the lettering flash across the screen.

As far as the computer knew, the Sharon Fry enquiries had so far not come across anyone of that description. A few minutes later they also knew that no employee of the Manor Park owned a Volvo.

'What about clients of the hotel?' suggested the researcher. 'We've got car details of most of the residents from the registration numbers.'

His button pressing identified two regular Manor Park clients who owned Volvos.

'Have we contacted them yet? Where do they live?'

The researcher read the details off his screen: 'One lives the other side of Bath, the other's a Bristol address.'

'Right, then, issue a High Priority Action to interview and eliminate. Get details of where they were that Saturday night, any witnesses, and find out if they've visited London between then and Christmas Eve.' The Incident Room Operations Manager started checking on the present whereabouts of suitable teams on the big blackboard that hung on the wall opposite the map.

'What about the restaurant clients?' William asked the researcher.

'We've only got as far as identifying addresses from the telephone numbers. No car details from them as yet.'

'What about addresses in the Bruton area?'

More button pushing produced several possibilities, including

Tony Mason at the Hotel Morgan, some seven miles away, and permanent resident there,George Prendergast. Both had eaten at the Manor Park several times.

More Actions were issued for further enquiries to be made, Tony Mason's name being deleted after William informed Grant he was dead.

Whilst this was being organised, the photo-fit officer brought in a picture of the car driver James Dent thought he'd seen pick up Sharon Fry the night she was murdered. As he laid it on the table in front of Grant, Pat James entered, still clutching the handbag. The picture caught her eye. 'That's Max!' she said.

'Max?' enquired Grant.

'Max Saunders, at the Hotel Morgan. Don't you recognise him, William?'

'There's certainly a strong resemblance,' said the sergeant slowly.

'Would you like to fill me in on this young man?'

William gave the inspector brief details. 'About two weeks before Christmas, we met him and his half-brother in a pub during our enquiries. We showed them Sharon's snapshot but both denied knowing the girl. Max lives in London, I think he'd only driven down that day.'

'No reason why he shouldn't have also been down on that Saturday. Find out his address, check Criminal Records for any previous convictions then pick him up for questioning. And I'll get the Superintendent to organise an identification parade for that chap, James Dent.'

'There's just one thing, sir,' began William but he was not allowed to finish. The Operations Manager had answered the telephone and now called Grant over and handed him the receiver.

'The caller asked for Sergeant Pigram, sir, but I think you should take it. She wants to report a murder.'

A spider of apprehension crawled up William's spine.

After a brief conversation Grant replaced the receiver and looked at his sergeant. 'Your little friend is in trouble once again,' he said. 'Some woman's been found strangled at that place she's working at, Hotel Morgan.'

Chapter Twenty-Three

They were a crowd in the small room, made smaller by the king-size bed that took up most of the floor space. The body lay on the bedroom floor clad only in a diaphanous robe that had fallen away from the limbs.

On the bed a rumpled duvet and dented pillows bore witness to its active occupation for at least part of the previous night.

The setting could not have been more different from the leaf-strewn ditch where Sharon Fry had been found, yet the state of the body bore an immediate resemblance to that other victim.

William forced himself to examine her. There was little trace in the splayed limbs and congested face of the girl who had flirted and danced the previous night. Now her face was engorged with blood, her lips and ears vivid blue. Last night her chiffon dress had teased and tantalised. Now the victim offered her bodily treasures without concealment to any hungry eyes but observers could summon little appetite. The pale globes that had thrust for attention against the soft material were flaccid and shapeless, the cinnamon-hued aureoles devoid of titillation.

'Strangled, of course,' said the doctor kneeling beside the body. 'And by the hand, clear thumb and finger marks.'

'Estimated time of death?' asked Grant.

'The usual question,' the doctor sighed but he was prepared. 'Roughly, very roughly, between nine and eleven hours ago.'

It was now just before midday. William counted back. 'Between one and three in the morning?'

'Very roughly.'

'Any sexual interference?' enquired the inspector.

'No bruising suggestive of a forced entry but intercourse undoubtedly.'

206

Grant turned to Pat James. 'How many guests are there at the hotel?'

'Most have already left, the special Christmas break ended this morning. There are still two couples here,' she consulted her notebook. 'A Mr and Mrs Chubb and the Misses Parker and Adamson. I've asked them to wait.'

'You'd better take preliminary statements from them first, then start on the hotel staff. You should get reinforcements shortly. Bill,' he turned to his sergeant. 'You can take Miss Lisle through her story.'

William sat Darina down in the hotel office. Today her hair was plaited in a thick braid looped underneath itself. The style left her face stripped for action, the skin pulled taut at temple and cheekbone, increasing the signs of strain in her face. Smudges of tiredness were feathered underneath the grey eyes.

'I thought Ulla was just lying in,' she began. 'You saw last night how much she was drinking. The rest of us were just about managing with breakfast and the bills and there seemed little reason to disturb her, though some of the guests were sorry not to be able to say goodbye. Most of them had left when Dawn, the girl who does the rooms in the stable block, rushed across. She was quite distraught. I thought first of all Ulla might just have collapsed from too much alcohol; we had a guest it happened to only the other week. So I went across to see.'

Darina swallowed hard, put her left elbow on the desk and leant her forehead against the tips of her fingers, pressing the skin as though to relieve some tension.

William waited quietly.

'As soon as I saw her I knew she was dead. And that I must call the police. I wanted to speak to you but instead they put me on to Grant.' She tried to smile. 'I think he could hardly believe I was involved in another murder case. I don't think he's ever got over that business with my cousin.'

'Don't worry about Grant,' said William. 'Let's just go through all the details of last night and this morning, shall we?'

Step by step he took her through the sequence of events, stopping her at the point where she said there could have been someone in the shrubbery as she and Max crossed the yard to the stable block. 'It was only an impression,' she repeated, 'but

207

we both thought there could have been someone there.'

'This was two o'clock in the morning?'

'About then, yes.'

'Male or female?'

'It didn't look like either. I mean, it was just an impression, someone moving.'

'Could it have been an animal?'

She hesitated. 'I don't think so. I know it was just an impression but I think it was a person.'

'We'll search the area,' said William. 'If someone was there, there may well be traces. What happened after that?'

'We went into the stable block.'

'Is the door kept locked?'

'No. All the rooms have keys but the main door is left on the latch.'

'And then?'

'I said goodnight to Max and he went to his room.'

'Which is where?'

'First on the right as you enter the stable block.'

William thought about the layout of the annexe as they'd seen it this morning, Ulla's apartment perched above the renovated stables like a clock tower with middle-aged spread. It was reached by a staircase that rose from the centrally placed entrance hall. On the ground floor a series of rooms ran off from either side of the hall, linked by a long corridor that ran along the back of the building, much like the original equine accommodation.

'Then I went to mine,' continued Darina, 'which is the second room on the left. Alex has the first.' She suddenly caught her breath and stared at him with eyes that had grown enormous.

'What is it?'

'When I went into my shower room, I thought I heard George Prendergast's video – his room is on the other side of mine – but I've just realised that the shower is between mine and Alex's, not his at all. The noises I heard must have come from Alex's room.'

She obviously did not like the implications of that fact.

'What sort of noises were they?'

Darina replied by recounting the tale of ex-civil servant George Prendergast and the blue movies.

'So you heard sounds of sexual activity.'

She looked at him with distaste. 'I heard people making love.'

William mused briefly on the way the human mind categorised information. The same sounds could be given different interpretations simply by the mind changing its perception of the noise's source. William filed away in his mind Darina's own change of interpretation.

'Who do you think was in his room?' He knew what she had thought, he had to hear her say it, unprompted.

'Why, Ulla!' It was obvious to her.

'But she'd just told him she wouldn't do what he wanted, that is sell the hotel. He left the table looking as if he hated her.' He waited to see what she would make of that.

'Remember the way she went after him? There's always been something electric between those two.' Darina was thinking it out as she spoke. 'I was beginning to believe one of the reasons Ulla wouldn't sell the hotel was because it kept Alex here, dependent on her.'

'Couldn't he get another job?'

'He showed no signs of looking for one. He kept on saying how he detested Ulla but, since his father's death, he's hardly left this place.'

'Protecting his interests?'

'He's been writing a book,' she said slowly. 'Maybe he hasn't even realised what was keeping him. Maybe last night Ulla made him admit just how much he was attracted to her. Attraction need have nothing to do with liking.'

Ulla last night had exuded sexuality, an animal on heat. William picked up his notebook. 'Let's go and look at both your rooms. Where is Alex, by the way? How has he taken the news?'

'He doesn't know. He and Max went out just before Dawn came over. They've gone walking on the Mendips. I said we didn't need them for a bit, I was well capable of bringing down the last of the luggage, and they should get some fresh air.'

'How did he seem?' William put the question casually as they started over to the stable block.

'Tired, overhung, as you would expect. Max was the same. Neither had much to say for themselves.'

'What did they do this morning?'

209

'The usual routine, boiler, fires, morning tea, breakfast, bills, luggage.'

'No time for idle chat, then?'

Darina nodded. Her energy seemed to be seeping away. Her dark blue dress, high necked and long sleeved, hung from her shoulders. She had lost weight over the last few weeks. A tiny chink of love opened in William's mind but it wasn't the moment. He pushed a gobbet of investigation into the crack.

'Is that where you thought you saw someone?' He pointed towards the shrubbery.

Darina was rubbing the upper part of her arms with her hands against the chill of the winter day. He wished he'd insisted she put on a coat before they left the warmth of the hotel. She nodded. 'Just about there, where the bushes are thick.'

He noted the location, saw that it was closer to the hotel than the stable block.

As they resumed their brisk walk across the yard, they met an irate George Prendergast coming towards them escorted by a young policeman.

'Miss Lisle!' he said as soon as he saw Darina. 'This is quite disgraceful, I'm being turned out of my room – for how long is what I would like to know!'

Darina glanced at William.

'I'm not sure,' he said. 'We have a murder enquiry to conduct.'

'And that's another thing, they say they want a statement from me. As though I could have anything to do with Mrs Mason's death!' He was full to the brim with ire and self-righteousness.

'It's a formality, Mr Prendergast,' said Darina. 'And we'll make available a room in the main hotel, we have plenty free at the moment.'

'When this news gets about, you're likely to have them free for some time to come,' he said spitefully, continuing on his way.

'I'm afraid he's right,' said Darina sadly. 'Murder won't be good for business.'

They ran the gauntlet of the police constable barring the entrance to all not on official business and Darina led the way to her small bedroom.

'As you can see, it's fairly spartan accommodation. That's the shower room, just wide enough for one person without a cat. And just as well it doesn't have a bath, the water's never been more than lukewarm.'

William entered the small box which managed to accommodate a plastic shower unit, a loo and a basin. He tapped the wall between it and the next room. It seemed reasonably substantial. He come out and tapped the wall that separated the bedroom from the room on the other side. This seemed more flimsy.

'Let's go and see Alex's room.'

It was tidy, the few possessions neat, the bed, like Darina's, unmade. The housemaid, Dawn, must have started her activities with Ulla's room. William looked at the lightly rumpled bedclothes. 'Forensic will go over it but if two people had a night of wild passion on that bed, I'll hand in my badge.'

Darina said nothing.

Alex's shower room was identical to the other, the two fitted end on end, the two lavatories back to back, with a grill above each that no doubt connected to a ventilation shaft. It seemed to be the only mechanism for removing stale air, no motor started up when the light was switched on.

'Go back into your shower room and see if you can hear me,' William told Darina.

He retreated into the bedroom, briefly contemplated attempting to reproduce the sounds of mating and decided to go for poetry instead, producing a loud and lively rendering of 'Once more unto the breach, dear friends.' Then he banged on the wall that connected with Darina's shower. There came a couple of bangs in reply. He went and joined her.

'I hardly heard anything,' she said. 'It sounded like a low mumble. The sounds last night were different, of course, but they were so clear.'

William entered and looked round her shower room again. As he studied the plastic cubicle, noting without registering the way the curtain was peeling off its hooks, he heard a door open and Grant's voice say, 'We shall need the bathroom fingerprinted as well and the usual search made. Apart from this old bottle of aftershave, there seem no obvious signs a man is in the habit of using it but some chaps travel with a razor.'

There was a pause then, less clear but still quite distinct, came another voice, 'We've finished photographing the body now, sir.'

'Right,' that was Grant again. 'Has the pathologist arrived yet?' There was a click as though of a door closing and they heard no more.

'Ulla must have left her bathroom door open,' said Darina.

'Perhaps as a source of indirect lighting,' he suggested, blotting out the memory of a hotel room in the Lake District.

After a moment Darina said, 'Of course, it mightn't have been Alex I heard in her room.' William did not comment.

She thought some more then asked, 'Do you know when she died?'

He gave the doctor's estimate and asked her, 'Exactly when did you hear the sounds?'

'As I told you, Max and I came over about two o'clock. I made a few notes before undressing. I'd had some ideas about promoting the hotel, a market gap I thought we could fill, offering holidays to parents with small children. You know so many hotels ban them? Tony Mason did, said they disturbed the other guests. But I thought this Christmas there was something missing without kids getting excited about Father Christmas and opening presents. Not everyone wants to get away from them. We could have a special playroom for them, get someone to amuse them whilst their parents go off on their own. Do special meals.' She blinked rapidly, 'It's hard to realise I'll not be able to discuss that or anything else with Ulla now. Anyway, there was that idea and some odd things I'd noticed about the organisation and food and things that I thought I'd forget if I didn't write down. And it helped me unwind a little. I suppose it must have been about two twenty, two thirty when I went into the shower room but I couldn't be sure, it might have been earlier, or even a little later.'

She sat on the unmade bed and looked out of the window. 'If Max and I did see someone in the shrubbery, could they have been coming over to Ulla?'

'Do you think there would have been time for him to have got upstairs, met Ulla, gone to bed with her and, if you'll forgive the expression, got into position by the time you went into the shower room?'

Darina looked doubtful, then said, 'If they'd made an assignation earlier, she could have been all ready . . . What about Adam Tennant?'

'Did you see him leave?'

'I poured him out of the front door about one o'clock, told him it was time he got back to his own hotel. I thought he might be hanging around waiting for Ulla to reappear but he went without protest. Could he have been waiting for a rendezvous time? But that was about an hour before Max and I went across.'

'I thought I heard your voice, Bill.' Grant stood in the doorway of Darina's room. 'I was coming across to the hotel to find you. I've just had a call from the Incident Room. Your chief suspect in the Sharon Fry murder was breathalysed at about three in the morning halfway between here and the Manor Park. I think we should go and interview him, don't you?'

Chapter Twenty-Four

Detective Constable Pat James took the statements of the four remaining hotel guests with care. But they proved to have nothing useful to tell.

She took the preliminary statement from Dawn, the house-maid who had found the body, putting the girl's halting story into sentences that formed a logical progression. Later Grant and William would interview her in more depth.

She took statements from the women who did the rooms in the main hotel. Also brief, also unilluminating.

At one stage, walking round the hotel looking for her next interviewee, she glanced out of an upstairs window and saw William and Darina Lisle walking over towards the stable block. She watched them stop and study the shrubbery. Pat's gaze lingered on the back of the man she worked with, saw the careful way he didn't touch the girl beside him. The little dream she had been indulging in faded.

Really she'd known the previous evening it had no hope. She was not proud of the way she had behaved. She hadn't seemed able to stop herself.

As soon as she'd been introduced to Max, she'd known she was intended as his partner. She hadn't disliked him, indeed right from the time she'd been introduced to him at the pub, he had interested her. His eyes were so blue and open, his face so frank, like the old type of clean-cut hero, really attractive in fact, not at all cynical like his elder brother. But she'd met young men like him before, brought up sheltered from life, with no idea of how it was for ninety-five per cent of the population. And usually there was some reason they thought life had handed them out a raw deal, they never realised how lucky they in fact were.

Nor had Max seemed at all interested in her. But good manners had made him chat to her and she might have enjoyed the brief dance they had had together if her attention had not been fixed on her colleague and his tall partner. No, she had not behaved well. But not nearly as disgracefully as the pretty Scandinavian woman who now lay dead. Her behaviour had been so flagrant, Pat had felt hers could hardly be criticised. But why hadn't William explained why he was asking her. Instead, she had been allowed, for a few short hours, to think that . . .

She turned away from the window, went back downstairs and found her way to the kitchen.

A short, stout girl in blue check trousers and white jacket, her hair covered by a triangle of white linen, was chopping vegetables. She greeted the constable cheerfully and offered her tea or coffee. Whilst the coffee was prepared, Pat established that the girl was the chef, Sally Griffiths. And that she slept in the stable block. But she'd gone to bed at around eleven o'clock, totally exhausted, had fallen asleep immediately and known nothing more until the morning. She had noticed nothing untoward on her way over to the hotel and had just started work in the kitchen when Dawn arrived in a state of collapse.

Sally Grififths was shocked but not badly upset. 'I didn't know Ulla well, it was Darina who got me to come and work here. I can't help wondering what's going to happen now. This place hardly seems good news for chefs. By the way, the previous one was here last night.'

Pat James looked up, 'You mean Ken Farthing?'

'Is that his name? Looks as though his face hit the electric mixer at high speed? Said he'd been in London but didn't like it.'

'What happened?' Pat James carefully controlled her excitement. This was the man who had worked at the Manor Park, who had had a brief affair with Sharon.

'She'd known him before,' Shirley had told Pat and William. 'They came from the same village. He spun her a great line about what a famous chef he was on the way to becoming. How he'd soon have his own television programme. His face would have put me off but Sharon though he was great. Had visions of them running a famous restaurant together. That was before she found

215

out he was unlikely to run anything smarter than a greasy spoon. The moment he was fired, she dropped him like a ton of bricks, wouldn't have anything more to do with him.'

William asked if he had threatened Sharon.

Shirley looked doubtful. 'He came round one night and wanted to see Sharon alone. There was a lot of shouting but she didn't seem at all worried, said that was just the way he was and she'd told him she'd finished with him.'

As far as Shirley knew, he hadn't bothered Sharon again.

Pat now asked Sally Griffiths what had happened the previous evening.

Ken Farthing had come to the back door, invited himself in, had had a few words with Angela, the little waitress, when she brought out a tray of dirty crockery, then asked Sally if there couldn't be a job for him in the kitchen.

'I felt a bit sorry for him, he looked so depressed. But apart from the fact there wasn't the work, he'd been on the fiddle.'

'The fiddle?'

'I told Ulla and Darina I thought he'd been signing for under-weight quantities of meat, then splitting the difference with the suppliers. When I placed the Christmas orders, they offered me the chance. It was put in the most oblique way possible, if I hadn't known what goes on, it wouldn't have meant anything. I declined to play ball, that's not my scene, but I told Ulla because it's the sort of thing you've got to watch out for. If you're not careful, you can lose a lot of money that way.

'Anyway, just as I was telling him it was no go, Ulla came into the kitchen. She saw him and really let fly. Told him if he ever showed his face here again she would contact the police.

'He went quite white and the way his face started to look made you think it had been almost pleasant before! But she'd done the trick, he went off without another word.'

'Do you know where to?'

'Haven't a clue. Ask Angela, she seemed quite chummy with him.'

The waitress had the day off. Apparently the hotel wasn't expecting to do any lunch business, the only cooking Sally had to do was for the staff and the one residential guest.

Which reminded Pat she hadn't taken a statement yet from

George Prendergast. He had been moved from the stable block and was now established in the library with a quantity of typescript. She went and found him there.

He was unctuously cooperative, happy to do anything he could to help the police investigations. He knew something of official matters, did the constable know he'd been a prominent civil servant in his day? Perhaps she'd like to hear something of his experiences some time?

Carefully Pat steered him on to his experiences of the previous night.

'Let's see,' he said, folding his small, white hands over his protruding stomach, leaning back in his chair. 'I think I went to bed about midnight. Wasn't it a splendid evening? I've so enjoyed this Christmas. Last year the Masons didn't have much of a party, they were in the middle of renovations. You don't know what a difference they made to the place. It was so ordinary before. But quite comfortable, and I found it very convenient for a number of reasons. The prices have risen considerably but the additional cost is well worth it.'

Pat got him back on to the previous evening. Had he heard anything after he'd gone to bed?

George Prendergast claimed to have slept the sleep of the just. 'Like a baby, in fact. Are babies just? When do we start the accretion of sins? By now I should have enough to make sleep impossible,' he gave a rich chuckle. 'But I slept. I woke at around seven, my usual time. I make myself a cup of tea when I wake. I keep an electric kettle and a box of Lapsang Souchong bags in my room. There's nothing like that tarry, scented flavour to start the day. You must be generous with the bags, though. I use two in a large cup and allow it to steep for five minutes before I add milk, I take some from the kitchen each evening. Keep it in a small thermos. One learns these little tricks that make such a difference to one's comfort. In many ways I miss the service flat I inhabited during the time I was in town.'

'Town?' Pat asked. 'Which town?'

He was shocked. 'London, my dear.'

Of course. Where else would he have been? Yet there must be civil servants working in Bristol, in Bath, in Exeter and further afield, Manchester and Edinburgh. Why should town necessarily be London? Why should Pat feel so at a disadvantage?

'Do you often go to London?'

'Not often, no. But every now and then I see old comrades at my club, sometimes catch a show, do some shopping.'

'When was the last time you went?'

'Last time? That would have been about three weeks before Christmas, I think. Yes, just about then.'

Pat could get nothing more from George Prendergast; the murder seemed to have taken place without impinging on his consciousness in any way.

In the afternoon Grant and William returned from interviewing Adam Tennant.

'He claims,' William told Pat as they settled down with a tray of tea in the hotel lounge for a discussion on progress so far, 'to have had a bit of a snooze in his car. Hoped he'd absorb some of the alcohol he'd drunk. After an hour or so, he says, he woke up and needed a pee so nipped out into the nearby bushes. Then heard someone coming out of the back door, we assume it was Darina and Max, and worked his way further into the shrubbery. Having relieved himself, he climbed back into his car, slept a bit more then started off for home, having the bad luck to run into Sergeant Pocock on the way, who had him up for driving without due care and attention. Pocock says he was making lace out of the verge, couldn't keep a straight line. The breathalyser was a mere formality.

'We've matched one of his shoes with a footprint in the shrubbery but there's nothing else to confirm his story.'

'So,' said Grant, 'he's now connected with two murders. I don't like it, it's too much of a coincidence. But even when we told him the DNA tests prove he's the father of Sharon's child *and* that he had intercourse with her the night she died, he didn't budge from his story, only said he'd forgotten they had had intercourse before going to the pub. As if that was something he could forget!'

'Can we build a case on the circumstantial evidence?' asked Pat.

'Difficult,' said Grant.

'And have both crimes been committed by the same person?' she asked again.

'The pathologist thinks so. On preliminary examination he thinks the bruising looks identical. Be interesting to know whether the DNA test will produce a match. If only those scientific boys could speed up the time it takes to get a result. As it is, we have to wait at least three weeks.'

'Any chance it could be a copy cat killing?' asked William.

'Possible,' said Grant after a while. 'Possible but unlikely, I think. There are not enough distinctive features.'

Pat doodled on her notebook. 'What do we think the motive for this new murder is?'

'Bill, what are your ideas?'

'A desire to get her out of the way?'

'Because of the hotel?'

'Could be. But I think there may be something more to it than that. Maybe she taunted someone, drove him just that bit too far. It's what could have happened with Sharon as well. Neither girl may have realised just what they were dealing with.'

'A pervert?' Grant looked sceptical.

'There doesn't seem to have been much planning about either killing. Everything suggests a sudden loss of control, perhaps after intense sexual activity.'

'It's early days on this one yet but the murderer, whoever he is, was damned lucky not to leave us anything to get hold of on the Sharon Fry case,' complained the inspector. 'Let's hope we can get some results from the fingerprint boys in Ulla Mason's room.'

'Alex Mason's car, the Volvo that was in the garage, may provide us with a link with Sharon Fry,' said William quietly.

'Sounds unlikely so far but the links between this hotel and the other case are building into something beyond coincidence,' grunted Grant.

Pat added some curlicues to her doodle, thinking hard. 'Do you think Ken Farthing's reappearance could be significant?'

'So far we have nothing to link him in with the Sharon Fry murder. He certainly wasn't the motorist who picked her up outside Bruton. On the other hand, it could be possible she was dropped at home alive and Farthing went visiting there later that evening.'

'Just as Adam Tennant could have,' said William.

Grant opened his mouth to make some comment but at that moment a constable knocked at the door and announced that Alex and Max were back from their walk.

Chapter Twenty-Five

Alex knew he'd reached the end of the line when he saw the police cars gathered round the Hotel Morgan.

He and Max had had a fine walk along the Mendips. The sun had shone and the bracken had been crisp and golden beneath their feet. They had a good talk and Alex began to think that maybe the army would suit his young brother. He needed roots and rules to live by; service life would give him that. There would be opportunities for sport and travel. And he would meet young men very like himself, it would help him socialise. Alex could not imagine a more stultifying life but Max was different from himself.

He was happy about Max's change of career by the time they got back to the hotel. And then he'd seen the police. Even though he'd known they would be there, it was still a shock.

A uniformed constable took both of them to the lounge. There were William and the pretty woman constable with an older man had announced himself as Inspector Grant and who stared at him and Max in considerable surprise. Then he turned to the sergeant, 'Why the hell didn't Pat or you tell me there were two of them matching the photo-fit picture.'

'Sorry, sir, I was just about to mention it when the call from this place came through and there hasn't been an opportunity since. And Pat was dancing with Max last night, no doubt he came to mind first.'

'Not what you could call identical but alike enough to cause problems.'

'I thought it might.'

It had made no sense to Alex but then the inspector told them both to sit down and broke the news of Ulla's murder.

Alex wasn't aware of reacting. He was only conscious of Max, of how white he'd gone.

'Ulla?' he cried. 'No, not Ulla! It can't be true!' The silence in the room must have brought some sort of confirmation for then deep sobs started to rack his frame.

Alex put a hand on his shoulder and pressed his brother into a chair. The boy held the back of his hand against his eyes, his mouth working as he tried to control himself. Then the policewoman brought them hot cups of sweet tea. He thought what damnable bad luck it was for Max. Ulla might have been, Alex stopped himself from thinking what Ulla might have been, but she had brought love and light into the youngster's life. Where was he going to find a surrogate mother now?

The inspector waited until the sobs had lessened, then he said, 'I have to ask both of you to accompany me to the station. We wish to question you and ask you to take part in an identification parade.'

The last part of his statement was a shock to Alex. Identification parade suggested there was a witness to something. A witness to what? He thought rapidly. Would it be as well to tell at least part of the truth?

'We shall also require intimate samples for DNA testing.'

'Can we refuse to give these?' Alex asked carefully.

'You can,' William answered, leaning forward. 'That will mean we shall have to obtain a Superintendent's Authority, which will cause some delay. Or we can tell you we intend taking a sample of your hair. Like this.' He suddenly reached out and plucked a couple of hairs from Alex's head with a quick yank that was surprisingly painful.

'Sorry,' said William, carefully inserting the hairs, roots and all, into a small plastic envelope. 'We really can't afford any delay.' He turned to Max. 'Are you going to object?' The boy shook his head. He looked shell shocked.

'Max,' said Alex. The boy turned and looked at him with the brilliant blue eyes that were so like his own. 'Before they start questioning us, we shall be read our rights. They include the right to remain silent. Don't feel you have to say anything you don't want to. And we can ask for a solicitor.'

The blue eyes looked bewildered. 'But I haven't anything to hide.'

'Then you don't need to worry,' said Grant cheerfully.

At the station they were fingerprinted, photographed and separated. After an interminable wait, they were brought together again but only to stand in a line with fourteen other young men all about six foot tall and with fair hair, all dressed casually, most in jeans and anoraks. Alex and Max were offered the opportunity to object to any of the young men but Alex could think of no good reason and neither, it appeared, could Max. Then they were allowed to choose where they would stand. Alex slotted himself about three in from one end, between a youngster wearing a pair of jeans identical to his own and someone whose hair was more or less the same length. He saw Max find a place towards the other end of the line.

A senior looking policeman Alex hadn't seen before brought in a short, chunky man and read out a statement from which it appeared the man had seen someone matching Alex and Max's appearance pick up Sharon Fry at about ten thirty p.m. just west of Bruton on the night she was murdered. Alex let out his breath in a long, slow sigh.

The man walked along the row looking hard at each face. He paused beside Alex, then passed on. When he reached Max, he looked back at his half-brother in a bemused way, then passed on again. Having reached the end of the line, he came back and paused, this time in front of a strange young man with straight fair hair that flopped over his forehead. Once again he moved on. When he regained his starting point he looked back along the line, his glance lingering first on Alex, then on Max and then on the other young man he had paused in front of. Then he turned to the officer and gave a slight shake of his head. His face said it all. He couldn't be sure.

The identification parade was dismissed and once again the brothers were separated. Alex could only surmise that Max was being interviewed first as he was ushered into small, bare room furnished with nothing more than a chair and a table and then left with a constable and his thoughts.

What seemed hours later he was taken into another room. He noted dark, absorbent material lining the walls, like a broadcasting studio, and listened as the procedure for recording the interview was explained to him by Grant, who broke open a new pack of two cassette tapes and loaded twin machines. At the end of the interview, he was informed, one would be used as a working copy, the other would be sealed in his presence and lodged securely for verification purposes.

Alex watched the little spools going round as the interview got under way, preceded by details of date, time and participants. He had wondered whether to ask for a solicitor. But the only one he knew was his father's smart London lawyer. Alex couldn't see him, no doubt dyspeptic from Christmas celebrations, taking kindly to a trip down to the West Country to advise a penniless youth on his rights under police interrogation. He was capable of guarding his own rights anyway, wasn't he?

The identification parade had given him a hint of what was to come but somehow he had still expected them to ask about Ulla and the events of last night. When they began by asking about the night Sharon Fry had been murdered, Alex knew he was in real trouble.

What had he been doing that evening? he was asked.

He took time to think. Asked them again what the date was. Finally said, 'I expect I was working.'

'The waitress Angela says it was your evening off.' There was a note of warning in William's voice.

'Then I expect I went out to some pub or other.'

'You didn't have a date?'

'I may have done, it's a long time ago.'

'Not too long for you to remember, I think.' Grant was curt.

Then they started. Suggested he had met Sharon Fry at The Feathers, taken her to some quiet spot, had quarrelled over the paternity of the child she was expecting. They told him she had jumped out of the car, run off. He had turned the car, followed her, she had got in again and he had started to drive her home but stopped in the layby, where they had quarrelled again. She had threatened him, he had lost his temper and strangled her. Then had placed her body in the ditch.

Steadfastly Alex denied everything. Even while denying each

suggestion, he shuddered at how well they had worked out the story. There wasn't much the police had got wrong. But they had no evidence. They couldn't have, otherwise he would have been arrested. The one piece of luck in the whole business was the failure of the chunky man to identify the driver he had seen. Alex blessed the resemblance between him and his brother and the presence of the other young man with fair hair that flopped over his brow. No, the police had no evidence. He allowed this belief to strengthen his resolve to admit nothing.

The hours wore on, cups of coffee were brought, jackets discarded, ties loosened, questions rephrased. Alex found himself being worn down with a deadening sense of familiarity. But not to the point where he failed to deny every accusation or offered an alternative scenario for that fatal evening.

Finally the police turned to the murder of Ulla Mason.

Here they seemed to be on firmer ground, had more facts to question him on. They asked him to tell them exactly what had happened after he left the table the previous night. Had Ulla found him? What had she said? What had he said? What had happened then?

By now he was very tired. The events of the previous twenty-four hours had been physically exhausting. Now the mental effort that had been called for ever since his arrival at the police station was taking its toll. At first he parried the questions, told them Ulla had merely said she would think again about selling the hotel, then he had gone to bed and not known anything more until the morning.

They took him through it again and again. Asking questions in a different way, approaching details from a different direction. Even though he knew how important it was that he remember exactly what he'd said, they caught him out, not once but several times.

He blustered, told them they were confusing him. He appealed to William as a chum. But William wasn't a chum now, he was a policeman investigating murder.

'Look, Alex,' he said as the questioning paused for a moment, 'we shall be sending your hair roots for DNA testing. The results will be matched against the code obtained from the semen present on the victim. We shall then know without a scintilla of doubt whether you had intercourse with Ulla last night or not. In your own interests, tell us the truth now.'

225

Alex sat and stared at him, the full implications of DNA testing brought home to him. What samples had they taken from Sharon Fry? What chance had he there?

Perhaps the time had come for being economical with the truth.

'All right, I'll tell you exactly what happened.' He paused, sorting things out in his mind, remembering the previous evening with total clarity but as if he was looking at the action through the wrong end of a telescope, dissociated from the actual events. A vivid picture of Ulla in her chiffon dress rose before him. He closed his eyes briefly. 'She was such a flirt,' he said and looked full at them. 'She caught me up in the back corridor after I left the table and stood right in front of me, moving slightly so that that damn dress swayed and shifted. Then she just reached out, grabbed my lapels and pulled me towards her.' Alex closed his eyes again, shutting out the sight of the detectives. 'She was like one of those dark liqueur chocolates, bitter at first bite then suddenly your mouth is full of sweet, fiery liquid. There was no question as to what was going to happen.'

There was a short silence.

'You went to her room,' suggested William.

Alex opened his eyes. 'You can have no idea what a night with that woman was like. She was overwhelming, unforgettable. I completely forgot all about her having been Dad's wife.' His mouth twisted bitterly. 'It would have been better for me if I had remembered.'

'You aren't the first stepson to fancy his father's wife,' said Grant dryly.

'And from Phaedra onwards it's usually been pretty disastrous.'

'Is that why you spent so much time away?' asked William.

'Do you know, until last night I truly thought I couldn't stand her, that Dad had violated Trudy's memory by marrying her. And all the time it was because I fancied Ulla myself!' He was almost consumed with contempt for himself.

'And I suppose you are going to tell us you didn't strangle her?' Grant leant back in his chair, balancing it on its two back legs, clicking a pencil against his teeth. Dark shadows had appeared on the jowls of both detectives but all signs of tiredness had suddenly fallen away, they were as alert as hounds hard on the heels of a fox whose speed has slackened and whose escapology has failed.

226

Alex looked at the little spools whirring busily round. 'This is the truth,' he said and allowed a little pause to build a certain amount of tension.

'We must have been together two hours or so. We'd made love, dozed for a little, made love again, then Ulla had gone to sleep but I wanted a leak. So I went to the bathroom.'

'Had you had the bathroom door open?' interjected William.

'Yes, how did you know?'

'Never mind, carry on.'

'We had the bathroom light on and the door partially open so there was just a subdued glow in the bedroom. Well, I had my leak and then I thought, why not take a shower. Make myself all fresh and clean and go back to Ulla like a new man. You understand?' He saw that William, at least, understood. 'So I had a shower. God, I felt good, the blood tingling through my veins, the water pounding on my back – and for once the water was hot. I felt like a god, an ancient hero, a crusader who'd do battle for his mistress. I sang, God knows what. There was a bottle of shampoo in the shower, so I washed my hair as well. I dried myself, found some aftershave of Dad's left in the bathroom cabinet. At least,' he said wryly, 'I think it was Dad's. I anointed myself, wrapped the towel around my waist and came back into the bedroom.' He found himself unable to continue for a moment.

Then he swallowed hard. 'The first thing I realised was that the central light was on, the room was bright, too bright, no more romantic glow. Then . . . ' he stopped once more.

'Then?' repeated William.

Alex ran his fingers through his hair. This was the difficult bit. 'Then I saw her lying there, on the floor, dead.'

'You mean,' said Grant slowly, 'you are trying to tell us someone came in and strangled her while you were in the shower?'

'It's what must have happened.'

'There was a telephone by the bed, didn't you think to call for a doctor, the police?'

'Come off it. What would you have done? The woman was dead, absolutely no doubt of that. How was it going to look? Everyone knew we were at loggerheads over the hotel. It was going to seem as though I'd gone to bed with her to try and persuade her to change her mind. And that she'd refused so I'd strangled her in a fit of passionate rage.'

He saw the inspector and sergeant exchange glances.

'I thought no one could know we'd made love and that if I didn't say anything, just collected up my things and left, it would look as though it had been the murderer who had gone to bed with her. Or someone else. It wasn't as if there weren't sufficient candidates. Most of the men there last night would have given their eye teeth to have been in that bed. DNA tests never occurred to me.'

'And in the morning?' asked William.

'In the morning?' For a moment he couldn't see what the man was driving at.

'Why did you take Max off this morning?'

'I couldn't stand the strain of waiting around for her body to be found. Once all the chores had been done I suggested we went off. And I wanted to spare Max the initial shock, he might have insisted on seeing her, Ulla meant so much to him.'

'Did your brother come down to see you earlier in the month?' Grant interjected.

Alex stared at him, what new line was this? 'Max hadn't been down for a couple of months until he arrived about ten days or a week before Christmas. He was working too hard.'

'You didn't see him the night Sharon Fry was killed?'

'Max? Of course not. He was in London.'

'Do you know that for certain?'

'Of course I don't. I hesitate to be biblical but I am not my brother's keeper, certainly not my half-brother's.'

'Did he know Sharon Fry?'

'How the hell would I know if Max knew her?' Alex flung at them in exasperation.

That wasn't the end of it. Backwards and forwards the two detectives went over both murders, like knitting, picking up stitches and working them into patterns that changed with each new approach.

More tape packs were broken open. The piles of labelled cassettes grew. Alex could feel disorientation begin, could sense he was beginning to lose his grasp of what he had told them and what he hadn't.

That was when he refused to answer any more of their questions. And stuck to his refusal.

Chapter Twenty-Six

The morning after Ulla's body had been discovered, Darina met an estate agent specialising in hotels. She had found his name in the industry's bible, the *Caterer and Hotelkeeper*, had rung and asked him to call round as soon as possible. That proved to be the following morning.

It seemed to her a sensible move. Alex was obviously going to sell. If she could find out what the price was likely to be, she might be able to work out whether she could afford to keep her dream of building Hotel Morgan into the sort of place she would be proud to run.

The agent was small and bustling with a businesslike air that inspired confidence. He asked about turnover and advance bookings. She was able to show him last year's figures and some bookings for the coming spring and summer, mostly repeats from the previous year. He went into her projected figures and the restaurant returns. She showed him a plan of the hotel and its grounds and Tony Mason's plans for renovations. Then they toured the establishment, including the derelict Elizabethan hall.

Finally he asked to see the outbuildings and grounds. Darina explained she was unable to show him inside the stable block but he looked at it from the outside, then surveyed the rest of the property.

'What about planning permission?'

'Mrs Mason told me they thought it would be possible to obtain permission for an extension or annexe to the hotel, or to rebuild the stable block, but they hadn't applied for it as yet.'

'What about selling off some of the land for a housing development, any chance of that?'

'No, apparently it's not in a scheduled development area.'

It had been a possibility the Masons investigated as soon as they had purchased the hotel; to have sold off part of the land for building would have produced some useful capital for their renovation programme. But they had been told there was no hope. 'Mrs Mason said there had been attempts by various of the villagers to create building plots, all of which had failed.'

'Pity, that area there is sufficiently near the village to be ideal for building if it was decided to allow development. And the road from the A37 offers perfect access. Could always be a chance, you know. Somerset is growing so rapidly they are rescheduling some areas.'

They walked towards the field he had indicated. It extended to several acres and lay behind what had once been the formal garden of the house and was now something of a wilderness. There was a ha-ha separating it from the field, which was regularly let to one of the local farmers for grazing cattle. Running around the field's boundary was a thick hedge with several mature trees. Beyond could just be seen the roofs of several bungalows on the outskirts of the small village. In earlier years the hotel would no doubt have been the local manor house. Darina could see that a development here would provide a natural extension to the village. Grow a screening hedge the other side of the ha-ha, and houses would not cause much of a disturbance to the atmosphere of a country hotel.

They started walking back. The agent went into details such as current price per bedroom, effect of community charge, desirability of country properties, swamping of the country house hotel market, the hotel's enlargement potential and its acquisition possibilities by a hotel chain, plus specialist considerations and a wealth of other factors to be considered, finally giving Darina a figure which he said represented 'what might be called the going price but much depends on market forces and these are somewhat uncertain at the present time. It should not be too far out, though, and I have some clients who could be interested if Mr Mason does want to put it on the market. You would do well, though, to investigate planning permission for that field. If that was obtained the price of the estate could well double.'

Darina explained her position and received his assurances that he would be happy to act for her if she decided to make a bid.

They said goodbye outside the hotel. Darina stood clutching his card while the agent got into his car. Her mind was as busy as a calculator, taking the price he'd given her, adding on the £75,000 plus Chris Chubb had said a new central heating system would probably cost, and the possible sums needed for renovating the stable block and refurbishing the first-floor bedrooms of the main hotel. It was an alarming total. And at the back of her mind was the nagging possibility of planning permission inflating the basic price. Of course, if she was able to buy the hotel at its current valuation, then found it possible to sell off that field for building, she would solve much of her capitalisation problems at a stroke. But she couldn't do that to Alex. There were, though, others who would. A whole new train of thought was started up in her mind.

The agent's car drove down the drive and Darina walked round the hotel towards the stable block. There were some notes she wanted to collect from her room, if the police would let her.

She passed through the yard and saw the wood pile. There had been no Alex or Max to cope with chopping logs and making fires today. She had struggled with those on her own after managing to light the boiler, thankful there was only George Prendergast in the hotel.

How long would the police question the two brothers? She refused to contemplate the possibility that either had been guilty of murder. Then her eye was caught by the rubbish bins, untidily put back after being emptied of their Christmas débris. A little shutter opened in her mind and she saw hanging out from one of the bins the pair of pants that had caught G.P.'s eye. The pants Max had found in Alex's car.

And it all fell into place. It had been Pat who had said on Boxing Day night that what the police really needed was to find Sharon Fry's panties. Why hadn't she remembered about them then? Had it been an inner reluctance to admit their significance that had blocked her memory until now? Then she asked herself why she thought the worst without proof? They might, just might, have belonged to Olivia after all.

Darina abandoned her quest for the notes and went back into the hotel, sat down in the office and looked at the telephone.

Should it be the police? Or should she check with Olivia?

She looked up the Brownsword number in the telephone book, reached for the instrument, then hesitated again. A bald query as to whether the girl had left a pair of pants in Alex's car was going to get a pretty dusty response.

She found the ordnance survey map and her car keys, told Sally she might not be back for lunch and drove off, resolutely refusing to stop for the army of press clustered outside the drive.

Northwood Hall was an imposing Victorian house surrounded by immaculate lawns, specimen shrubs and a wide variety of trees. Darina wondered who did the gardening. She parked in front of the house and rang the doorbell. Olivia herself answered. 'Hello,' she said as though she'd expected someone else. 'What are you doing here?'

'I wondered if you had heard that Alex is in custody,' said Darina.

The girl lifted a hand to her mouth. 'No!' she breathed.

'In connection with Ulla's murder. You know she was found strangled yesterday?'

'It was all over the television. They haven't arrested him, have they?' she sounded horrified but not totally surprised.

Darina hesitated. 'Could I come in?' she asked.

'If you want.' Olivia retreated from the door ungraciously. 'But you've got to tell me about Alex.' She led the way through a hall furnished with polished antiques into a back sitting room with sofas draped in dark Indian bedcovers which were thickly covered with dog hairs. Magazines and newspapers were scattered everywhere, many with headlines on the murder. A large television set invaded one corner. The furniture was heavy, late Victorian and covered with a hectic assortment of ornaments, photographs, books and bronzes of dogs and horses. On the walls were hunting prints hung without a hint of arrangement. A wood-burning stove provided warmth.

Olivia crossed the room, opened the doors of the stove and flung in an extra log. Then she drew her long cardigan around herself and sat in a corner of one of the sofas, tucking up her legs on the seat and shrinking into the corner. She was wearing a pair of baggy grey flannel trousers and a sloppy brown turtle-neck sweater underneath a black, over-large cardigan. Her hair could have done with a good brush; it looked as though dust had dimmed the shine of the coppery strands.

'Now tell me what's happened with Alex.'

'There's not much to tell. The police took both him and Max down to the police station for questioning yesterday afternoon. I expect they'll release them quite soon. After all, Alex and Max knew Ulla better than anyone, they must have a great deal of useful information for the police.' Darina tried to sound confident and matter-of-fact.

Olivia said nothing. Her eyes were tired and ringed with dark circles, undisguised by any attempt at make-up. Her face was pale, innocent of lipstick. Without her warpaint and chic clothes, she looked ordinary, not worth a second glance. 'It's possible the police will want a statement from you as well, about what happened on Boxing Day night,' added Darina.

'Not the best of parties.' Olivia reached for a packet of cigarettes from the table beside her. She shook one free, lit it with a gold lighter, inhaled deeply, then flipped up the cigarette between her fingers and looked at the wisp of smoke that rose from the gently growing band of ash. 'And I don't know what happened after I left. Though I can imagine. Ulla had her eyes on him all evening.'

She took another deep drag at the cigarette and blew smoke towards the ceiling, blinking her eyes rapidly. 'He's a real shit, isn't he?'

Darina said nothing.

'He's been playing with me. I thought I was getting somewhere, that we had something going, something good.' She drew again on the cigarette, then knocked off the ash into the saucer of an empty coffee cup sitting on the table in front of her. 'I don't know where it went wrong. We had such fun in the beginning. Even when I heard all the rumours about other girls, I still thought I was the one who meant something. But he's a real S.H. one T.'

'You're pregnant, aren't you?' Darina asked gently.

Olivia blinked quickly, glanced at her then turned her head away and looked first at one of the hunting prints, then back across the room at the fire. She didn't need to answer.

'Have you told Alex?'

The girl stubbed out the cigarette with a fierce movement

and pushed a hand through her hair. 'Not in so many words. I
hinted and that was enough. Alex said, straight out, he'd never
allow any woman to do that to him . . . ' She shook out another
cigarette, leaning forward from her hunched position on the sofa,
lit it, then pressed herself back into her corner, pulling the sweater
even tighter. 'He was so cold. His eyes were like that sky you see
while skiing, a sort of frozen blue, but underneath he was boiling.
It was as though he might explode. I was frightened. That's when I
ran off the dance floor.' She dragged quickly on the cigarette. 'I've
been frightened ever since. And when I heard about the murder,
I didn't know what to think.'

'You think Alex could have killed her?'

A tear squeezed itself out of Olivia's left eye and her nose
started to run. She gave an ineffective sniff then reached behind
herself for a box of paper handkerchiefs. 'He looked at me on the
dance floor as though he could murder me.'

'Hardly the same thing,' murmured Darina.

Olivia blew her nose hard.

'Have you told your parents about the baby?'

Olivia shook her head and reached for another handkerchief.

'What are you going to do?'

'I don't know.' It came out as a whisper interrupted by a gulp.
'God, it's such a mess. When I first found out I was almost
pleased. I thought he'd have to marry me. And if Daddy managed
the hotel business, we'd have some money and could buy a nice
house.'

'What do you mean,' asked Darina sharply. 'What hotel business?'

Olivia stopped her snivelling. She looked panic stricken. 'Did
I say that?' she whispered. 'I only meant that he thought if the
hotel was sold, Alex would have money. Daddy knows I want
to get married and that we can't if Alex hasn't any money. He
hasn't any to give me, not at the moment.'

'But it doesn't sound as if Alex wants to get married,' said
Darina remorselessly.

'He must, he must! I can't have this baby alone. And I don't
want an abortion. I've had one already. I felt awful afterwards,
I was depressed for months. They said I should never have been
allowed to get rid of it.' The eyes were now dark holes in the

pale face. Gone was poise, sophistication, worldliness. This was a badly frightened girl who didn't know where to turn. 'God, what a bastard he is.' She threw back her head and gazed at the ceiling.

'You weren't on the pill; why didn't you make him take precautions?'

Olivia shot her a resentful glance and said nothing.

'By the way,' Darina reached into the pocket of her jacket, 'have you by any chance lost these?' She drew out a pair of panties and casually tossed them on to the table between the two sofas.

Olivia glanced at them without the question seeming to register. 'I always wear French knickers,' she said.

Darina picked up her own pair of Marks and Spencer's pants and thrust them back into her pocket. 'Well, these can't be yours, then,' she said.

'Look here,' said Olivia suddenly. 'What on earth is this, why should you think they could be mine?'

'I just like clearing up odd questions,' said Darina with absolute honesty. 'Have the police been in touch with your father yet?'

'Not as far as I know.' Olivia's eyes suddenly grew larger. 'What are you getting at? You don't think he could have been involved with Ulla Mason, do you? That was all over months ago.' Then she drew in her breath on a sharp gasp and brought her hand to her mouth.

'Don't worry,' said Darina dryly. 'I am sure it will just be a formality.'

'Mummy's not going to like it.' Olivia stubbed out her second cigarette beside her first. 'She runs things around here, you know. But Daddy and I stick together.'

'Won't she help you?'

'If I tell her, she'll think of something incredibly efficient, then spend the next ten years flinging it up in my face.'

Darina watched the nervous hands shake a third cigarette out of the pack then fail to ignite the lighter.

After the fourth attempt, Darina reached for the lighter, flicked the flame alight and then held it whilst Olivia drew on the cigarette.

'Thanks.' She pushed the greasy hair away from her face and

235

leant back in the sofa again. 'I suppose I shall have to hunt all I can and hope for the best.'

Darina took in Olivia's casual casuistry without comment and got up to go. As they went back into the hall, the front door opened and in came Major Brownsword followed by two other men. Olivia's father was laughing.

'He'll sell, no doubt at all. We should be in possession by the time the new structure plan is common knowledge.' He saw Darina and stopped abruptly.

She looked at the Major, at Adam Tennant and at the man with a face like a weasel.

'Don't start counting your chickens too soon,' she said sweetly, turned to take her leave of Olivia and departed, conscious of a profound silence behind her.

Chapter Twenty-Seven

Darina drove straight to the police station. She asked for Sergeant Pigram. He was unavailable. Instead Pat James came down and took her up to the small, tidy offices where the CID worked.

'Do you have some information for us?' the constable asked, sitting behind a desk and gesturing Darina towards a chair. Her manner told the tall girl as plainly as if she had uttered the words she was intruding on a very busy office. The constable seemed at home and very sure of herself.

Darina hesitated. It was difficult to know where to begin with this briskly efficient young woman. She took a long look at the glossy brown hair, discreet make up, understated wool dress and jerkin and the brown eyes. Brown eyes that, for all the warmth of their colour, were frosted with antagonism.

Here was a girl with none of Olivia's wiles but one that looked just as determined to get her man.

'I take it you haven't just come to pass the time of day? We are in the midst of a murder investigation, you know.'

Darina heard herself take a sharp, inward breath, then steadied herself. Part of her sympathised with the other girl, could understand her feelings. 'I came to give you some information,' she said quietly.

'Information?' Pat raised an enquiring eyebrow.

'I know you've got Alex and Max here, that you're questioning them. Well, I think I can help.'

'Interested in Alex are you? Those blue eyes seem to have attracted a great many of the local females.'

Darina's sympathy began to evaporate. Pat James was being more than tedious and less than helpful. It was the first sign of non-professionalism she had seen in the girl and revealed just how involved she had allowed herself to become with her detective sergeant colleague.

And how involved had he become? Something churned with sickening jolts inside her. Darina wondered if she had made the greatest mistake of her life. William's love had seemed so secure, something she could depend on, ask to wait at her convenience. Had he grown tired of waiting?

Then she wrenched her mind back to the matter in hand. This, certainly, must not wait any longer.

'It's a matter of . . . ' she started, then stopped as William entered the office followed by Grant. Both looked exhausted.

'Ah, Pat,' said the Inspector, 'how have you got on with that handbag and have we got the results of the London enquiries yet?'

The girl rose, 'We have a visitor, sir.'

'Darling!' William appeared delighted to see her. Grant rather less so. He gave her a brief nod and asked again for Pat's information.

The constable gave a tiny shrug of her shoulders. 'I got onto the manufacturers of the bag. They gave me a list of outlets. One was in Bath so I went there this morning and they identified it as identical to one sold to a Mr Adam Tennant.'

'No great surprise,' grunted the inspector. 'And London?'

'The team has just returned. Max Saunder's alibi for that Saturday evening has stood up. He was in a pub in Chelsea until just before eight o'clock.'

'So he could hardly have been outside The Feathers at seven-thirty,' said Grant slowly.

'No, sir.'

The inspector turned his attention to Darina. 'And what brings you here, may I ask?'

Darina said, 'I think I have some information for you.'

'Think? Don't you know?' He looked at his watch and sighed. 'We've only got another couple of hours with those two before our twenty-four hours are up and we have to decide whether an arrest can be made or we let them go. I must have another session with Mason, he's holding out on us, I know it. What we need is another angle, some other way to get to him. Constable, work with one of the researchers and find as many links between the Sharon

238

Fry case and this one as possible. Guests who may have stayed at or visited both hotels, staff who could have worked at each, hotel suppliers, any common denominators you can think of.'

Pat left the office without a backward glance.

'Miss Lisle,' Grant continued. 'I get a nasty feeling in the pit of my stomach when you tell me you think you have information. You'd better give the details of whatever it is to Bill here.'

Grant left and William sat behind the desk, running a hand over his tired face. Then he gave her a faint smile. 'No breath of spring could be more welcome and I'd love to sit and chat but I have to ask you to give me whatever information you have as quickly as possible, this is a critical phase.'

'You look terrible, what have you been doing?'

'We've been questioning Alex and Max and when we had to stop, we spent most of the night reviewing the evidence, trying to find something to challenge Alex on.'

'Do I gather you haven't got very far?'

He sighed again, 'We know Alex is being less than open with us. Max has answered every question frankly and his account of his actions on that Saturday night seems to have checked out. But for the last few hours Alex has refused to answer any questions at all. I know he's connected with this Sharon Fry case, it's gut instinct, but there's nothing, absolutely nothing, to tie him in.'

Darina quashed a comment on detectives who said they never worked on hunches and instead started on her tale.

William listened quietly while she went through the story she had pieced together. 'As soon as Olivia told me the pants weren't hers, it all seemed horribly clear,' she finished.

He sighed. 'But the evidence has disappeared?'

'Buried on some waste tip. If only I'd known.'

'No way you could. We shall have to see what we can do without the actual garment. At least it gives us something new to work with. I'll see you out.' He rose from his seat.

Darina rose also but remained where she was, 'I'd rather wait.'

'It could be a long one.'

'I don't mind.'

He smiled at her, his warm, personal smile. 'You don't have to get back to the hotel?'

She shook her head, words had deserted her.

239

'Right, then.'

He took her down to a bare room with a table and chair and left her.

Darina sat, then wandered restlessly around. This was no waiting room with magazines to distract. She had nothing to do but go over and over such details of both murders as she knew. Would the information she had brought provide a breakthrough in the case? With part of her mind she hoped desperately it would prove a red herring, hoped that she had constructed a house of cards on shifting sands and that one word from Alex would bring the whole edifice crashing down.

And beneath the revolving cogs of her mind she was aware of still feeling the pressure of William's hand on her arm. If the case did break, would he be free to spend some time with her? Would he want to? And if he did, what exactly were her feelings?

In a seeming non-sequitur, Darina remembered her mother's goodbye the previous morning. Ann Lisle had looked around the Hotel Morgan's hall with a keen, assessing gaze, glanced at her final bill, brought out her chequebook and paid the account with a flourish.

'I shall enjoy watching what you do to this place, my darling. I can see you are going to make it somewhere I can bring my friends. Gerry and I will certainly be telling everyone we know to come and eat here, won't we Gerry?' The general grunted assent as he handed over his own cheque. 'I shall enjoy helping you put it on the map.' And her help was not to be underestimated. Ann Lisle knew most of the county, was involved in arranging charity lunches, dinners, balls, could drop recommendations for wedding locations and places for friends to stay.

Darina was grateful and said so. Her mother's face lit up in a way her daughter had rarely seen. 'It will be such fun to be involved in a small way with what you are doing. Now, come on, Gerry, if we're to make that lunch at The Castle in Taunton you promised me, we must get going. We've got to drop off our things at home first. 'Bye darling, tell Mrs Mason we were sorry not to be able to say goodbye. Though I'm hardly surprised she's not made an appearance,' she added caustically. 'If she's to be your partner, you will have to watch her drinking.'

Darina called to Max to carry their bags and watched her

mother and the General leave the hotel feeling for once in her life a certain rapport with the woman who had borne her. And also a certain guilt. Perhaps the General understood more about people than she had thought. After all, you didn't rise to high rank in the army these days without a certain level of intelligence and ability to judge character. But could it really be that she herself had shut her mother out of her life rather than the other way round?

Now she thought that relationships were a two-way business. Her mother had surely set in motion the divergence of understanding. By the time she had realised what a small part she played in her daughter's life, it was too late, Darina never considered including her mother in any of her activities. Perhaps, though, there was something that could be rescued if both of them tried. It would require hard work, the old patterns would re-establish themselves all too easily. But it would be worth it to rediscover a mother.

Darina thought about the alienating power of non-communication, how easy it was to drift away from loved ones. How important not to shut people out.

Like hamsters round a wheel, her thoughts chased each other up and down her tired mind while she waited alone in the bare room.

Finally William came back.

'He knows you are here and says that if you're present he'll tell us everything but only if you are there. Will you come?'

Wordlessly she rose and followed him into the quiet of an interview room, questioner and respondent next to a pair of recording machines.

The fair hair fell over a brow white with weariness, the blazing blue of the eyes was dimmed, the handsome face slumped over the lean chest.

Grant sat on the other side of the table. He acknowledged Darina's entrance with a brief look and recorded her presence in the room on the tape.

William sat her in a chair.

Darina looked at the exhausted figure. 'Hello,' she said gently. 'Would you like to tell me all about it?'

He raised his head and looked at her. 'You aren't like the others, are you?'

241

'Like whom?'

'Like those bitches!' Venom snapped in his voice.

'What did they do?' Darina asked. Beside her both detectives were silent.

'Betrayed me, betrayed my brother. They didn't deserve to live. And I did it for my father. He should have killed her.' He fell silent.

Darina reached out for his hand and held it while she waited.

After a moment he said, 'I was so excited that evening. I'd made up my mind what I was going to do, what the right path for me was. It was as though a weight had fallen from my shoulders. I knew it was the right decision. I went to the local, met a few friends, had a beer or two. But it wasn't the same as sharing it with my brother and . . . ' his voice broke for a moment, then he continued, ' . . . and Ulla. I decided that it was still early enough to drive down and spend the night with them, then come back late on Sunday.

'I turned off the A303 to cut through Bruton, I think it's a better way than the Castle Cary road. Just after Bruton I saw her. Sharon Fry, I mean. I'd met her with Alex in a pub several months ago. We spent the evening together, us three. She was very pretty with long, lovely legs. But she wasn't interested in me, it was Alex she wanted to be with. Anyway, suddenly, there she was, just walking along the road, thumbing a lift. I stopped the car and called to her. At first she just shouted at me and made a rude gesture then went on walking. I got out and went towards her and afterwards she told me that that's when she recognised me. She'd thought I was Alex before, you see, our cars are very similar, both Volvo's, and in the dark she couldn't see any difference. Anyway, Sharon told me she'd had a quarrel with Alex and I said I'd drive her home, well, it wasn't far away and I couldn't leave her like that.'

Max was leaning earnestly towards Darina how, engrossed in the story he was telling. 'She started telling me what a sod he was, what a bastard. Well, I know how Alex can be with girls and at first I was sympathetic. I saw a layby and suggested we stopped as I was finding it difficult to drive and listen to her. I was quite tired by this time.' He gave a sigh. 'So I stopped and she talked. For a little while I didn't understand what she was saying. The moonlight was on her face and her hair was shining like sunlight on a waterfall. It was how I remember my mother, before, before . . . ' he broke off.

No-one said a word.

He started again, 'Then I realised she was talking about Alex, that she was saying she'd told him she was pregnant and he wouldn't have anything to do with the baby.' His voice rose in indignation, 'She was saying my brother had seduced her, that all he thought she was fit for was fucking, that he'd even fucked her that evening in his car but he wouldn't do the decent thing. She kept on repeating that word, again and again. I wanted to tell her that my brother had treated her exactly as she deserved but I thought I should make sure I knew exactly what she was. I wanted to be certain.' He looked at them with a certain amount of pride. 'I told her how pretty she was, how she excited me and if she'd allowed my brother to, well, wouldn't she allow me?'

His face flushed now and voice hoarse, Max said, 'And she smiled at me and told me she wasn't wearing pants, they must have got lost in Alex's car. She took my hand, guided it beneath her skirt. Then I saw my mother in her face and I found my hands were round her neck and everything went red.

'Afterwards,' his voice grew matter of fact, 'I wasn't sure what I should do next. Then I thought what my father would have done. The simplest course of action is always best, he used to say, don't complicate things. So I put her in the ditch and drove back to London. I knew no-one could connect her with me.'

There was silence. The little spools whirred on.

Then Darina asked softly, 'What about Ulla? I thought you loved her?'

The blue eyes looked candidly at her. 'I did, like I loved my mother. No, not like I loved my mother. But I loved both of them so much. And they were both whores. I was too small to kill my mother and my father wouldn't do it. He told me again and again what a wicked woman she was, how wrong the thing was I found her doing, how I must never behave like the man she was with and must never, never have anything to do with women who were like her. But he didn't kill her.' His voice was puzzled. 'When I found Ulla was like that, it was like before, something in me snapped.'

'What made you go to her room?' Darina asked, afraid to glance at William in case it deflected Max's concentration and stopped him talking. She could only hope this was the right line to take.

'I couldn't sleep. I wanted to talk to Alex, I knew he was unhappy. I thought perhaps he couldn't sleep either, so I went along to his room. He wasn't there. I went into his bathroom to relieve myself and heard sounds, they were . . . disturbing. I listened. And I knew. I knew what must be happening.' His face and voice distorted. 'But I couldn't believe it. I thought it might be a nightmare. I sat on Alex's bed and tried to think of something else. But it was no use. All I could think about was, was what I'd heard. And I had to go and see. See for myself.

'I went up to her room. The flat wasn't locked. I thought it might be, if it was I was going to barge the door down. But it wasn't locked. Odd that,' he considered the matter for a moment then continued. 'I must have made a noise because as I entered the living room, the bedroom door opened and she was standing there, wearing a flimsy robe, it hardly covered her at all. I think she wanted me to see her. See her pointy breasts. I pushed past her into the bedroom. I thought Alex would be in the bed, like that other time,' he closed his eyes briefly, 'but the room was empty. For a moment I was so relieved, I thought I must have been mistaken. But she came up behind me and said that Alex was in the bathroom and I must leave, we would talk in the morning. She put her hand on my arm, the robe was all hanging open and she called me darling Max.' His voice broke and the wide mouth twisted in an odd way. 'Suddenly my hands were round her neck, just as with Sharon.' He gave a strangled sob.

For a while there was silence.

'What happened then?' asked Darina.

Max caught his breath, he looked puzzled, 'I don't know. Next thing I knew I was back in my room – so I went to bed and when I woke up it was as if nothing had happened. So I thought I'd dreamt it all. When the inspector said yesterday afternoon that she really was dead I couldn't believe it.

'They've been asking me so many questions. I didn't think

244

I should tell them about Sharon and Ulla, I didn't think they would understand. But I thought you would, you've been so nice to me. You're not like those others.' He sighed and closed his eyes, leaning back in his chair.

The little spools stopped whirring.

Chapter Twenty-Eight

Much later William drove Darina and Alex back to the Hotel Morgan.

Before then the police had taken Max Saunders backwards and forwards through his statement, checking details, filling in gaps. Max had been unfailingly courteous and helpful, his eyes set in hollow sockets of exhaustion, their expression dead. He showed no remorse.

Yes, he'd found Sharon's pants in Alex's car. 'I knew they must be hers, she'd told me she'd left them there. Alex can't have known they were there, otherwise he would have got rid of them. I thought of taking them up to London to dispose of, like I had the handbag. I found that in my car after I returned from Somerset. I emptied it and put everything bit by bit in different rubbish bins. I didn't want to throw the bag away, it looked too good, someone might have been suspicious. Finally I thought I would bury it in Hyde Park, then no one would find it. But there were too many people about, they would have wondered what I was doing. Then I saw the compost heap and thought I could hide it there. No one could trace it to me anyway, I'd wiped off all my finger prints.' But he'd missed the two tiny labels tucked at the bottom of one of the bag's side pockets.

'And I'd cleaned the car,' he added with pride. 'Father would have approved, I'd thought about everything.'

'Is that why you offered to clean Alex's car?' Darina asked.

'No, that was the funny thing, I just thought it would be nice for him. I hate things to be in a mess. It was only when I found the pants that I thought he could be suspected of the murder. When I heard him tell the police that night in the pub that he'd never met Sharon, I knew he was afraid he wouldn't be able to prove he didn't do it.

'I wondered how to get rid of them without arousing suspicion. Then I thought of what father said, about the simplest course of action being always the best, so I threw them into one of the hotel's rubbish bins.'

And that was about it.

After Max had been removed to a cell, Alex was brought in and asked to give them his side of the story. He took the news of Max's arrest very quietly. 'Poor sod,' he said. Then he was silent for a long time.

Finally he told them the details of his meeting with Sharon the night she was murdered. 'She rang me at the hotel from The Feathers. She sounded in quite a state. I was supposed to see Olivia that evening but she'd started getting far too possessive and I thought it would do her good to be ditched for a date.'

'How long had you known Sharon Fry?' asked Grant.

'Oh, several months. Max and I were out pub crawling one evening and ran into her. Blondes have always been a weakness of mine and her legs were really sensational. First I tried to get Max and her together, I was always trying to get him off with girls. His damned father had instilled some extraordinary Puritan ethics into him, he only went for modest little numbers who hid everything, I wouldn't be surprised if he'd decided he should remain pure until marriage. I felt if only he would loosen up, have a few flings, he'd find life much easier. Anyway, it was patently obvious that Max was too young for her and she was only interested in me, so finally we made a date for her next night off.

'God, we had some good times together,' a fleeting, reminiscent smile passed over his face. 'She was amusing and a great lay and I thought she was like me, just in it for the fun of the thing. I knew she was calculating, ambitious, out for a rich man. I told her I didn't have any money and I thought she looked on me as her bit of slumming, a relaxation from the main hunt. I'd pick her up, we'd go to a quiet place and drink whatever beer or wine I'd brought from the hotel and have some fun,' he paused. 'She invented some highly original positions in that car.'

'What happened that evening?' asked William colourlessly.

'I picked her up at The Feathers. She'd got over whatever it

247

was that had upset her and was in fine form. Randy as anything, would hardly let me drive. But I insisted we went somewhere quiet, away from the road; we'd had one or two narrow squeaks when impatience got the better of us.' Alex hesitated briefly then continued, 'Anyway, I drove up a little lane I know and at first it was business as usual. Then she said she was pregnant. Stupid bitch, she'd told me she was on the pill.'

'You hadn't used protection?' asked Grant.

'Should have done, I suppose, she was enough of a good time girl to be a risk of some sort. But I hate those things and after America it was such a relief not to have to worry. You know over there girls ask if you've been tested for Aids? I reckoned down here one was pretty safe. We're all fools over some things. But I'm not foolish enough to be taken for a paternity suit.'

'What did you tell her?' asked Grant.

'That she could do what she liked with it. That there was no way she could persuade me the child was mine and even if it was I had no money and refused all responsibility.'

'How did she take that?' There was no expression in William's voice.

'Flew into a rage. It turned out she'd never really believed me when I'd told her I had no money. And now that she knew, God knows how, that Tennant had offered to buy the hotel, she thought I was going to be loaded. She accused me of treating her like dirt then stormed out of the car and said she never wanted to see my face again. Well, that suited me.'

'So you just let her walk off?'

'Not quite, I ran after her. Bit difficult because my trousers tripped me up as soon as I opened the car door, I'd forgotten they were round my ankles. Then I caught her up and tried to persuade her to come back to the car. She spat at me like an angry cat, told me not to come near her. Said I owed her some respect. Respect! I thought she needed to cool down a little and a bit of a walk would probably do her a lot of good. I went back to the car and finished the wine I'd brought. I really expected her to be back asking to be taken home. After about twenty minutes or so I thought I'd better see if I could catch her up so I reversed up to the road and set off in what I thought was the direction she must have taken. When I didn't come across her, I tried the other way and then decided she must have hitched a lift so I went home.'

He sat thinking for a little while. Then he looked at William.

'When you showed me that snapshot in the pub and told me she'd been murdered, it was as though some automatic pilot took over. I heard myself saying I didn't know her without any conscious decision on my part. I'd forgotten Max had met her. I remembered immediately he denied knowing her and reckoned he'd followed my lead. As he had done so many other times.' For the first time deep distress showed itself.

'I haven't been much of a brother to him. I should have insisted he saw a psychiatrist as soon as his father died. Before that it was impossible, the old boy ruled the suggestion out entirely.'

'You thought he might be unstable?'

'I thought any boy faced with finding his mother in bed with a lover, brought up by a manic disciplinarian and two Victorian left overs needed a little help coming to terms with life. I tried to do what I could by showing what a normal home life could be.' He reflected for a moment. 'Maybe if Trudy hadn't died, things would have turned out differently. Or maybe if I had been around more often, tried to give him some real understanding instead of playing the big brother who could show him a good time.' He shook his head dispiritedly and fell silent.

Then he asked, 'What's going to happen now?'

Grant said, 'Now comes the hard work of preparing the case. We have to assume that your brother's solicitor will get him to plead not guilty.'

'But he's confessed,' Darina said, her voice edged with surprise.

Grant looked at his most sardonic, 'Juries have heard enough tales about confessions being extracted under police persuasion of one sort or another to be open to the suggestion it need carry no weight.'

'But surely it won't come to court, the boy's insane,' protested Alex.

'Not for us to say,' said William. 'And it's a tough business proving someone's unfit to stand trial.'

'The forensic examination of his car may provide something, and the scrapings from Sharon Fry's fingernails have shown traces of skin other than hers. Tests may well prove it to belong to Max Saunders. Which will take some explaining away by defence counsel. And we may find similar traces under Ulla Mason's fingernails, though I can't see any scratches on the defendant.'

'Pity that the chap who saw the victim being picked up outside Bruton couldn't be sure of identifying the driver,' regretted William.

'I thought it was all up with me when I was in that identification parade,' said Alex. 'I knew I hadn't approached Sharon the way he described but I thought he'd got confused. At first I was grateful Max and I looked so alike. But then I started thinking. All the while you were questioning me, odd little thoughts on Max kept popping up in my mind. And I thought anything more I told you might incriminate him if it didn't me.'

There were a few more formalities. Alex rang his father's solicitor and asked him to handle Max's defence. Darina found herself back in the little room she had waited in earlier, her mind now wiped clean of all thought while Grant and William followed through Max's arrest and released Alex from custody.

Finally the sergeant was allowed to drive them back.

'Come in,' said Alex when the Bentley drew up outside the hotel.

'You wouldn't have some food available, would you?' asked William as they entered the hall. 'I managed a shave this morning but I can't remember when I last ate.'

'That's a police suggestion I can approve of,' said Alex. 'You don't exactly overfeed your guests.'

Darina led them through to the kitchen. It was late evening and Sally had long gone. She checked the fridge and found some chicken breasts and bacon. While she prepared a meal, Alex brought through a bottle of whisky and some glasses and served them all a hefty slug.

'We need it,' he said.

There was nothing to toast. The breaking of the case had brought only grief, no satisfaction, and the ghost of poor Ulla hovered around them, a restless spirit.

Alex drank deeply. 'What I still don't understand, my God, that's classic detective novel stuff, still, I have to ask the question. Darina, when you saw Max find those pants in my car what

250

made you think that it was he who had murdered Sharon rather than me?'

Darina turned over the bacon wrapped breasts in her pan and added mache lettuce to the salad she was preparing.

'Right from the first I could see that they worried Max and I found that a bit of a puzzle. When I finally put two and two together, long after I heard the police were looking for Sharon Fry's panties, I realised that he knew they were important. That they could implicate Alex in her death. And how did he know that? Only the police and the murderer knew they were missing at that stage. If Max had known nothing about the killing, he would have thought, as I did, that the pants were Olivia's and teased his brother about them, probably handed them back. That would have been the natural reaction.' She gave the chicken a slight press with her finger to see if it was done.

'Then I remembered something else. When Max had spoken to me about wanting to talk to Alex and Ulla about his decision to join the army, he started to say something then seemed to change the direction of his sentence. I thought it possible he might have been going to say he had been coming down to discuss it with them but then stopped himself. What if that had been the night Sharon had been killed?

'And his relationships with his mother and Ulla worried me. They weren't normal. He'd allowed any feeling for his mother to be totally repressed and built Ulla into some sort of angelic all-woman, mother-cum-dream-lover. Nobody could live up to that, it could only be a matter of time before she disillusioned him in some way and I couldn't see how he was going to handle it. So I wondered if on Boxing Night he had seen Alex leave her room and realised they had been lovers, whether it would have tipped some balance in his mind.'

She looked across at Max's half brother. 'I was sure it couldn't have been you that killed her.'

He lifted his glass to her, 'Thank you for that.'

'You needn't be, it wasn't that I didn't think you capable, but because I couldn't see why Ulla would have put on her robe to be murdered in unless someone had come unexpectedly into the room.'

'That thought had occurred to us also,' said William quietly.

251

'From the way you were questioning me, I was convinced you thought I was the murderer.' Alex refilled his glass, the other two were not half way through their drinks.

'We knew you were holding out on us, that you hadn't told us anything like the whole truth,' the sergeant said peaceably.

Darina placed the cooked chicken breasts in a serving dish, tossed the salad, took the plates from where she had put them to warm and went through to the staff room. There she found knives and forks and rapidly laid three places at the table.

There was silence for a little as they ate. Then William gave a small sigh of satisfaction and asked Alex what he was going to do about the hotel.

'Oh, sell, of course. What about it, Darina? Do you want to buy?'

'I don't think I will be able to afford the price,' she said quietly. She was conscious of William looking at her. 'It's probably worth a great deal more than you thought.'

She told Alex of her conversation with the estate agent and Major Brownsword's remark. 'I think he's got together a little consortium. Weasel face is Chairman of the Council Planning Committee. He was lunching here with another councillor that Monday we came.' She looked across at William, 'Remember the man with the growth behind his ear? He was drinking with Adam Tennant the night we went to the Manor Park. Weasal face also rides with Major Brownsword's hunt. They all know each other quite well.

'I think the new Area Structure Plan will schedule this village for development. Which means houses can be built on the large field behind the hotel garden. So, if the estate agent I spoke to is right, the value of this place could double. Neither councillor could offer for the hotel without it looking extremely odd. But it would look quite natural for Adam to buy it. His only difficulty is money, which the other two were apparently going to provide, I should think they both have excellent credit ratings.

'The plan was probably for Adam Tennant to buy Hotel Morgan at its commercial value, less if possible, the offer he made Ulla was not particularly generous according to the estate agent I spoke to, before the new structure plan scheduling development in this area came out. That would then mean they could sell off some of the land for building, recoup the capital expenditure and perhaps a bit on top as well. Adam could then set about reorganising this place. We discussed briefly the possibility at our first meeting and he told me then he would put in a good manager to run it for six months looking to sell it on at a profit. At that stage, all three of them would have had a healthy return on their original investment.'

'You mean,' said Alex slowly, 'I stand to make quite a lot of money out of this place after all?'

'It looks like it.'

'But,' said William, 'surely you could sell off the land separately and offer Darina the hotel?'

She was filled with a joyous surprise.

'Of course. How about it, Darina?'

She shook her head, not looking at William. 'No. Thank you, but no.'

'I don't blame you, I don't think I shall ever want to see this place again. It took my father's life and, in a way, Ulla's. Hotel Morgue is about right.'

'There's something else I should tell you,' said Darina after a moment. 'Major Brownsword apparently intended his share of the profits to enable you to marry Olivia.'

Alex sat rigid. 'What the hell does that mean?'

'Olivia's in love with you but she knows you haven't got any money.'

He laughed shortly. 'It'd take more than a share of the profits from this place to finance Olivia's lifestyle.'

'Do you know she's pregnant?'

'You mean it's true? God damn it. Bloody females. I thought she was trying it on. After Sharon, I couldn't take it.'

'What are you going to do?'

He flung his fork down and reached for the whisky again. 'I sure as hell am not going to marry her. And that's for her sake as much as mine. Can you see the wreck she'd be after a couple of years marriage to me?' He sighed deeply. 'I suppose I shall have to accept a certain responsibility for the child. At least now I shall be able to afford to give some support.'

'Support doesn't end with money,' said William. 'Don't think you can make out a banker's order and forget you have a child, children need parents, in the plural.'

The ice blue eyes looked across the table. For the first time Darina saw their gaze falter. 'You think I'm a shit, don't you? And you're right. But I suppose I can't go on evading responsibility for ever.' He pushed his plate away, the meal unfinished. 'I'm sorry, Darina, food's lost its appeal. I'm going to my room. Help yourself to anything you want to drink, I've left the keys in the locks.' He picked up his glass and the bottle of whisky, now half empty, and left the room.

'Kind of him to give us the run of the bar,' said William dryly.

Darina sat taking in the realisation that she was no longer part of Hotel Morgan. The keys to the bar and everything else now belonged to Alex. She had been playing at hotel proprietor and the game was over.

'Miss Lisle, I thought I heard you in here.'

George Prendergast stood in the doorway, a cardigan badly buttoned up over wrinkled trousers.

'I need to know what the position is over the hotel. Will you be continuing to run things now Mrs Mason is dead?'

Darina looked at him and decided there was one more act she could carry out before relinquishing the reins of Hotel Morgan. 'For the moment, Mr Prendergast, I am indeed in charge and I have to tell you you are no longer welcome here. Please make other arrangements. Shall we give you twenty-four hours to find somewhere else?'

'Twenty-four hours?' he stuttered. 'But that's outrageous. I can't possibly. This is my home.'

'Not any more, Mr Prendergast.' She held his gaze and watched with satisfaction his discomfiture grow. But as he glanced away and rubbed a hand across his mouth, then turned, stumbling into the door frame before finding his way out of the room, she felt pity. Almost she called him back but then she remembered how Dawn day after day had had to put up with the noises from his video and how Angela had been assaulted. Without much effort she stifled the instinct to tell George Prendergast he could stay after all.

'Coffee?' she said brightly to William. He nodded. 'And why don't we have a brandy? Can you get a bottle from the bar? We'll stay here, I don't want to run the risk of meeting up with G.P. again.'

'Are you really sure about this place, that you don't want to try and buy it?' he said a little while later as they sat drinking coffee and sipping Courvoisier.

She nodded.

'Have you another hotel in mind?'

'The Manor Park perhaps?' she asked on a gasping giggle. Then she shook her head. 'I haven't exactly given up my hotel ambitions but I think there are other things that need my attention more at the moment.'

He looked up from his contemplation of the brandy in his glass. 'Dare I ask what?'

'First tell me what your feelings for Police Constable James are.'

'Pat? What on earth do you mean?' His stare of astonishment was all the reassurance she needed. 'You can't be jealous, surely?'

'It was just I've seen so little of you the last four weeks,' she apologised. 'And before you say anything, I know it's not been entirely the police's fault.'

He took her hand in his, placed a gentle kiss in her palm then folded her fingers over the spot, 'Are you saying you will marry me?'

She caressed his cheek with her other hand. 'No, my darling. I meant everything I said when we lunched here. I'm not ready to settle down. But I do want to spend as much time with you as I can. I had a letter the other day from my cousin's publishers. Apparently since his death demand for his cookery and food books has risen dramatically and they are thinking of reissuing one or two of his early works. They have suggested I edit them, bring them up to date. I thought I might take that on, stay with my mother and work down here.'

His mouth twisted. 'For one sublime moment I thought you were going to move in with me. I should have known you would have some other project in mind.'

She looked steadily at him. 'You mustn't try to rush me.'

He sighed, 'It's difficult, especially when you look like that.'

She leant towards him and planted a gentle kiss on his mouth, resisted his attempt to turn it into something more passionate and

255

said, 'I have a better idea. Why don't we take the rest of the brandy upstairs to my room?'

He rose immediately. 'I thought you would never ask.'

'Yes, you did, otherwise you would never have been drinking spirits.'

He groaned, 'How am I going to curb this eternal detecting instinct of yours?'

She laughed, 'Any attempt is doomed to failure. You will have to learn to live with it.'

She gave him the brandy bottle and picked up the glasses. As she led the way out through the kitchen, along the passage and into the hall, she turned out the lights. Then locked the heavy front door. Finally they climbed the stairs. Hotel Morgue was closed.